WELCOME
TO THE
FAMILY

WELCOME TO THE FAMILY

CATHRYN GRANT

bookouture

Published by Bookouture in 2025

An imprint of Storyfire Ltd.
Carmelite House
50 Victoria Embankment
London EC4Y 0DZ

www.bookouture.com

The authorised representative in the EEA is Hachette Ireland
8 Castlecourt Centre
Dublin 15 D15 XTP3
Ireland
(email: info@hbgi.ie)

ISBN: 978-1-80550-236-4
eBook ISBN: 978-1-80550-235-7

For Don: The heart of my family.

PROLOGUE

Her body lay on the ground at the bottom of the stone staircase.

At first glance, she looked serene, as if she were sleeping there. Her pale blue dress spread around her, shimmering in the ghostly light of the wine cave. The fabric looked so soft, as if it were made of expensive silk, but the design was simple and casual—a sundress for a summer picnic. The strands of her hair were equally silky, light brown with streaks of blonde. Her arm, resting on the bottom step, was relaxed, with three gold bracelets dangling from her wrist, one with a heart charm attached.

But when I took another step down, her face was all wrong. It wasn't filled with pain or torment, but at the same time, it didn't have a look of rest about it, like it should if she were peacefully dreaming. It was blank and cold. Her skin was too white with a sickly gray shadow. Her lips were too dark, parted slightly with a stiff quality to them. Her eyes were closed but they appeared sunken and almost glued shut.

Her toes were pointed in a way that didn't look natural. Her chest was motionless.

The air caught in my own chest and for several seconds, I

couldn't breathe. I didn't scream or gasp or cry. I stared, the edges of my vision growing dark.

Looking at her was the second most horrifying experience of my life. And gazing at her lifeless face, I knew that if I didn't uncover the secrets this family was hiding, it was only a matter of time before someone looked with horror on my own lifeless body.

PART ONE

ONE

CLAUDIA

The driver was standing outside the baggage claim area holding a cardboard sign with my name on it, just as Daniel had said. He took the handles of both my large suitcases and wheeled them outside to the curb where a black sedan was waiting.

He opened the back door, and I slid onto the creamy leather seat. After loading my bags into the trunk, the driver settled behind the wheel. "It's an hour and a half to the winery, so make yourself comfortable. There's bottled water in the console, and snacks if you're hungry."

I thanked him, buckled my seatbelt, and checked my phone. No messages from Daniel. I sent him a text to let him know I'd landed. He replied with a heart. Daniel would be meeting me at his family home where I'd be meeting his mother and siblings for the first time. I was nervous, but excited. While I was here for five weeks, we would plan our wedding, and his family and I would get to know each other.

He'd assured me I would love his family, and they would feel the same about me. I shouldn't be intimidated by the fact that they owned and operated one of the largest, oldest, award-winning wineries in the Napa Valley. *My mother will adore you.*

Don't think about how powerful she is. She's all about family. You shouldn't worry at all.

Ninety minutes later, the car turned down a long, straight road lined with palm trees. The San Francisco skyline and the shimmering water of the bay were far behind me. Except for the buildings of the winery itself, which weren't visible from their family home, there was nothing but acres of vineyards in every direction. I was used to gazing out my apartment window at the lights of Seattle.

We drove for another quarter of a mile or so before I saw an enormous concrete wall that seemed to stretch for miles. Two black iron gates opened as the car approached and we pulled inside. It felt like I was entering a prison or a compound of some kind. I looked up, half expecting to see towers along the walls with guards watching the surrounding area.

As the gates close behind me, a chill ran down my arms. The driveway was a massive sand-colored brick parking area. In front of us was a long, rectangular pool of water with fountains, surrounded by grassy areas and trees.

Standing behind the fountains and gardens was a three-story chateau. Ivy grew over the walls, making the windows look as if they were peeking out from copious amounts of hair. There were two enormous wings, an arched front door large enough to allow ten people to enter at once, a red tile roof, and a small tower on top of the center section.

I shouldn't have been surprised at the massive, lavish house for a family of four adults, but why were they protecting it with these twelve-foot walls surrounding the estate? I rubbed my arms to ease the chill.

I pulled out my phone. I had a decent signal, so that was good. I texted Daniel to let him know I was outside. There was no response.

The driver stopped the car, turned off the engine, and got out. He opened my door, and I climbed out into the hot afternoon sun. The temperature was nearing ninety degrees—hot, even for the Napa Valley in June. I put on my sunglasses. It might not be the best image for meeting Daniel's family, but the glare was intense, and neither did I want to meet them squinting like a shady character out of a 1950s B movie.

The driver unloaded my bags and carried them to the arched doors. He placed them on the ground and returned to the car.

I checked my phone. Nothing from Daniel. Was I supposed to ring the bell? That was awkward. He'd promised he would meet me, and we would enter the house together.

"Enjoy your day." The driver got back into the car, closed the door, and made a long, sweeping turn toward the gates. They opened in front of him, and he drove out. The gates closed behind him with a clanking sound that echoed off the walls and resounded through my bones. An involuntary shudder that I couldn't explain ran through my body.

I sent another text to Daniel.

> The driver just left. Are you coming out or should I ring the bell?

He still didn't answer. I started walking toward the door. It was so hot, I could already feel perspiration as thick as oil on the back of my neck. My skin felt like it was on fire. Even with that, I walked slowly, feeling like I didn't quite belong here.

Meeting his mother, or whoever might answer the door, without Daniel beside me, wasn't what I wanted. This wasn't at all how I'd imagined it.

I touched my fingertips to my cheeks, patting them to get rid of the moisture that had built up while I was standing in the sun, surrounded by all that brick. I felt like Dorothy wandering along the yellow brick road, but without the courage she'd had in the form of a sweet, anxious lion trying so hard to be brave.

I tipped my head back, shaking my hair loose from the sides of my face and neck. I took a deep breath.

Before I could lift my hand to ring the bell, one side of massive arched doors swung open.

A woman with dark, almost black hair, swept into an elaborate updo stood there. She wore no makeup except burgundy lipstick and black mascara, but her skin, despite the fact she was in her early sixties, was flawless. She wore a white dress that fell loosely to the middle of her calves and white cowboy boots with fringe. From pictures Daniel had shown me, I knew it was his mother—Janice Keller.

"May I help you?" she asked.

I extended my hand. "Hi. I'm—"

"How did you get in here?"

I stared at her. There wasn't a shadow of recognition or welcome anywhere on her face.

TWO

CLAUDIA

I gave the woman in front of me a warm, apologetic smile. I wanted her to know it was probably a mix-up. Maybe Daniel had the day wrong. He'd sent a heart when I said my plane had landed, but maybe he hadn't read my message. Maybe he just saw the words and sent a heart because he was busy. His job was demanding. He and his brother and sister had a lot of responsibility running a winery the size of Chateau Noir. He worked long hours and there were lots of high-pressure meetings, lots of critical decisions and VIP guests that consumed his time.

Soon, I would be involved. Once we were married, he wanted me to be part of the family business.

"The driver Daniel sent dropped me off. He had to get back to the airport to pick up a VIP for a wine tasting."

"Why are you here?"

"Oh." I laughed. "Sorry. I'm Claudia. Daniel's—"

"I know *who* you are. I asked *why* you're here."

This was really confusing. Had Daniel forgotten to tell her I was coming? I was supposed to be here for five weeks. No one wanted a houseguest for that long without advance notice. I could feel my luggage around me, like I was a homeless waif looking to move into their luxurious home and leech off them for an indefinite amount of time.

Why hadn't he told her? I wanted to check my phone, but that would look rude. She was already glaring at me as if I were the rudest woman she'd ever met.

"Daniel said you were expecting me."

"Did he?"

"He was going to be here when I arrived, but I guess he's late."

"Is that right?"

"I'm here to meet you." I smiled. "To get to know you, and the rest of your family. To plan our wedding."

She stared at me. I wouldn't call her look cold, but it wasn't warm. It was nothing. Blank. Almost as if she hadn't heard what I'd said. As if she hadn't understood me, or didn't want to talk about it.

My cheeks were starting to hurt from smiling, from trying to look relaxed when I felt anything but that. *Where* was Daniel? I would have felt my phone buzz if he was texting me back. Besides, he should be here, not texting. Even though I knew no one was there because the air around us was completely motionless, I turned to look behind me. All I saw was sunbaked brick, the steadily dancing fountains, and those tall iron gates that looked impossible to open without a specially programmed device. There were no visible locks or handles.

She continued to stand there, not speaking. She stared at me as if she'd asked me another question and was waiting for my answer. I had no idea what I was supposed to say or do. Should I offer to leave? Should I take out my phone and call Daniel? Should I tell her to call Daniel herself?

Even if she hadn't known I was coming, why was she acting like this? She knew who I was. Did she not want me staying in their house? Was she upset that we were getting married? But why? My heart started beating faster. I could feel it tapping too hard against my bones, making me wonder if she could see it jumping around inside my chest, going slightly sideways, starting to take flight.

It made me feel like I was a tiny bird and any minute she could reach out both her hands, wrap them around my chest, and squeeze the life out of me. I could feel the air caught in my throat. It was hard to breathe. I wanted to gasp in a big, deep breath of oxygen, but that would make me look like I was having a panic attack, which it probably already looked like.

What was I supposed to do? Should I ask if I could come inside and call Daniel? Should I ask her if she wanted me to leave? Where *was* he?

She still hadn't said anything. She hadn't smiled, hadn't moved. I wondered if she'd even blinked. I hadn't noticed because I'd been too busy trying to breathe. She must have blinked, but right that minute, she was only staring.

"I wasn't aware of this. It's totally unacceptable." Janice took a step back. She didn't ask about my luggage, and she didn't invite me inside.

THREE

CLAUDIA

Tears pricked my eyes. Even if she hadn't known, why was it unacceptable? My hands shook as I pulled my phone out of my pocket and sent another message to Daniel.

While I waited for a response, I gave Janice a look that I hoped was friendly but was probably needy more than anything else. "May I bring my bags inside? And sit down? It's really hot, and I'm—"

"Let's not get ahead of ourselves," Janice said.

I sucked in air as if I'd been punched in the chest. What did that mean? Was she going to send me away? I didn't understand what was going on. Why didn't she want me here? Maybe Daniel hadn't told her about me at all. But she'd said she knew who I was, so that wasn't it.

My phone finally vibrated with a message from Daniel.

> I'm so sorry, babe. I'm on my way. I was held up. I'll be there in ten minutes.

There was a kiss emoji.

I felt my body relax. Then I looked at Janice and all my muscles tightened again.

The glare from her eyes, watching me text, felt hotter than the afternoon heat that splashed across my back. I ignored the intensity of her gaze and sent another text to Daniel, asking him why Janice hadn't known I was coming.

> There's been a lot going on. Maybe she forgot.

> She definitely forgot. What's been going on?

> We'll talk when I get there. Soon. xx

> She won't invite me inside. Does she even know we're engaged?

He didn't reply. I heard the sound of the gates opening and turned to look. Daniel's black Mercedes drove through the open gates and stopped. He stayed inside the car, his head bent forward, looking at his phone. Why was he checking his phone? Didn't he understand what was happening here? His mother was acting like I was an uninvited guest, as if she didn't even want me to marry him. She was acting as if she hated me for some reason I couldn't begin to figure out.

I needed him beside me. But I couldn't very well walk over to the car and open the door, begging him to get out. That would make me look worse—like I knew I didn't belong here. But right now, that was exactly how I felt.

He'd told me his family was different, they were very close and very private, but it had nothing to do with money. They were just protective of each other. Their dad had died when he and his brother and sister were small. Because of that, they'd clung together to comfort their mom, and each other. That, and running a family business.

They might seem standoffish, hard to get to know, but it had nothing to do with money. It was their closeness, their bond that formed a shell around them. I couldn't take it personally. That's why my visit was planned to be five weeks. It would take time to get to know them.

I shouldn't be shocked by the lavish house or the presence of people who worked to care for their family. It was necessary because their work running a successful winery was demanding.

But that wasn't the vibe I was getting from Janice. She was making me feel as if she didn't want me here. She was making me feel that my slightly worn suitcases, which she kept glancing at, were soiling her historical estate. She wouldn't even let me inside her house, as if I might stain the furniture.

It couldn't have anything to do with who I was because she didn't know me. Unless she thought I was only interested in her son for his money.

But I hadn't even known about the winery until Daniel and I had been together for six weeks. We'd met at a yoga retreat. I was there because my sister insisted it would help me cope with my roller-coaster emotions and occasional anxiety. He was there, I learned after a while, because he thought it would give him an edge in his career. The first two weeks we were together, we didn't mention our careers at all because it was one of the rules of the retreat—no talking about anything from the outside world.

After that, we'd had a long-distance relationship for a few weeks. We mostly texted and had video calls to talk about trying to keep up with the yoga and meditation techniques we'd learned at the retreat.

I turned back to Janice, attempting another smile. I wondered if my cheeks would literally crack from the effort of forcing my lips to curve again. "I'm excited to talk about our wedding plans with you. I'm looking forward to hearing your ideas."

Why wasn't Daniel getting out of the car? Didn't he see me

standing there like a stray cat while his mother blocked the doorway?

"About this fiancée thing," Janice said. "I don't see a ring on your finger. So, it would be better if you don't pretend you're someone you're not." For the first time, she appeared to smile slightly. But had she really? Her lips were straight, with a tiny softening of her upper lip that suggested a smile. But maybe I'd imagined that cruel smile.

FOUR

CLAUDIA

As if he'd been waiting for his mother to deliver that cold message, I heard the car door open as soon as Janice finished speaking. The door closed with a thud and a moment later Daniel was beside me, his arm snaking around my waist pulling me against him.

"Mom, this is Claudia." His arm tightened around me. "The woman who rocked my world. She's the kindest person you'll ever meet. She's smart and so talented. I can't wait for you, and everyone, to get to know her."

I felt my skin grow even warmer as his words slid through me. All my anxiety dissolved in a single breath. I smiled at Janice, eager for a fresh start.

"Yes, we've met," Janice said. "I'm delighted to have you here." She gave me a sparkling smile, then came toward us and lifted her cheek to Daniel for a kiss.

His lips lingered on her skin, and I inhaled the aroma of her fresh scent that I hadn't noticed until then. She turned to me and held out her arms. "Welcome to our home, Claudia." She placed her hands on my shoulders, squeezed them gently, and pulled me toward her in a warm hug. I felt her hands move and her thumbs press into my collarbones. I was relieved, hungry for air, when she finally let go.

"Come inside. Let's get you settled." Janice took my hand and turned to Daniel. "Ask Greyson to take Claudia's bags to your rooms. I'll get her something to drink. And then she can freshen up for our cocktail party. Doesn't that sound good?" She gave me a beaming smile.

With that, she led me into an entryway facing a sweeping staircase with a plush red carpet that rose to the second floor far above us.

I hardly had time to take in the massive staircase, before she hurried me through a living room that looked out on the back patio, turning right down a wide hallway decorated with framed oil paintings to a shockingly modern kitchen that was larger than my apartment. The center island included a curved granite breakfast bar with chairs featuring what I hoped was faux zebra upholstery.

Janice took a glass out of the cabinet and filled it with water from the spigot in the fridge, chattering the entire time to Daniel, asking detailed questions I couldn't understand about his business meetings. She opened the fridge, took a wedge of lemon from a dish with a pair of tongs, and placed it in the water.

I thanked her and took several grateful swallows.

"So, Daniel and I will catch up on business, Claudia. Greyson will show you to Daniel's rooms. You can shower and get dressed for our cocktail party." She smiled. "Then we can all get to know each other a little better."

Better? We didn't know each other at all. And what I did know so far, was making me think she had a multiple personality disorder. What was happening here? I wanted to talk to Daniel. I wanted to tell him how she'd treated me. I wanted to know why she'd acted as if she didn't want me around until he showed up, and why she didn't seem to believe we were engaged.

As if he'd heard his name through hidden speakers, a man who introduced himself as Greyson appeared in the kitchen. He wore a pale blue button-down shirt with the cuffs rolled back to show nicely muscled forearms. His hair was brown streaked with blonde, styled with gel, and he had a light stubble across his face. He looked more like a model than a butler. A chief of staff? A personal assistant? I had no idea, and I wasn't told.

He gave me a sympathetic smile, a smile so out of place, I wondered if he didn't know who I was. His gaze flicked briefly toward Janice, anticipating something from her. When she ignored him, his lips tightened and he turned away.

Daniel took the empty water glass out of my hand. He touched my face, lifting my hair away from my forehead. "How was your flight?"

"Nice," I said. "No bumps."

"Enjoy your shower," Daniel said. "You'll feel better after." He kissed me softly. "I'm glad you're finally here."

His kiss made me feel better, but I wanted him to come with me. I didn't want to be alone with Greyson in this enormous, unfamiliar house. It was so lavish, so dark and filled with furniture and artwork that looked old and expensive, beyond anything I'd ever seen, much less lived in. Now, this was my home for five weeks. Deep inside, something was whispering to me that there might be things about Daniel that I didn't know.

I followed Greyson back through the living room with its two statues of women who looked like Greek goddesses, into the entryway with three more statues, and furniture that looked like it might have come from a museum. Greyson didn't say anything as he led me up the grand staircase, past a few closed doors, and stopped at another creamy white door.

"Here you are." He opened the door and stepped to the

side. "There's a cell phone on the desk in the sitting room. Press one to reach me if you need anything at all. There's no password. It only works on the property." He stepped in front of me and waited for me to make eye contact. "I mean it. Anything. Don't hesitate to call."

It was such a strange comment. I knew I wouldn't. Why would I call a man I didn't know when I had Daniel with me?

The bedroom had pale gray carpet and gray walls. The chandelier was black with lights like candles, and the bed was covered with a gray and white fur throw. I wondered if I would ever feel at home here. I sent a text to Daniel and asked him to come see me.

Daniel:

> I need to update my mother on my meetings. Talk soon. xx.

I dropped my phone on the bed. A shower would make me feel better. Daniel was right about that.

When I was showered, my hair dry, my makeup fresh, and wearing a flowered sundress and pink flip-flops, I wandered out of the bedroom and down the hallway to the stairs. It was easier to retrace my steps than I'd thought.

Greyson was waiting for me in the living room. "How is everything?"

"Fine. Thank you."

"It will take some getting used to," he said.

I nodded and gave him an appreciative smile. I wasn't sure if he meant the house or Janice, or something else.

Greyson ushered me out to a stone patio that spanned that back of the chateau and overlooked a large black-bottom swimming pool surrounded by rocks, with several small waterfalls splashing into the pool.

Daniel and his mother sat at a table covered by a dark green umbrella. Beside them was a cart with wine and liquor bottles on the bottom and an assortment of glasses on top. Trays of appetizers covered the surface of the table. The other family members were nowhere to be seen.

Daniel stood and kissed me on the lips. He pulled out a chair for me and I settled beside him.

After we'd selected our drinks—beer for Daniel, a martini for Janice, and a glass of white wine for me—Greyson left us alone with far too much food for the three of us.

Janice took a sip of her drink then raised it toward me. "Welcome to our family, Claudia. We're so glad to have you here."

"Thank you." I touched my glass to hers. "Are the others joining us?"

Janice smiled and plucked one of the olives off her stir stick. She ate it.

Daniel took a sip of his beer. "What did you think of my rooms?"

"They're comfortable. Luxurious."

He laughed and reached for my hand.

"Tell me about yourself," Janice said.

It sounded like a command, but she was smiling, eating another olive. "Try some of the calamari. It's the absolute best," she said.

I took a calamari ring and ate it, although it wasn't my favorite thing. I followed it quickly with a grape and a sip of my wine. I smiled to show pleasure. "I work in PR."

"Yes, Daniel told me. For a non-profit. Not a perfect fit, but I expect you have skills we could utilize."

"Daniel and I haven't really talked about it." I glanced at Daniel.

He took a sip of his beer and smiled at me, then turned his attention to his mother. "Claudia would be a huge asset. She's smart and creative. She has an instinct for what captures people's interest."

"We'd love to have you join us," Janice said.

I nodded, hoping it didn't look like I was committing to anything yet. Daniel and I hadn't discussed it seriously. I'd almost wondered if he was simply being nice, wanting to make me feel welcome. I loved working for the wildlife protection organization I'd been with for two years now. I liked living in Seattle. We hadn't even talked about where we were going to live. Daniel had an apartment in Seattle, and as I watched his mother studying me over the top of her martini glass, I realized we hadn't gotten very far in talking about what our lives were going to look like after we were married. We'd only been engaged for a month, and everything had been about our wedding—where and when, with most of that involving dreams more than any actual planning.

"And your family?" Janice asked.

"One sister," I said.

Janice smiled. "Your parents?"

"I told you." Daniel placed his hand on my leg, squeezing it gently.

"Oh, right," Janice said. "So sorry. Your father was never in the picture. That must have been difficult. And your mother is sadly gone."

I said nothing. I felt cold, numb. I wanted the day to start over. I wanted her to stop asking so many serious questions. She was acting as if I owed her every detail about my life, that I had to tell her my most personal thoughts without any casual conversation to get to know each other first. I took a long swallow of wine.

She changed the subject then, asking more about my job, what I liked to do in my free time, wanting to know more about how Daniel and I had met and what I liked about her son. When we were finished, I'd had two glasses of wine and a few sips of water. Most of the food remained untouched on the table.

Janice stood. "Dinner is at eight. We won't be able to join you. It was delightful to get to know you." And then she was gone.

Daniel and I went up to his rooms. I didn't speak until the door was safely closed behind us. I kicked off my flip-flops and collapsed onto the bed. It felt comforting. Heavenly, actually.

He lay beside me and took my hand. "My mother really likes you."

"I'm not so sure about that," I said.

He squeezed my hand. "She does. I know her."

"She almost kicked me off your property when I first got here. She acted like she had no idea who I was." I told him everything she'd said.

"You caught her off guard, that's all. I told you; there's a lot going on."

"What's going on that she treated me like a stray cat?"

He laughed. "She didn't treat you like a stray cat."

"Worse."

"Please don't overreact."

"I'm not overreacting."

He sat up, releasing my hand. He got off the bed and went to my suitcases, dragging the largest one toward the walk-in closet. "My mother doesn't like drama."

I sat up. "I don't think I'm being dramatic."

"I told you that was a deal-breaker for me. No drama."

"When did you say that?"

"I'm sure I did."

"Well, this isn't drama. All I told you is how she treated me. She was cold and, actually, rude."

"Please don't do this."

"Do what?"

"All this drama. She doesn't like it. I don't like it."

"I'm telling you what happened. I'm not being dramatic. It was really upsetting."

"No one likes drama."

"I'm not being *dramatic*. I'm just trying to—"

"Good." He came to the bed, pulled me to my feet, and put his arms around my waist, holding me close. He gave me a long, deep kiss until I felt myself sinking back down onto the bed, with Daniel on top of me.

In the end, my body felt good, but my head did not feel good at all. I knew what I'd seen and heard. It felt as if he was trying to tell me my own experience was wrong, that it hadn't happened that way. After everything I'd been through, I'd learned to trust my own self. I'd learned not to let other people make me doubt my own perceptions.

FIVE

CLAUDIA

After a romantic dinner alone on the patio, during which I resolved not to spoil our first evening by complaining about his mother anymore, Daniel and I returned to his suite of rooms.

We made love, more tenderly than we had earlier, when all my feelings from being rejected and left standing in front of that imposing front door had poured out of me and into Daniel's body.

As we lay beside each other, I burrowed my toes into the fur throw Daniel had assured me was fake. I opened my eyes and gazed up at the chandelier, the candle-like lights set to glow dimly, making the room look soft and slightly blurry.

"Did you tell your mother we were engaged before I arrived?" I asked.

He sighed softly.

"Daniel?"

"I'm almost asleep."

"I just wondered. She said something strange."

"I know you were upset. And I told you there's a lot going on. I'm sorry you had a rough start, but everything's fine now." He propped himself up on his elbow and brushed his lips across mine. Then he turned to the nightstand, picked up the remote, and the lights in the chandelier went out. The room was so dark, I felt as if I was inside a cave. The coverings on the windows didn't let in a single flicker from the outside lights or the moon.

"She didn't believe we're engaged. Because I don't have a ring."

"We need to take care of that," he said.

"But she acted like not having a ring meant we aren't engaged at all. A ring shouldn't matter."

"It doesn't."

"She said it did."

"She's old-fashioned. Don't worry about it."

"She told me I'm *getting ahead of myself*."

He sighed, in a louder, more deliberate way this time.

"Did you tell her we're engaged, or not?"

"Of course, I did."

"Then why did she say I was getting ahead of myself?"

"I don't know. Maybe you misinterpreted what she said."

"How could I misinterpret that? It's pretty clear."

"Not really. What does it mean?"

"When I said I was looking forward to getting her input on our wedding, she said I was getting ahead of myself. That means I shouldn't be planning our wedding."

He turned toward me and pulled me close. He put his hand on the back of my head and pressed my face against his chest. "Shh. You're tired from your trip, and the pressure of meeting my mother, of being introduced to a different lifestyle. Please don't overthink everything."

"I'm not overthinking." My voice was muffled. I tried to pull away but the pressure of his hand on my head was firm. I liked feeling him hold me, but I wanted him to explain why his mother would say something like that. I wriggled free from his arms.

"Let's go to sleep," he said.

"What do you think she meant?"

"I don't know. But she knows we're engaged. She talked about you working for the winery. I don't know why you're so upset. When we had drinks, she fell all over you. She couldn't have treated you better if you were her own daughter."

"Then why did she make a big deal over not having a ring and getting ahead of myself?"

He kissed my nose. "Let's not get paranoid, okay? Day after tomorrow, we're going to go out and get you a big, flashy ring. How does that sound?"

"That's not what's bothering me. I don't need a ring."

"The biggest diamond you've ever seen. That way, the whole world will know how much I love you, and that you belong to me." He kissed me lightly and moved onto his back.

"It's not about the ring. It's what she said."

He laughed softly, but it sounded hollow. Was it the large room, or something else? It didn't sound like him.

"My mother likes things done properly. I'm sure that's all it was. Now let's get some sleep."

A moment later, his breathing changed, telling me he was asleep. I was more awake than ever. I didn't want a big flashy ring.

Daniel and I had been together for nearly six months, I thought I knew him inside and out. But in a little more than six hours, I'd started to feel as if I hardly knew him at all.

SIX

CLAUDIA

The following evening there was a formal meal at their twelve-foot stone dining table. The dining room was another huge room with twenty-foot ceilings. One wall was a series of square mirrors divided by intricate metalwork forming a larger square. Two sets of French doors opened onto the front gardens, but seated at the table, there wasn't much of a view of the garden or the pond and its ever-dancing fountains. The room was dark and quiet, with burgundy walls and a charcoal gray ceiling.

The chair where Janice sat at the head of the table was black crushed velvet, looking very much like a throne, with wings at the side that hid her entirely when I first entered the room. The back of the chair extended almost a foot past the top of her head. An identical chair at the opposite end of the table was empty.

Daniel's brother, Elliot, and his girlfriend, Faith, joined us for dinner.

"Sadly, Abigail isn't feeling well, so she won't be with us this evening," Janice said.

"I'm sorry to hear that," I said.

Janice didn't respond and no one else said a word about it.

Daniel and I took our seats and the first course, chilled cucumber soup, was served.

"How do you like the wine country?" Elliot asked.

I laughed. "I can't see any vineyards with all these walls around the property."

Elliot raised his eyebrows and hesitated a moment before answering in a clipped tone. "We need to keep our little oasis safe," he said. "Has Daniel shown you the lake?"

"No." I took a sip of water.

"The lake is the family jewel. The crowning achievement. The—"

"Stop with the lake," Daniel said.

"How many families own a lake?" Elliot looked at me, giving me a smile that appeared smug, or maybe something else. I wasn't sure. I felt like he wanted me to react to the lake, but I wasn't sure how. Maybe I was supposed to ask Daniel to show me the lake right away.

"Is it man-made?" I asked.

Elliot laughed.

Why was my question funny?

I glanced at Faith. She was staring at her soup. She looked up at me with a quick flash of her eyes, then returned her attention to her soup. As far as I could tell, she'd only taken a single taste.

"You really need to see the lake," Elliot said. "There's a gazebo. Perfect for looking at the water and contemplating the meaning of life. And death."

"Let's talk about something else," Janice said.

Elliot picked up his wineglass and leaned back in his chair. He swirled the wine and eyed me over the top of the glass. "Why is a gorgeous gal like you settling for my brother?"

I started eating my soup. Why was he doing this? Daniel was very good-looking. Better looking than Elliot, so I didn't understand his point. I felt my face getting hot. I wanted Daniel to say something, although I wasn't sure what. There was nothing that would make this not feel embarrassing. What was Janice thinking? Did she consider me rude because I hadn't answered? But there was no way to answer.

"Did I embarrass you, Claudia? You must know you're very nice to look at," Elliot said.

I glanced at Faith again. She acted as if she hadn't heard him. In fact, everyone was acting that way. I felt as if Elliot and I were the only two people in the room. Me, with my face and neck on fire. Elliot smirking at me. I couldn't swallow; I couldn't talk. My head was filled with a buzzing sound.

I was not considered beautiful. I had good skin and a nice smile. I was always grateful for my silky, thick medium brown hair with a hint of red highlights, my blue eyes. But I looked more wholesome than hot. And it almost felt as if he was mocking me. In the cliché of who was marrying *up*, it was probably me, not Daniel, in the looks department.

"Talk to me," Elliot said. "You're here so we can get to know you. Don't keep secrets. I want to know all about you."

I gave him a limp smile. Did they all think I was keeping secrets? Did they know things about me I wasn't aware of? How much had they looked into me on the internet? I hadn't checked in a while. I tried not to worry about things like that. My sister said it was better not to obsess about things you couldn't control. Everyone said that.

"What hasn't my brother told us about you? What will shock us, what will make us fall on our knees with respect?"

I looked at Daniel. He'd settled back in his chair because Greyson was clearing our soup bowls. Daniel didn't look at all uncomfortable.

"I work in PR," I said.

Elliot nodded as if that were the most fascinating career he'd ever heard of. "I bet you're a star."

"Not really."

"Too humble. Give us the highlights. What are you the proudest of?"

Was this a job interview? Janice had mentioned that PR was a useful career skill. Hadn't she?

"It's for a non-profit," I said. "It's a million miles from the world you all work in."

"My ex-wife was like you, very secretive. It's alluring." Elliot gave me a smile that looked like a come-on.

I knew I was not imagining it.

"Secretive until the end. Took them with her."

The end? What did that mean? Was she dead? Or did he simply mean she'd left their marriage with her secrets? It wasn't clear, but somehow, he made it sound like she was dead. I looked at Janice, then back at Elliott, not sure if I was supposed to ask about his wife or assure everyone that I didn't have secrets.

"Look at those eyes. Deep as a lake," Elliot said. "Lots of secrets buried there."

"I'm not secretive." My voice sounded weak and uncertain. It seemed like the wrong thing to say, but I didn't want Janice to think I was sneaky. I didn't want Daniel to think that. Why was his brother doing this? Maybe it was some kind of test.

Greyson returned, pushing a cart with the main course—prawns, black rice, and miniature glazed cherry tomatoes, the size of small marbles.

While he served us, Elliot continued talking about my eyes, speculating about what kind of secrets I might be keeping. I wanted Daniel to tell him to stop talking, to defend me, although I wasn't sure what he would defend me from.

Finally, our food was served, Greyson was gone without anyone having spoken to him or acknowledging his presence at all. The man was like a ghost, moving around the edges of the family, tending to their needs, ignored by them except when they spoke his name.

Elliot had finally grown tired of talking about me. All of them, all but Faith, began discussing the winery. I couldn't understand much of what they were saying, so I tuned it out as much as I could. I didn't completely zone out because I didn't want to be caught off-guard if someone asked me a question, but I knew nothing about the workings of a winery. I needed more time to think about whether a career change was what I wanted.

In the little over twenty-four hours since I'd arrived, I felt as if my thoughts hadn't been my own. I'd been swept into Daniel's childhood home, his family's possessions, and the ever-present aura of his mother. Even when she wasn't in the room, we'd been talking about her, or I was thinking about her, gazing at photographs of her, her children, and her ancestors, looking at artwork she enjoyed.

I'd eaten unfamiliar food and felt the lurking presence of Greyson, and other staff members, although I'd hardly seen them except an occasional disappearing back around a corner when I stepped out of a room.

The world beyond the walls surrounding their home didn't seem to exist.

Later, in our rooms, I kicked off the high heels I'd worn to our fancy dinner. I pulled my navy-blue dress over my head and tossed it on the armchair, too exhausted to hang it in the closet. I went into the bathroom, scrubbed my face and teeth and brushed my hair, my mind buzzing with wine and confusion.

Daniel was already in bed, and I slid in beside him, feeling like a horrible person for complaining during our second night together with his family. But I couldn't let things start piling up.

He ran his hand up my thigh and over my hip, moving more slowly up my body. I placed my hand on top of his. "Did it seem like Elliot was flirting with me?" That wasn't at all how I'd planned to say it. There was no doubt in my mind his brother had been flirting with me, but now I'd made it sound like I wasn't sure, like I wanted Daniel to confirm it for me, that I didn't trust my own instincts.

He yanked his hand away from me as if I'd bitten his finger. "Of course not!"

"He was. Talking about my eyes. Telling me I had secrets, and—"

"Oh my God, Claudia. He was just being friendly. He wasn't flirting. Faith was sitting right there."

I wanted to ask if Elliot's ex was dead, but I could see that question wasn't going to land well at all. "He was absolutely flirting."

"He was not flirting with you. I have no idea why you would think that. You never struck me as someone who needs attention."

"I don't need attention."

"Then why are you taking a few friendly comments and turning them into something crude?"

"Because the things he said were—"

"You're reading into it. And you're absolutely looking for attention if that's what you think it was. He's a friendly guy without a lot of filters and he was trying to get you talking. You looked nervous as a cat sitting there. He was trying to get you to relax and warm up to my family."

"I didn't see Faith warming up to your family."

"What does that have to do with anything?"

Maybe Faith could tell me if his ex was dead. I wasn't sure why I cared. Maybe because it was so strange. He talked about her as if she was, but he didn't come right out and say it, so I wasn't sure if I was supposed to tell him I was sorry for his loss. But he'd called her his ex. People don't do that when someone dies.

"I told you drama is a deal-breaker for me. First my mother, now my brother. You weren't like this before. What's going on with you?"

"I'm not creating drama. And why do you keep saying it's a deal-breaker? Are you having second thoughts?"

"No, of course not." He moved closer and wrapped his arms around me. He nuzzled his face into my neck, kissing it until I giggled.

"I just felt—"

"He wasn't flirting. If you want more attention, just say so." He put his mouth over mine and pulled me on top of him, kissing me so that I couldn't speak. Soon, I forgot what Elliot had said that made me so uncomfortable.

But I wondered whether Daniel's family was causing him to have second thoughts about marrying me.

SEVEN

CLAUDIA

When I woke, Daniel was leaning over me, smiling. He took my hand and kissed my fingers. "Are you ready to go shopping for the most fabulous bling that's ever decorated a woman's finger?"

I laughed. "I don't need fabulous bling. I have you."

"And now, the whole world will know." He scooted out of bed. "I thought we'd have a quick breakfast and head out. After we've made the selection, I'll take you out to lunch."

My head was spinning, thinking of our last words before we'd fallen asleep. Were we just going to forget that he'd called me dramatic? Again? That he'd said I needed attention? It wasn't very flattering, and I didn't like it. Almost as much as I didn't like that his brother had absolutely flirted, or played some kind of game with me. Elliott's behavior was not normal, whatever you wanted to call it.

But did I want to bring all that up now when we were going shopping for my engagement ring? It would forever spoil this day in my memory, and his. That wasn't what I wanted. We could talk about it later. We had five weeks to talk about it. I didn't need to hash out everything right this minute.

For all his casual attitude about getting an engagement ring, it turned out Daniel had planned something that took my breath away. It also gave me a glimpse into how much money his family had, as if the walled chateau with its enormous, antique-filled rooms and luscious pools of water and palm trees, and the promise of its own lake hadn't already done that.

When we arrived at the jewelers in San Francisco, which he described as their family jeweler, something I hadn't known was even a thing, we were taken into a private room. A selection of twelve diamond rings in various cuts and settings, already sized for my finger were displayed on black velvet cloth. It turned out that Daniel had taken a ring out of the bowl on my dresser weeks earlier, had it measured, and arranged for the rings to be custom fit.

This way, I would be sitting at lunch wearing my new ring, the ring I would wear every day for the rest of my life.

I felt overwhelmed by his outlandish effort to make me feel cherished. At the same time, I felt as if I was stepping into a world where I didn't belong. Until now, the fact that his family owned a world-class winery had been almost a mirage, some-thing slightly unreal, out there in the distance, something that didn't affect me or our relationship. It was his job. It was work that he did, which kept him challenged and engaged.

What did all of this mean for our future? I wasn't sure I wanted to live in a house where someone served me dinner and washed my dishes and clothes and cleaned my bathroom. I didn't know what I would do with a *family jeweler*. I wanted to laugh, even thinking the words.

Was this why they were treating me so strangely? Were they testing me? Inspecting me to see if I measured up to some standard they had for their lifestyle? Daniel had never said a word about any of this. He was starting to seem like two different people. Yet, he acted as if he was the same person, and I was confused if I thought anything different.

We drank champagne at lunch, celebrating our engagement

for the second time. I couldn't stop staring at the teardrop diamond on my left ring finger. I took a picture of my hand, holding my champagne glass, then our hands together. I wanted to send it to my sister.

She was currently unreachable. She was doing a sort of *Eat, Pray, Love* type of thing in Thailand and had left her phone with a friend while she traveled. She wanted to experience life without technology for a year, so we hadn't spoken for the entire eleven months she'd been gone so far. Even so, I emailed her and sent her photos regularly. When she returned from her spiritual journey, she would have a diary of my life to catch up on. She'd promised to use a notebook and pen to keep track of her experiences so I would have the same.

She didn't even know I was engaged.

It was disappointing, but the thrill of asking her to be my maid of honor when she returned would make up for it. And I kind of liked writing to her, making up her reactions in my own mind. Most of the time, I already knew what she would say. That's how well she and I knew each other. Growing up the way we did, we had to stick together. We both had to learn to know what the other one was thinking at all times.

As Daniel drove through the gates of his family estate and they closed behind us, I felt a light pressure on my chest, almost as if I were being locked inside the walls of their property. It was silly to feel that way, but I hadn't seen any way out, and I couldn't help thinking that if I wanted to go out by myself, it wasn't possible. I didn't want to, but the thought crossed my mind, uninvited.

We walked into the living room. A woman who looked a few years younger than I was sat on one of the sofas. She had full lips that were highlighted with pale pink gloss. Her hair was swept up with a few tendrils falling around her face. She had gray-blue eyes that were outlined in dark gray with thick lashes.

She wore white flowing pants and a white tunic top. She gave me a cool look.

"Abigail." Daniel crossed the room and kissed her cheek. "This is Claudia. My fiancée."

"I know," Abigail said.

I walked toward her and held out my hand. "Nice to meet you."

She stood, took my fingertips, pressed them briefly between hers, and let go. "Hello, Claudia." She reached for my left hand and turned it so she could see my ring. "Very nice." She let go and gave me another cool smile. "How are you liking the Napa Valley?"

Why were these people so fixated on the Napa Valley? I supposed they were simply being polite. But it wasn't as if I was visiting from another country. I'd been to the wine country before.

"It's a gorgeous place," I said.

"Please excuse me." She smiled and walked toward the hallway leading to the kitchen.

Daniel took my hand, smiling. "That went well."

I gave him a puzzled look. Why did it need to go well? And what happened? All she did was say it was nice to meet me, and that my ring was nice.

"Do you want some water?" Daniel asked.

Before he could move, Elliot appeared in the room, headed toward me with such intensity I wanted to move out of his way. Had Abigail sent him to look at my ring?

"I heard it's official," he said. "Let me see." He reached for my hand.

"It was *already* official." I glanced at Daniel.

"Let's see the ring," Elliot said, his tone more insistent, his voice at a slightly higher pitch.

I held out my hand.

He took my fingers, holding them tightly, drawing my hand

up as if he meant to kiss it. I tried to pull it back, but his grip was strong, pinching my fingers. I wanted to cry out, but the look in his eyes suggested he was pretending to be playful, and he would make me look hysterical if I did.

I tugged again.

His thumb stroked the top of my ring finger, barely moving, a gesture so slight I was sure Daniel couldn't see. At the same time, he still managed to keep a tight grip on my fingers. His face was so close to mine I could smell the hint of an orange on his breath. "Why are you pulling away?" he asked. "Are you afraid of me, Claudia?"

"Should I be?"

He laughed.

My throat felt tight. I tried taking a deep breath, but the air was too dry.

In a louder voice, Elliot said, "Very nice ring. Good job, bro."

"Thanks," Daniel said. "Claudia chose it."

Elliot dropped my hand. "Nice."

He left the room as quickly as he'd entered, headed toward the kitchen where Abigail had gone. A moment later, I heard the murmur of low voices coming from the kitchen. I strained to hear what they were saying, but it was impossible to make out.

EIGHT

ELLIOT

"I feel sorry for Claudia. I really do. This is not an easy family to break into. It's almost impossible to find your way into this family, ya know?"

I looked at Faith, sitting beside me in the gazebo, then turned my attention to the lake, spread out before me, a wide expanse of deep blue that made my eyes hurt, my heart too, it was so deceptively beautiful.

"We're close. Abnormally close. Some might call us pathologically close. Psychotically close.

"You don't run a winery that rakes in a healthy nine figures a year... gross, obviously... and not develop a tight relationship. It's either that or kill each other. It's a business that can have a dark side. Everyone knows that. Most businesses can. If you don't keep the family tight, and an even tighter rein on your employees and your business practices, things can go off the rails very quickly. You need good financial people you can trust with your life, sharp people who know what they're doing. The entire family needs to agree on hiring practices, and getting two people to agree is difficult, bringing four of us into agreement is not an easy accomplishment. We've worked relentlessly to build trust, to stay close. A family that's going to thrive in this business needs to trust each other to the core. They need to understand each other, and they need to be loyal.

"It's hard for newcomers, for friends and lovers to break in. Marrying into our family is a different kind of commitment than it is for most families.

"My former wife can attest to that. You probably have a few comments on that, right, Faith?"

She didn't answer me. She was a little tipsy. Drunk, to be honest. I knew that, and I knew she hadn't processed a word I'd said.

Even at four in the afternoon, she was out of it. There was plenty of very nice wine, obviously, as well as some excellent liquor in our house and Faith sometimes took too much advantage of that. I didn't mind. I wanted her to enjoy herself. She loved making fancy cocktails and taking pictures of herself beside our pool or one of the fountains, or anywhere around the estate, and posting it on social media.

My mother was fine with that, as long as she never mentioned the winery or gave telling details. Or mentioned my name. I'm not on social media. No one in our family is. Not that we're too good for it, but my mother always felt we shouldn't get involved with that. Someone takes care of social media for the winery, but we've always stayed away from the personal stuff.

"There are other things that have made our family closer than most. I should probably talk to you about that, Faith, but I'm not sure our relationship is there yet. It's for your own protection, honestly."

She didn't respond. Her sunglasses hid her eyes. Her head rested against the back of the chair. It had a relaxed, slightly untethered look to it, as if it might roll right off her neck. She was out. Passed out or simply dozing in the afternoon breeze, I wasn't sure.

There was no reason to stop talking. I sometimes did that.

People that are gone might hear you. No one knows for sure that they don't. So why not speak to them? That's why I came out here to talk to my father. With Faith so out of it, I could easily talk to him. Maybe he could hear me.

"You disappeared when we were so young, Dad. We had to stay close. Maybe we were close before that. I honestly can't remember. I can't remember anything at all before that day. It's like a blur of unfocused photographs that might be showing scenes from someone else's life. That's how I feel.

"Did this happen? Did that happen? You could probably tell me, but you won't, obviously.

"My life, the life I remember, started after you disappeared.

"And we were close. We kids had to stick together because Mom was shattered. We were the glue. We grabbed ahold of her and kept her from coming apart. She needed to touch us, needed to feel us in her arms and press her face against our heads, breathing in the life of us.

"For a few years, we were never apart. Our teachers came to the house. We ate every meal together. We took trips together—all over the world. The four of us became a single organism.

"Our thoughts became synchronous. We finished each other's sentences.

"There was some space when we got older, but we're still close."

I closed my eyes, not speaking for a few minutes.

"Does that annoy you, Faith? I'm not sure. You've said you love me. You've said you like to take things as they come. You like my family, and you love being here with me. Maybe you just like being here. Maybe it's only the luxury you love, since you grew up not having much.

"I don't know. It's working, for now. Right?"

She still didn't answer. I didn't wake her to ask.

I stared at the lake, narrowing my eyes to shut out everything but the water. I watched it ripple in the breeze, the sun shimmering across the surface. It looked so peaceful, so content. So blameless.

Faith said she feels safe here. The walls make her feel safe. I think our money makes her feel safe. But this is not a safe place. She probably needs to wake up, and if I were a better person, I would tell her that.

NINE

CLAUDIA

It felt like I might be doing serious damage to our relationship if I complained again to Daniel about his family but pretending everything was okay wasn't an option. His brother was giving me the creeps.

The way he'd held my hand and rubbed my finger made me want to cry. Looking at his eyes, boring into mine, I hadn't known if he was trying to make me cry, or if he actually thought I would be interested in him. Did he think I was going to leave the man I loved and run off to one of the many dark, hidden bedrooms with his brother? What was wrong with him? Maybe he was trying to make me look bad. Maybe he *wanted* me to complain to Daniel, and if Daniel stood up for me, Elliot would deny it and make me look like I was the one trying to start something with him.

The whole thing was making me queasy.

I'd imagined doing all kinds of fun things with his family, talking about their childhood, learning more about Daniel by hearing stories from the past. I'd pictured all of us laughing together, playing board games, tasting wine, splashing in the pool, watching his brother and sister tease him with family jokes.

Daniel and I had gone for a swim in the pool, but I couldn't talk to him there. Multiple rooms from their sprawling house had windows facing that luscious, grotto-like pool. I couldn't risk someone hearing me, even if I kept my voice low as we drifted into the deep water, looking up at the stars.

We dried off and sat at the smaller poolside table sipping sparkling water, the balmy night air comfortable on my damp skin, but still, I couldn't find the right words to tell him.

"You're quiet," he said.

I smiled.

"Are you feeling okay?"

"Just relaxing from the water and enjoying the night."

He placed his hand over mine and squeezed it gently. My first instinct was to yank it away, remembering how Elliot had grabbed my hand, making me feel as if I couldn't escape. I forced another smile and curled my fingers slightly.

"You're sure?"

I nodded.

Now, when I spoke to him in the privacy of our room, he would know I'd been lying. Would that make it worse?

Later as I lay beside him in bed, the lights of the chandelier dimmed to almost nothing, I told him what Elliot had done. Daniel's reaction was predictable.

"Please stop doing this," he said.

"I'm trying, but I don't understand your family."

"You imagined it."

I sat up. "Don't tell me I imagined something I clearly felt. He rubbed my finger. Like he was coming on to me."

"Then you imagined his intention. Maybe he had a twitch or something."

"Do you really believe that?"

"I told you—"

"This isn't normal. He asked me if I was afraid of him. Who does that?"

"Are you? Because you're acting like you are. You need to stop."

"Stop what? Your mother acted like I didn't belong here. Your brother is flirting with me as if I'm a random, unattached female. And even if I was, he's out of line. *Afraid* of him? What does that mean?"

"I just wish you'd stop acting like my family is out to get you. I know we're tight and not as welcoming as we could be, but you need to give everyone a chance. You're not even trying."

I didn't like it that he considered the *we* in this situation to be him and his family, not him and me. "I wish you'd stop gaslighting me."

He let out a sharp laugh. "That term is so over-used. I told you my family was close, and it might take a while to get to know them. All you've done is criticize them. I thought you'd make more of an effort. I thought you'd give them a chance. That's not gaslighting."

I closed my eyes. I felt an ache in my heart that was growing more painful every hour. He wasn't listening to me. It seemed as if he thought my experiences with his mother and his brother were all in my imagination.

"You're different when you're around them," he said.

"So are you."

With that, both of us drifted to sleep.

* * *

In the morning, again, he acted as if there wasn't any trouble between us. He seemed to have forgotten what I'd said about his brother, or maybe he was choosing to forget. He took my hand, kissed my ring, held out my hand and admired the diamond, throwing off glittering sparkles in the morning light.

"I need to get to work." A moment later he was out of bed and the shower was running.

He gave me the briefest kiss goodbye and said he would see me at dinner. It wasn't clear if he was disappearing into one of the rooms in the house that functioned as an office, or if he planned to take his car and was driving to the winemaking facility adjacent to their estate, or to the corporate office in San Francisco. I sent him a text, asking the question, but he replied that he was on a conference call and would touch base later. The response was longer than it would have taken to simply answer my question.

I went downstairs to the kitchen. Fresh fruit, breads, and pastries were arranged on platters. I filled a plate with a few things and carried it outside to a small table at the corner of the patio. I put my plate down and returned to the kitchen for a cup of coffee and a glass of orange juice. On the patio, I scrolled through my phone while I sipped juice, then put my phone aside to eat, letting my mind drift and relax into the steady, peaceful sound of the waterfalls splashing nearby.

"Your man left you on your own?"

I heard Elliot's voice behind me. I didn't want him to know he'd scared me. I wondered if he'd noticed my arm jerk slightly at the sound of him speaking when I'd thought I was alone. I picked up my coffee and took a sip, hoping I appeared calmer than I felt.

"He's working," I said, without turning to face him. "I thought you would be too."

He walked around the table and pulled out the chair across from me. Rather than sitting. He put his foot on the seat, propped his elbow on his thigh, and rested his chin in his upturned hand. "How's the food?"

"Very good. Thank you."

"Glad to hear it. That's quite a stone my brother bought you."

I took another sip of coffee.

He reached toward my hand.

I pulled it away from him.

He laughed. "I just wanted a closer look, but I don't need one. It's just like my former wife's ring. Almost identical."

"Your former wife?" Before he'd called her his ex. Did this mean she *was* dead? Referring to her as his former wife?

I didn't like it that my ring was similar to hers. Could it be a coincidence? There wasn't a huge variety in engagement rings. It could happen easily enough. But I still didn't like it. Maybe he was misremembering. But if she was dead, I liked it even less. It shouldn't matter, but it upset me. I couldn't help it. The idea of it made me feel sad and uncomfortable. "Is she—"

"There's my phone." He yanked his foot off the chair and pulled his phone out of his pocket. Lifting his hand in a half-hearted wave, he put the phone to his ear and disappeared behind me.

I hadn't heard the phone ring. I hadn't been aware of it vibrating. Had it? Or did he not want to tell me about his wife?

I looked at my ring, tilting my hand to catch the light, wondering if I'd made the wrong choice. I tried to remember if Daniel had nudged me toward this stone, this setting, or if it had been solely my decision.

TEN

CLAUDIA

Janice sent Greyson to find me in a small sitting room on the second floor where I was working on a jigsaw puzzle that had been laid out on a table, only part of the border begun.

"They're waiting for you in the dining room," he said.

I looked up at him.

"She doesn't like to be kept waiting."

"I didn't know it was dinnertime. No one told me."

He nodded.

It was already seven o'clock. I hadn't noticed how late it was, completely swept away by the challenge of putting together the puzzle pieces to form an image of the Eiffel Tower.

When I arrived in the dining room, Janice, Elliot, Faith, and Abigail were seated at the table. The elaborate chair that matched Janice's was still empty. Abigail was in the seat to Elliot's right, across from me. Daniel's chair to my right was empty.

I stood in the doorway. I couldn't imagine eating dinner with these people without Daniel beside me. I took a deep breath. I shouldn't be thinking of them that way. This was his family. Soon to be my family. Calling them *these people*, even in my thoughts, was not helpful.

Daniel had said I wasn't trying hard enough. What about them? Was I so different from them, such an outsider, all they wanted to do was make me squirm? Maybe they thought I wasn't good enough for him, and if they made that fact obvious to me, I would remove my diamond ring and walk out the door. But every time I looked at those gates, I wondered if that was even possible. I would have to call Greyson to open the gates for me.

"Where's Daniel?" I asked.

"He'll be here soon," Janice said.

"Is he still working?"

"I said, he'll be here soon."

"I know. I just wondered—"

"Will you please take your seat? You're making us all feel a little anxious, standing in the doorway watching us." Janice gave me a pleading smile.

"We're starting without him?"

"It's dinnertime," Elliot said. "You need to chill. You're a grown woman. I think you'll be okay eating dinner without Daniel holding your hand. You managed breakfast on your own."

"I just..." I felt my throat close up and tears fill my eyes, turning their faces into blurs. Why did it feel as if they were always attacking me? I felt like I couldn't do anything right. I only wanted to know where Daniel was, but arguing with them was holding up the meal. It was going to turn them against me even more, and it wasn't going to bring Daniel any faster, wherever he was. I stepped into the room and took my seat.

As Greyson placed small salads in front of us, Elliot turned to his mother. "Did you see the fabulous ring Daniel bought for his bride?"

"Mm?" Janice pulled the fork out of her mouth and chewed carefully.

"Show her," Elliot demanded.

I held out my hand.

Janice nodded her head once, then returned to her salad. "It's almost identical to Tina's."

"Let me see," Abigail said.

I didn't want to hear any more about it. Abigail had already seen my ring. I wanted to eat my salad. I wanted Daniel beside me. I held my hand over my salad, angling it slightly in her direction.

"I can't see," Abigail said.

I moved my hand.

She stood and reached across the table, grabbing my fingertips and pulling my hand toward the center of the table, crushing my ribs against the edge as she did so.

"Oh. That's almost... you're right, Elliot. I feel like I'm looking at Tina's hand."

She let go of my fingers quickly, as if they'd scorched her hand. She gave me a pitying smile. "I'm sorry, Claudia. How on earth did you make a mistake like that?"

"I didn't make a mistake. I love this ring. Daniel and I picked it out together."

"Oh. Did you?" She settled back in her chair. She picked up her wineglass and took a sip, gazing at me over the top.

"I love it," I said.

Faith glanced at me, letting her eyes meet mine, holding my gaze for several seconds. She swayed her head slightly, letting a faint smile play across her lips.

"That's all that matters." Abigail took another sip of wine.

"I wonder if it was Daniel's subconscious," Elliot said. "Thinking about Tina."

"Could be," Abigail said.

I glanced at Faith again. She was sipping her wine. She held the glass up and looked through the liquid, her eyes slightly unfocused at first, then meeting mine.

"You could exchange it," Abigail said.

I began eating my salad faster, shoveling greens into my mouth.

"Hey. Sorry I'm late."

I turned at the sound of Daniel's voice. He kissed the top of my head and pulled out the chair beside me.

"How was the meeting with Harrington?" Janice asked.

"Excellent."

Before I could say anything to him, before Abigail or Elliot could make any more disturbing comments about my ring that, until that morning, I'd loved with all my heart, Daniel launched into a long description of his meeting, telling his mother and siblings about the other participants, describing their demeanor and their positions on topics I knew nothing about. He went on to repeat almost the entire content of the meeting in such detail I was awed by his recall of so many figures and regulations.

Ten minutes into his report, I tuned him out.

While he talked, Greyson removed our salad plates, and refilled our wine and water glasses. I noticed he poured more wine into my glass and Faith's compared to the others'. He served the main course—chicken breasts in a light cream sauce with roasted broccoli.

When the meal was over, Faith left the table without saying anything, taking her wineglass with her. The family was still talking about Daniel's meeting. I followed Faith's lead and excused myself. No one seemed to hear me, so I left the room.

I wandered into the living room, expecting to see Faith, but she was gone. I sat at the grand piano, lifted the cover off the keys, and brushed my fingers across them. As a child, I'd wanted to learn to play the piano but never had a chance. I wondered if anyone in Daniel's family played. He'd never mentioned playing it, and in the few days I'd been there, I hadn't heard

WELCOME TO THE FAMILY   51

anyone use it. Letting such a beautiful instrument sit there unused, serving only as a piece of art, made me sad. But it was possible I was reading it wrong. I hadn't been there long enough to know. I replaced the cover over the keys.

I needed to try harder. Despite their joint attack on my ring, I needed to try harder. Maybe it hadn't been an attack at all. Maybe my ring was identical to the mysterious Tina's, wherever she was. Maybe I didn't understand a family like this. I still had plenty of time to turn things around. It had only been a few days.

I loved Daniel with all my heart. That was one thing I was absolutely certain about. Until I'd walked into this house, I'd believed we were soulmates, destined to be together. We saw the world the same way. We liked the same movies and music, we enjoyed the same activities. He made me laugh and I did the same for him. From the moment I met him, I'd felt as if I could tell him anything. Almost anything. And eventually, I would tell him all my secrets.

I wasn't sure why that had changed inside this house. I was going to change it back.

I slid off the piano bench and walked back toward the dining room. It was silent. Had they all left? Just as I was about to step around the corner to check, I heard Janice speaking in a low voice.

"She's going to poison you against us. Trust me. That girl is a viper."

ELEVEN
CLAUDIA

I backed away from the doorway, walked quickly through the living room, and into the entryway before Janice had the chance to accuse me of being an eavesdropper along with a viper. Which was worse? I was pretty sure viper was worse. I ran up the stairs. I went into our room and grabbed my phone, then continued down the hall to the tiny sitting room where I'd worked on the puzzle. The room overlooked the secluded section of the patio where I'd eaten breakfast that morning, a breakfast that now seemed like it had been days ago. I closed the door and leaned against it, slowing my breath.

Settling into a huge armchair that seemed to swallow me, as surely as this family was swallowing me, I closed my eyes for a moment. I didn't want to see Daniel. I needed to think. I probably didn't need to worry about seeing him. I was almost certain he was the person Janice had been talking to when she called me a viper.

What did that mean? Did she think I was planning to marry my way into their family business to destroy it?

The Kellers were the vipers. I absolutely felt like I was living in a pit of snakes, despite the opulent furniture and pools of water, the lush gardens and the three-story chateau. Despite the expensive cars and jewelry and clothes.

If she had been talking to Daniel, why hadn't he defended me? Was he that cowed by her? I knew he loved me. Even though he'd tried to gaslight me, even though he tried to explain away the things I'd experienced with his mother and Elliot, I had no doubt that he loved me. I got it that his family was private and strange and difficult to connect with.

I was not going to let this intimidate me.

Janice was scared. Maybe something horrible had happened with Tina and she'd developed a deep mistrust in the women her sons chose to marry. It could be anything. Maybe she'd had some other devastating experience in her life. I knew absolutely nothing about her, except that she was a successful, powerful businesswoman, she'd lost her husband when she was young, and she'd raised three children by herself.

Still, the way she was treating me, no matter what her life had been like, no matter how she'd had to fight to make her way to the top in a world most likely dominated by men, I didn't deserve this. I was marrying her son. She should be treating me with love and kindness and respect. They should be gushing over my ring, not making me feel like it was something that had been plucked out of a dead woman's coffin, if that's what it was.

No one would even say. But Elliot seemed to be hinting around that fact.

I pulled my knees up to my chest, hugging them close. I wasn't going to tell Daniel I'd been called a viper. Of course, if he was the one she'd been speaking to, he already knew that. If he did, he probably wouldn't tell me. He wouldn't want me to start criticizing them again. I was going to double down on my effort to win their love. I shouldn't have to win it. I should have it given to me, but it was clearly not going to happen that way.

I picked up my phone and opened my email.

I tapped my sister's address and began tapping out my

thoughts to her, feeling as if she would be able to read them a few minutes from now. She would write back and make me feel better. Calmer. Safer.

> My future mother-in-law is a scary woman. I know I shouldn't think of her that way, but every time she looks at me, I feel like she might want to kill me. I know I'm imagining it, but I feel like she thinks I'm taking Daniel away from her. Or something. I don't know what it is. She called me a viper!

I put the snake emoji and continued tapping out my thoughts as fast as I could, telling her everything else that had happened since I'd arrived. By the time she saw it, all of this would be over. I might be closer to my future mother-in-law than I'd been to my own mother, although that wasn't saying much. It wasn't saying anything at all, really.

I might be feeling sisterly toward Abigail. Maybe she would be joining my own sister as one of my attendants in my wedding. Anything was possible.

I told her she should be proud of me because I wasn't running and hiding, or losing my grip like I often did when I was confronted with someone attacking me.

She knew that about me. But she was also the one person who had helped me see those weren't good ways to cope. And most of the time, some of the time, I listened to her.

When I was finished, the email was seven long paragraphs. I hit send. I smiled, picturing her connecting back to the world after she finished her trek and finding an inbox filled with messages that would tell the story of my life since she'd left.

I shoved my phone into my pocket, pushed myself out of the comfy chair, and went to the door. I opened it and looked out into the deserted hallway. Our bedroom door was closed. I wondered if Daniel was inside. Before I looked for him, I wanted a cup of tea. I needed to do something for myself. I was tired of Greyson bringing me food and coffee refills, snacks and bottles of water. I hadn't opened the refrigerator or folded a towel myself in three days.

I went down the stairs, thinking I might find some of the family members in the living room or see them through the back doors, gathered on the patio. The place was deserted. The soft music that often played through the recessed speakers in all the rooms had been silenced.

The kitchen was mostly dark, with two lights over the island on the lowest setting spreading a soft glow across the room, reflecting off the stainless-steel appliances. I took the kettle out of its cubby and filled it with water. I began opening cabinets, looking for tea. I found one cabinet with assorted loose teas and a fancy pot and cups. All I wanted was a bag for a quick dip into steaming water. I finally found some in a drawer.

When the water was hot, I dropped the bag into the mug, poured the water over it, and waited for the tea to steep. As I stood in the thick silence, I heard footsteps in the living room.

"I'm trying to talk to you," Elliot said.

"The conversation is over," Janice said.

"Wait," Elliot said. "I can't go through this again."

Janice didn't respond.

"You need to do something," Elliot said.

There was another moment of silence.

"There's nothing to be done," Janice said. "I told you, I have it under control."

"You don't. You don't have anything under control," he said.

I heard footsteps again, followed by silence.

Twice in the space of less than two hours I'd heard conversations I wasn't meant to. I supposed it was because they weren't used to visitors in their home. Another aspect of their tightly connected family. Although Faith lived in the house and it seemed as if she'd been there for a while.

I felt like I was prying into their lives. I didn't mean to be listening, but they seemed to assume no one was around. Maybe they were used to Faith staying in her room, or lounging by the pool, or walking out to the lake. I'd been told she spent a lot of time out there, although I hadn't seen it myself.

The property was huge. It boggled my mind that there was an entire lake that I couldn't see from the gardens and pool area, blocked by a few other buildings that were shrouded by so many lush plants I couldn't make out much of their features either.

But the size of their property wasn't the main thing on my mind. I wanted to know what Janice had under control. Was it me?

TWELVE

CLAUDIA

I carried my cup of tea downstairs and out to the patio. I had no idea what had happened to Daniel. I supposed he might be in the bedroom, waiting for me. But he hadn't come looking for me, and he hadn't texted. Maybe he was working. There might be details from that complicated meeting he was still sorting out.

It felt strange to be wandering around his house without him, but I'd been doing it all day and was getting used to it. I sat on one of the lounge chairs beside the pool, stretching out my legs, crossing my ankles, and taking a sip of tea. It had cooled to the perfect temperature.

I heard the door open and turned to see Elliot step outside. He stood there for a moment, staring at the swimming pool. Then, he appeared to be looking directly at me, but he didn't acknowledge my presence. It was impossible to believe he couldn't see me. The pool was well lit and there were small lights around the garden and fairy lights strung overhead.

After a few minutes, he walked around the edge, moving slowly, still not acknowledging me. He stopped a few feet away, grabbed a lounge chair, and dragged it close to mine. The scrape of iron on the concrete sent chills down my arms and legs.

"You look lonely," he said.

"I'm not."

"I'm good at reading women, and I say you are."

"You're reading it wrong."

"Am I?" He gave me a sad smile, as if he wanted to suggest that I was lying, and I could trust him with my secrets.

"You are." I took a sip of tea.

"If I were my brother, I wouldn't leave my beautiful fiancée sitting alone in the dark."

His comment frightened me. What was he trying to say? That I wasn't safe out here alone with him? I turned my head slightly, watching the waterfall.

"Am I making you nervous?"

"No." It was a lie, but I thought my voice sounded confident.

"Are you still upset about the ring?"

"I was never upset about the ring."

"No girl wants her ring to be a replica of someone else's. Especially her future brother-in-law's ex."

I took a sip of tea and uncrossed my ankles, shifting in the chair so I was sitting straighter, and turned to face him. "How long has it been since you split up, if you don't mind me asking?" To soften my tone, I added, "I hope it was amicable."

"It was abrupt." He laughed softly. "We never spoke again."

Why was he laughing? Who laughed over a breakup? And he hadn't said how long. Did his laugh, and never speaking again suggest that it wasn't amicable? I supposed it did.

"I probably shouldn't call her my ex."

"Isn't this cozy!" Janice's voice was shrill and loud as she walked up behind us.

I startled, causing tea to slosh in my mug, some of it splashing onto the back of my hand. I wiped it on my leg.

Why were they always sneaking up behind me, making me jump out of my skin? How was I going to make this work if every time I vowed to win them over, they did something creepy or unsettling or slightly scary?

"How are you doing, Claudia? Can I get you anything to eat?" Janice's voice remained shrill. "Something to drink? Oh, I see you have something. Tea? Did Elliot make you tea? He's quite the connoisseur with tea. But maybe you'd like a glass of our reserve wine?"

"I'm fine, thank you."

"May I join you? We've hardly had a chance to get to know each other, have we?" She put her hand on my shoulder and squeezed gently.

I wanted to tell her she'd interrupted, ask her to leave. I wanted to know whether Elliot's wife was alive or dead. Why wouldn't anyone come right out and *say*?

"What are you and Elliot talking about? You looked so grim. You should be happy and enjoying life. All the good things that are about to happen to you," Janice said.

I couldn't tell her what we'd been talking about. She was the cheerful, friendly Janice. Telling her might flip the switch back to the woman who thought I was a viper trying to poison her son. And possibly worm my way into her business. Although how she thought I might do that was impossible to figure out. Why was she suddenly so nice to me? Inside, was the woman who called me a snake. What was going on with her?

All of them, even Daniel sometimes, were making me feel as if I was losing my mind. Was this some kind of game they were playing? Did they want to find out whether I would fight back, or how much I would put up with? Were they all just moody beyond anything I'd ever experienced? Or was it something worse that I didn't even understand?

Daniel acted as if there was nothing unusual about their behavior.

"Cheer up," Janice said. "Don't look so worried. You're safe here with us. Our home is the safest place imaginable. No one can get inside these walls unless we invite them." She smiled, and in the watery light from the pool, washing across her thickly made-up skin, turning it ultra pale, she looked like a vampire.

THIRTEEN
CLAUDIA

The wavering light on the surface of the water seemed to grow more intense as Janice talked. She turned her attention to Elliot, and they began discussing staffing requirements at the winery. They talked about people I didn't know as if I'd met them and was thoroughly familiar with their work history. They discussed scheduling and management issues. As I had at dinner, I tuned them out after a few minutes. I watched the waterfalls and let the uneasy light wash over my eyes until I felt like my entire brain was immersed in a pool of dark liquid.

I wanted to leave, but at some point during the conversation, Janice had put her hand on my forearm. Now, she'd wrapped her fingers around it, holding me tightly as if she wanted to keep me in the chair until they were finished. Excusing myself, peeling her fingers off my arm, felt like a disruption that would anger her. I was essentially handcuffed to the chair, a captive to their conversation.

Where was Daniel? I longed for my phone to vibrate with a message, giving me an excuse to get free from her grip.

Finally, as my eyes began to drift closed, and my head

bobbed forward a few times, jerking back suddenly as I tried to stay awake, Janice let go of my arm.

"We're keeping you up, aren't we? The poor thing is tired." She patted my arm.

"She wants her lover," Elliot said.

"Her beauty sleep," Janice said.

It felt as if insects were crawling across my skin as I listened to their bizarre comments. I wondered if Janice could feel the goosebumps running across my arm. "I am tired," I said.

"I'll take care of your mug. You get yourself up to bed." Janice stood and picked up my mug.

I pushed myself out of the lounge chair, swaying slightly from the sudden movement after sitting for what now seemed like hours, but had surely been less than two.

When I opened our bedroom door, the lights were out. I moved the door wider so light from the hallway could enter the room. Daniel was in bed, sleeping. I supposed it was fair—he'd described a long and very intense meeting. Still, I felt a pinch of hurt that he'd never looked for me, hadn't wanted to go to bed together, hadn't cared about saying goodnight. That he'd left me to fend for myself with them.

I pressed the switch for the lamp on my side of the bed, closed the door, and made my way to the bathroom. When I slid in beside Daniel a few minutes later, he didn't move. His breathing remained steady. I kissed his lips. He didn't move. I lay on my back beside him, staring into the darkness, my eyes seeing undulating water for a long time.

I was woken while it was still dark by the alarm on Daniel's phone trilling.

He reached over, turned it off, and was out of bed before I could adjust myself to what was happening. "What time is it?"

"Shh. Go back to sleep," he said. "I have another all-day meeting."

"What time is it?"

"Five."

I sat up.

He came around the bed and kissed me gently. "Go back to sleep."

"I've hardly seen you."

"Tonight. I promise."

"But—"

"Tonight." He went into the bathroom.

I sat up, turned on the bedside lamp, and arranged the pillows behind me. I scrolled through email and social media while I waited for him to shower and dress. When he returned to the bedroom, I dropped my phone on the bed.

"Did Elliot's wife die?"

He stared at me as if my face had turned into a wavering mirage from the pool lights.

"Why would you ask a question like that?"

"It's a simple yes or no question."

"It has nothing to do with you."

"Why can't you just answer me? It's a simple question. What's the big secret?"

"I don't understand why you're so interested in something that's in the past and has no relationship to you at all." He walked to the nightstand and picked up his phone.

"Because he keeps saying strange things about her that make it sound like she might be dead. And I don't understand why he sometimes makes it sound like they're divorced and other times, he makes it sound like she's dead. It's really weird. And it's kind of—"

"Why are you doing this? I don't understand *you*."

"I asked a simple question about your brother's wife and

you're acting like I'm asking about his sex life. Is she dead or not?"

"It's a painful situation, okay? And I don't understand why you want to stir it up. I need to get going. I set the alarm because I have to be at this meeting at seven, and if I don't leave right now, I'll be late." He shoved his phone into his pocket and almost lunged at the door, flinging it open as if he couldn't wait to get out of the room.

I fell back onto the pillows and closed my eyes. I pressed my fingers gently against my eyelids. Why wouldn't he tell me if Elliot's wife was dead? It shouldn't be a secret. Why wouldn't Elliot himself tell me?

If it was so *painful*, I would be empathetic. I didn't need to know the details. I just wanted to know if the woman was dead. It wouldn't have been that important if they hadn't *made* it so important, if they hadn't tried to hide it from me.

Now, I wanted to know why they were hiding it.

FOURTEEN
CLAUDIA

After two cups of coffee, two slices of toast, and a bowl of strawberries, I returned to our bedroom. I curled up on the window seat in the sitting room and propped my phone on my knees. I opened a browser and entered *Tina and Elliot Keller* in the search bar.

The first hit, as I'd expected, was a marriage announcement. It was longer than the little snippets that most people have, but not a half-page spread like some families with the position and resources of the Kellers might typically get.

The announcement said Tina Curran and Elliot Keller had been married at the Keller family home two years earlier. It was a small gathering. Tina's parents were both deceased and there was no mention of any siblings. Abigail Keller had been her maid of honor and Daniel Keller was his best man. The couple had honeymooned for three weeks in Italy. There was no mention of her career and only a brief mention of the family being prominent in the Napa community. The winery wasn't named.

I clicked some of the other links, but the first few were all repeats of the wedding announcement.

As I scrolled through other hits, clicking links that looked promising, I was more disappointed each time. Most of them were about Elliot and the winery.

I changed the search terms to focus on divorce but found nothing. I changed them again to *Tina Curran death* and also came up with nothing. I searched for an obituary but none of them were the Tina Curran who had been married to Elliot. After exhausting the search engine, I turned to social media.

There were no profiles for Tina Keller. I tried Tina Curran and found a single Instagram account. The final post had been made ten months ago. It was a picture of a palm tree in front of a white wall that I was fairly certain was the inside the Keller's estate. The caption read: *Going off-grid for a while. Time to chill.*

The post had twenty-seven likes and four comments, all of them telling her to enjoy. There was nothing personal enough to give me insight into their relationship or whether they knew anything about her desire to go off-grid. I wondered what that really meant. Usually, people who went *off-grid* were completely disconnecting from society—giving up credit cards and often even a hookup to the electric company, growing their own produce and raising chickens. I was certain she only meant she wasn't using social media. It seemed a little over-the-top.

I looked out the window at the garden stretched out below me. Abigail was sitting on a bench. She was sipping from a water canister, gazing up at the branches of the palm tree above her. Or maybe, gazing up at my window. It was difficult to tell.

I tucked my phone into my pocket and hurried out of the room.

She was still in the same place when I got outside, still looking up.

"Hi," I said. "Mind if I sit here with you?"

She kept her head tipped back. "It's fine."

I settled on the bench.

She lowered her head and took a sip of water.

"I was wondering if you could answer a question," I asked.

"Oh? What's that?"

"Is Elliot's former wife dead?"

She tipped her head back again, which made her voice sound strained. "Why do you care so much?"

It was an odd way of phrasing it. Surely Daniel hadn't told her.

"I don't care so much." The minute I spoke the words, I regretted the way I'd said it. I sounded so cold. "I mean, I'm not prying. It just seems like something you'd mention, and people seem to be making a secret out of it."

"People?"

I sighed. Why wouldn't anyone tell me? Why was it such a secret? "Elliot talked about her as if they were divorced, but then he spoke about her as if she'd died. When I tried to ask, he changed the subject." It wasn't exactly the truth, but close enough. Hopefully they weren't comparing notes, although thinking about what she'd just said, maybe they were.

"We don't talk about her. For Elliot's sake. To spare his feelings." She stood. "You understand. It's not something he wants to think about all the time."

"He mentions her a lot."

"To spare his feelings, we don't mention her. What he chooses to talk about is up to him. I'm sure you understand that." She dragged her fingers through her hair, which was loose around her shoulders, down to the center of her back.

"I do understand. But—"

"If you know what's good for you, don't be so curious."

FIFTEEN

CLAUDIA

Daniel arrived home at six. I'd finished my swim just a few minutes before.

My swim had been both as pleasant and as unpleasant as I'd expected. The water was a perfect temperature, and the size of the pool made it feel like I was in a natural body of water, swimming without boundaries, which was an incredible feeling after being vaguely aware every so often over the past few days of the locked gates that I had no idea how to open. At the same time, I had to force myself to focus on the feel of the water, the movement of my arms and legs, and the rhythm of my breaths to keep from obsessing over the idea that one, or more than one of them, were surely watching me from inside the house.

Still, I was glad I'd done it. The feel-good part outweighed the swimming in a glass tank sensation.

I was wearing cut-off jeans and a tank top, painting my toenails pink when Daniel came into our room. He sat beside me and held out his hand. "Give me the brush. Let me do that."

I laughed. "Really? You won't make a mess?"

"I'll be very careful."

He took the brush, dipped it in the bottle, and ran a stroke of color over the middle toenail of my right foot. The pleasure of watching him do something so gentle made me feel as if my heart was turning to liquid, running through my body.

He painted the next toenail, then handed the brush back to me. "We're having a formal dinner tonight. Do you have any long dresses with you?"

"No."

"Okay." He stood. "I'll get you something." He disappeared out the door as quickly as he'd entered.

Fifteen minutes later he was back with three ankle-length dresses—two black and one burgundy.

"What's the occasion?" I asked.

"No occasion. My mom likes to do this sometimes."

"Oh." I'd thought maybe they were celebrating our engagement. But pointing that out to Daniel would begin another argument about his family. At the same time, it wasn't a good habit to start keeping all these things to myself. Wasn't that the road to trouble in a marriage? But talking about it only alienated him. I loved him so much. I wanted the man I'd known and fallen in love with. The man who had thrilled me to my core when he asked me to marry him because I knew, I absolutely knew we belonged together.

Now, I felt as if I was being asked to marry his entire family. It was complicated and messy and too much work. I didn't like how tangled up with them he was. I couldn't figure out if this was a huge red flag, or if things would settle out once the five weeks were over and we were back on our own. I didn't have a clear picture of how often his work required him to actually be in the Napa Valley. I was starting to realize, it might be all the time. All those months in Seattle might have been an unusual situation.

Why did he even have an apartment in Seattle? He'd never said, and I'd never asked because he'd made it seem like part of his lifestyle. In the time I'd known him, he'd flown down to

Napa every other week or so, for a day or two at a time. That seemed manageable. But I was starting to wonder if that wasn't an accurate picture of his life.

"What's wrong?" Daniel asked.

"Nothing."

"You looked like you were going to say something."

I shook my head. "Let me try on the dresses." I took the burgundy one first. It fit perfectly. It was cut low in the front, lower than I was used to, and open to my waist in the back. "Do you think it's too—"

"No." Daniel smiled. "You look awesome. Wear that one."

"I only have black shoes."

"No one will be looking at your shoes."

"But will your mother think—"

"These were her dresses. When she was younger. She'll be thrilled to see you wearing it."

I had a terrible feeling I was stepping into a hornet's nest. There were so many ways this could go badly for me.

When I walked out of the bathroom after doing my hair and makeup, and secretly admiring myself in the full-length mirror, I stopped, taking a quick, sharp breath. Daniel stood near the window wearing a tuxedo. He looked absolutely gorgeous. Without the aid of any hair product or the recent use of a razor, using only the mirror over the dresser, he'd made himself look like he was ready to walk along the red carpet at a televised awards ceremony.

"You look fabulous," I said.

"Not as fabulous as you." He walked toward me and gave me a long, lingering kiss. We stepped away from each other, smiling. Both of our smiles said we wanted to remove our fancy clothes and fall into bed.

Instead, he took my hand, and we went downstairs.

Dinner was a five-course meal that began with an appetizer of melt-in-your-mouth escargot in garlic butter.

Janice said nothing about my dress. She gave me a cool look, kissed both my cheeks as if she were European royalty, held up my hand to study my ring, then dropped it, also without a comment. She gushed over Daniel's stunning good looks and then announced to no one in particular that she had the most handsome sons on the planet. I couldn't argue with her.

"I had to look good for my fiancée." Daniel squeezed my hand. "I knew she was beautiful, but, wow! So many of our dates were outdoors. I loved it—exploring Washington state, being alone with her in such spectacular places. But now I see I missed out on another side of her." He lifted my hand to his lips and brushed them across my knuckles.

I felt my neck grow warm, but I didn't mind. It felt good to hear him talk about us in front of his family. I turned my attention to Faith. She wore a long navy-blue dress, as dangerously low-cut as mine. I wondered if it also belonged to Janice. And then I wondered if this was some kind of game she was playing with us—her future daughters-in-law. Was Faith that? I didn't know. Along with Elliot's ex, or possibly dead wife, no one had mentioned it.

A few minutes after we were seated, nibbling on our escargot, Abigail entered the room. Janice stood, again as if this was some sort of royal family.

"Hi, sweetheart." Janice walked around the table, took her daughter's hand, and kissed her cheek. "You look absolutely beautiful. As always." She gave her a warm smile, then stepped back to admire Abigail's long white dress featuring a choker collar studded with clear stones I assumed were rhinestones, but maybe they were diamonds. Anything was possible at this point.

We returned to our appetizers, enjoying the food in silence. Soft music played through the speakers, but the volume was so low, it was hard to make out what was playing. It was more of an annoying hum than it was actual background music to ease the uncomfortable silence.

"That dress was made for you, Claudia." Elliot said.

I ached for Daniel to tell him to stop, but he remained silent. Saying thank you felt as if it might open a door to something I didn't want to hear. All Elliott could see of the dress at this point were the strips of fabric that covered my breasts, leaving quite a lot exposed. I'd been so wowed by how I looked, I'd ignored my instinct. I'd felt in my gut this was coming, and I'd ignored it. I hadn't even tried on the other dresses, although maybe they would have been the same, judging by the dress Faith was wearing.

A sharp pain in my stomach was telling me that Janice had absolutely set us up to feel uncomfortable, if nothing else. I never wore clothes that exposed this much skin unless I was in a bathing suit. When I was standing up, it hadn't been as obvious, with all the fabric of the long skirt drawing attention away from the effect.

"Have I embarrassed you?" Elliot asked.

"No."

"I expected you to thank me. Usually, women bask in a man's attention and admiration."

I glanced at Daniel. He was sipping his wine. He had a relaxed, pleasant expression on his face. Could he not hear this? What was he thinking? I wanted to give him a sharp kick with the heel of my shoe, but the way we were seated made that impossible.

"I *am* making you uncomfortable," Elliott said. "And I don't think your fiancé is coming to your rescue. He's not a rescuing kind of guy, are you, bro?"

Daniel scowled but said nothing.

"Well, you look hot," Elliot said. "That's all I'm trying to say."

I looked at Faith. She gave me a sympathetic smile, then

picked up her wineglass. Was everyone unable to hear what he was saying? Was I somehow misinterpreting him? His words were plain. His intention was clear. What he was saying was crude and I hated it, but I had no idea what to say to make it stop without making them all turn on me, accusing me of rudeness, or something worse. I was terrified that anything I said would bring Janice's wrath raining down on me.

"I could sit across from you all night and not eat a bite of this scrumptious meal, but feel absolutely satisfied," Elliot said.

"Please stop," I said.

He laughed.

My eyes burned with tears. This was so unfair. I tried so hard to be what people wanted and it was never enough. They always wanted something I couldn't quite figure out. Why did it always have to be so hard? The tears grew thicker, making it hard to see. I willed them not to trickle down my cheeks.

Elliot didn't say any more. But he stared at me blatantly throughout the rest of the meal. I choked down my food, feeling as if it might come spilling back out at any minute. With every bite, I thought about leaving the table. I wanted to cry. I wanted to beg Daniel to get me out of there. But he ate and smiled and looked as if he were having the time of his life.

Later, in our room, Daniel tried to kiss me the moment the door was closed. I pushed him away.

"What the hell was that with your brother? Why didn't you say anything?"

"What?"

"The things he was saying to me! About my dress, telling me I looked hot, trying to make me uncomfortable. It was awful. And everyone just sat there like they couldn't even hear him. Especially you."

"Why do you keep doing this? Are you into him? Is that it?"

He looked genuinely hurt, and slightly concerned. As if he hadn't heard the things Elliot had said.

"Did you *hear* him?"

"Hear what?"

"He might as well have asked me to take my top off."

"God, Claudia. What are you doing? You're making me feel terrible. What's been going on here when I've been gone?"

"Nothing! I'm not interested in your brother. But he makes all these flirty innuendos and you just sit there like it's okay."

"I admit, I'm used to tuning him out. But if you think he's flirting, or whatever, it takes two people to flirt."

"I didn't do a fucking thing!"

"Shh. Lower your voice. Don't talk like that."

"At least you can hear what's being said now."

"What's that supposed to mean?"

"You let him say those things to me and you didn't defend me."

"I didn't know you needed a defender. And I don't know what things you're talking about. He said you looked great in the dress. And you do."

"He's either coming on to me, or trying to embarrass me, to make me do something that will upset your mother. Whatever it is, I don't want to be around him."

"He's my brother. You have to take him as he is. He's had a tough time of it." He shrugged.

"I have to take him as he is?"

"Do you love me or not?"

"Of course I love you. I adore you." *Of course* I loved him. But I also felt betrayed. And abandoned. I felt like he was asking too much. Was I supposed to let his brother degrade me and say nothing? Was I supposed to let his whole family do whatever this was? I didn't even have a word for it.

"I want it to stop," I said.

"Then tell him that."

"I did."

"Yes. And whatever it was that upset you so much, he stopped."

"But he kept staring at me."

He looked at me as if I were a child, crying hysterically because I'd been given a yellow cup instead of a red one.

He came toward me and put his arms around me. I stiffened, but he tightened his grip, resting his head on top of mine. "I love you so much. My brother is messed up, okay? He had a really bad time when our father died. I'm not sure he completely recovered from that. And then his wife..."

He was quiet.

"What about his wife?"

"Let's think about us, not Elliott," he said. "We're going to make this work."

His words made me shiver.

Make it work?

Did he mean my relationship with his family? Or did he mean us?

SIXTEEN

CLAUDIA

When I woke in the morning, Daniel was sitting up in bed beside me, gazing down at my face, his eyes damp with emotion.

We'd made love after our disagreement last night, and he'd been more tender than ever before. Had he thought that would fix things? Honestly, it had, for a few minutes. But all the feelings of betrayal returned the moment he moved onto his other side, and I heard his breathing shift to something deeper.

I saw myself again, sitting there like a pig on a spit, Elliot staring at me with drool on his lips while Daniel sat beside me, smiling and enjoying his meal, ignoring my humiliation. I'd lain there for an hour or more, feeling the heat on my skin, wishing Daniel would wake and tell me how terribly sorry he was, that he would find a way to explain why he'd behaved as he had.

Now, he took my hand and pressed it to his chest. "I'm sorry," he whispered. "I'm so sorry. I didn't know what to say. I shouldn't have acted like it was nothing. It... well, there's no excuse."

"I don't understand why you just sat there and let him talk to me like that. And I don't understand why he's doing this to me." I wanted to say more. I wanted to tell him I found it almost frightening. But he was apologizing. I should appreciate that and not start complaining. It wouldn't help anything.

"Elliot's in a bad place. And when someone's been traumatized, it comes out in strange ways, you know?"

"Yes, I know. But if he's feeling so awful, why is he already with Faith? And is Tina—"

"It's more than that."

It sounded like he was making excuses. What did those crude comments have to do with trauma, anyway? And how did they make Faith feel? Although she hadn't seemed to notice either. And was his former wife dead, or not?!

"Why is everyone so secretive about—?"

"Elliot is so sensitive."

I laughed.

Daniel looked hurt.

Were we talking about the same person? Or was he remembering someone who had existed in the past and he didn't recognize the person Elliot had turned into? It felt like nothing but an excuse for despicable behavior. But I couldn't say that. He was being so nice, so sweet, trying to apologize, to explain.

"When my father died, my mother didn't want us to wallow. She said it was really important that we not give in to our feelings and constantly talk about how sad we were and how awful it was."

"You need to talk about your feelings."

"People over-indulge their feelings."

"Okay."

He leaned over and kissed me. "Anyway. I'm sorry I didn't tell him to stop. He's always acted out. He likes to make people squirm, I guess."

"That's perverted."

"He doesn't mean to be a creep. He... I can't explain it. I'll ask him to stop." He kissed me again and scrambled out of bed.

"But I still don't understand about his wife. Is she dead? Or what—"

"Gotta shower." The bathroom door closed so hard, I almost wondered if he'd slammed it deliberately.

I fell back on the pillows and closed my eyes. I didn't want him to *ask* Elliot to stop. I wanted Daniel to *tell* him to stop. I also wanted Elliot to know he should stop. To not even think that way. But apparently that was too much to ask.

I drifted back to sleep. When I woke, Daniel was gone—another early meeting at a winery north of Calistoga.

I started another email to my sister.

It's scaring me how Elliot keeps looking at me, and talking to me like he wants to fuck me or something. I'm afraid to be alone, and I'm afraid something will happen that will make Daniel angry with me. Or Janice.

And Daniel doesn't even notice. I don't know what's going on. It's so confusing, I feel like crying every day. I wish I wasn't telling you this, because I know you'll love Daniel. You will. It's just hard right now. I hope you get that.

I told her all the other details of the awful evening. I imagined her sitting in my chair, listening to Elliot's words. Of course, she wouldn't have sat there taking it.

My sister would have stood up and tossed her wine in his face. Although, she doesn't drink alcohol, so she would have tossed her water. Or maybe she would have taken her escargot fork, leaned across the table, letting him see even more of her body, and stabbed his cheek with the tines. That's my sister. She doesn't take anything from anyone. And she would not have allowed her fiancé to apologize so quickly. She probably wouldn't have forgiven as quickly.

But she didn't know Daniel like I did.

The moment I met him, I knew he was a good man, an

amazing man. And even though I'd felt slightly gaslit since I'd arrived at his mother's home, even though it felt as if he took his family's side over mine, I knew he was crazy in love with me. He'd proved that a hundred times.

I knew he was a good guy even before I met him.

I'd arrived at the yoga retreat and was standing in line at the registration table. I turned to look around the room while the woman at the front of the line asked too many questions about the rules for disconnecting from technology, wanting everything explained to her personally, even though it was all explained on the website.

Standing near the table where they'd placed bottles of smoothie drinks, whole-grain muffins, and bowls of fruit, was a good-looking man who appeared to be trying to decide what flavor of smoothie he wanted. A woman who had not yet entered the frame of mind for a yoga and meditation retreat came barreling through the doors yanking her wheelie suitcase behind her.

She rushed to the food table, reached around the man, who I later learned was Daniel Keller, and grabbed a smoothie from the side of the stacked pyramid of bottles. This caused the entire pyramid to collapse. Bottles tumbled everywhere, and as some hit the floor with too much force, the containers exploded, sending thick red, green, and orange juice spraying across the woman's beige pants, her sandals, and Daniel's jeans and shoes.

Daniel gave her a disappointed look, which told me everything I needed to know about this patient, gentle man. In fact, I'd wondered why he needed a retreat that was billed as helping people find inner calm and detachment, enabling attendees to learn skills that would keep them from over-reacting to life's stress. He clearly already possessed that inner calm.

The woman lost it. She let out a string of curse words at the imbecile who would stack bottles like that. She cursed the mess, Daniel's *choice* to *block her way*, the decision to provide smoothies as a snack, the traffic, the rules of the retreat, and several other unrelated upsets from her life.

Daniel went looking for a staff member and helped them mop up the mess.

I think I started to fall in love.

As I recalled my first impression of my fiancé, I imagined my sister emailing me back, telling me I needed to tell Daniel to get his creeper brother out of my face. She might even tell me to end the visit. I'd met his family, now it was time to move on. But Daniel desperately wanted me to know them, he wanted us to form a close bond. So, I ignored the sisterly voice in my head. Besides, I didn't know for sure that was what she would say. It was only my imagination.

Writing to her had reminded me of my vow to try harder to get to know Janice. To give her another chance, to try to understand her.

I went to the kitchen, grabbed a bottled iced tea out of the fridge, and wandered through the rooms on the first floor, looking for her. Maybe she was working. After all she was the CEO of their company, the one in charge of the whole operation. She was basically the boss of her sons and daughter. That alone probably made for an unusual family relationship.

Still, despite her title, she seemed to be around the house most of the time, as were Elliot and Abigail. Daniel was the one who was off at meetings.

I found Janice in the massive library, filled with serious, ancient-looking books. She was working on a laptop, her phone propped up against a pillow on the chair beside her, and her feet resting up on a footstool to keep her laptop steady on her thighs. She wore black leggings and a black tunic. Her hair was combed into a tight, wavy bun on top of her head that still showed her curls, and her feet were bare, displaying freshly pedicured black toenails.

I knocked on the doorframe. "Can I get you a cup of tea? Or some coffee?"

She looked up at me, startled. "Greyson takes care of that."

"Oh. Okay." I took a step back.

"Did you want something?"

"Not really."

"Yes, or no?"

"I don't want to interrupt your work."

She held my gaze, suggesting that I'd already done that.

"I just wondered if you..."

"If I, what?"

"About the tea. Or coffee."

"If you want to talk or ask me a question, why don't you say so?"

"I don't have a question, I just thought..."

She sighed and closed her laptop. "I prefer it when people are direct."

Did she? She hadn't been very direct when I'd first arrived. Her comments were more in the category of passive aggressive. But maybe she thought that was direct—telling me I shouldn't assume I was engaged to her son until I had a diamond on my finger.

"I don't know you at all," she said. "I knew Elliot's wife quite well before they were engaged. And I've known Faith for years."

"How did you—?"

"Knowing absolutely nothing about you, I hope you won't hurt my boy."

"Did Tina hurt Elliot?"

She picked up her phone and glanced at it, although I wasn't aware that it had vibrated with a message. Without looking at me, she asked, "What are you suggesting?"

"I wasn't suggesting anything. You were talking about Elliot's wife, and Faith, and then you said—"

"Don't connect dots that aren't related to one another. All I said was, don't hurt my boy. I'm a protective mother."

I wanted to tell her I'd noticed, but I didn't think she would take that as the humorous comment I intended, so I lifted the bottle to my lips and took a sip of cold tea.

I thought about my vow. She wasn't making it easy. But I'd also interrupted her when she was working. I shouldn't have knocked on the doorframe, even though the door had been open. "I'll let you get back to work," I said.

She smiled.

I walked away, wondering what Tina had done to *hurt* Elliot. Maybe those dots *were* connected. Maybe this was the reason no one wanted to talk about Tina.

SEVENTEEN
CLAUDIA

That night I told Daniel I needed time alone with him. Outside the walls of his family home.

An easy web search had brought up lots of hiking areas within a half an hour drive. I'd found one that looked the most appealing with ten miles of trails through redwood forests, including some creek-side trails.

I thought he might object. I worried he would think I was trying to escape from his family, that I was retreating to my life-long habit of hiding from people and situations that scared me. I'd told him a little about my mom and the rages that consumed her when she was drunk. Not a lot. He didn't need to know all the horrifying, nightmarish details. Just a blurry picture of it so he understood that part of me, so he understood that I spent my childhood looking for places to hide. That my sister had been my hero who stood up to the monster in our lives and protected me. That it took me a long time to fight back.

But he didn't say anything like that.

He was thrilled that I wanted to explore his home state.

"I'll ask Greyson to pack us some sandwiches," he said.

"I can do that."

"It's his job. He doesn't mind."

"Neither do I."

"Let Greyson do it." He kissed my cheek.

The next afternoon, we had a bona fide picnic basket to put in the trunk of Daniel's car. We were both wearing good walking shoes, shorts, and tank tops, with sweatshirts tied around our waists, and ball caps on our heads.

I settled in the front seat of the car.

As Daniel walked around to get into the driver's seat, he looked at his phone. He stopped. He glanced at me, held up one finger, then walked toward the front door and disappeared inside. He was gone for five minutes, then seven, then nine.

Just as I opened the car door to go look for him, he emerged. Behind him was Abigail. Her hair was in a ponytail, threaded through the opening in the back of a ball cap. She wore shorts and walking shoes. They started toward the car, Abigail almost bouncing with excitement. Daniel opened the back door and Abigail slid onto the seat. Daniel closed the door and got into the front.

Abigail reached forward and rested her hand on my shoulder. "Thank you for inviting me to come along. I love hiking." She removed her hand and settled back.

Daniel started the car, made a wide turn, and headed toward the gates, which opened for him as if by magic.

"A hike was a great idea," he said. "I'm glad you thought of it."

"Me too," Abigail said.

They talked to each other during the entire twenty-five-minute drive. I joined in once in a while, but mostly, my mind was circling around our surprise guest in the backseat. I wondered how it had happened that she'd been invited. Had she asked where we were going and invited herself? Had Daniel gone looking for her and invited her along so she and I could get to know each other better without the hovering presence of their mother? But why would he do that? I'd told him I missed him, that I wanted time alone with him. I couldn't understand why he'd invited her without even asking me what I thought of the idea. This wasn't what I'd wanted at all.

I was looking forward to hiking. I was excited to be outdoors, away from the gardens and the house. But I was utterly depressed that I wasn't going to have Daniel to myself.

The hike was gorgeous. The towering redwoods were refreshing and peaceful. The picnic was delicious. Daniel shared his sandwich with Abigail. Even so, there was more than enough food.

Abigail began packing up the leftovers. "I don't know if my mother mentioned this, Claudia, but she might need a few pieces of information from you for your background check."

"What?"

"Just your social security number. Previous addresses. Things like that. Nothing major."

"I mean, what background check? What are you—"

"We don't need to talk about that," Daniel said. "Why did you bring that up now?"

"I thought she knew. It's not a big deal."

"Knew what?" I asked.

"It's nothing," Daniel said. "Abigail shouldn't have brought it up."

It was a very big deal. And he had never said a word. Why would she do a background check on me? Didn't they trust me?

"If you're going to work for the winery," Abigail said.

"We don't need to talk about it," Daniel said. "We haven't even discussed her role."

"Well, she'll still—"

"Not now," he said.

Abigail had an expression on her face I couldn't read. Triumphant? Like she'd pulled one over on her sibling? Or something else? Suspicion? I wasn't sure. It didn't matter. I felt sick. They could not run a background check on me. What kind of family did something like that? What did that have to do with falling in love and getting married? What was wrong with them?

Until she mentioned the background check, we'd had a good time. Although, when we arrived back at the house, I didn't feel I knew Abigail any better than I had when she'd popped into the backseat a few hours earlier. We'd mostly talked about the scenery and wildlife. They'd talked about the winery and some new technology for fermentation tanks. Abigail went on and on about her workout routine and how great her personal trainer was, so I guess I learned that about her—she liked to keep in shape. I didn't talk much about my life and we didn't discuss our wedding at all. The only thing I'd learned was that they trusted me far less than I'd ever realized.

That night, I felt more than my usual discontent squirming in my stomach. If I mentioned it again, Daniel was definitely going to be upset, but my feelings wouldn't go away. I'd been there for a week now, and I still felt like no one wanted me there. His mother made me feel like a pariah one minute and gushed all over me as if she were putting on a show for Daniel the next. His brother was beyond disturbing. Abigail was cool and distant, even when she seemed to be friendly. Faith walked around like a ghost. Literally. And now this! A background check.

The gates made me feel as if I couldn't leave if I wanted to, and the things Elliot said, that all of them said, made me feel I was being set up. But for what?

I couldn't understand what the purpose of my visit was. Four more weeks of this was intolerable. I could only imagine things getting worse.

As we lay in bed, Daniel already running his hands over my body, I let out a deep sigh that clearly communicated displeasure instead of what he was expecting.

"What's wrong?" He rested his palm on my belly.

"I had a really good time today, but I wanted to be alone with you."

"Abigail wanted to come."

"I get that. But it was supposed to be—"

"The entire reason you're here is to get to know my family."

"I understand that but you and I haven't had any time to talk. We need a little time alone. And when we do talk, our conversations end with sex. We never resolve anything."

"What needs resolving? And what's wrong with sex? I thought you loved it?"

"I do. That's not... it's just..."

He moved his hand away from me. "What's the problem now?"

"You make it sound like I'm... I don't know. Why does your mother—?" I was almost relieved when he interrupted me. I wasn't sure I wanted him to know that the suggestion of a background check terrified me.

"I feel like you don't like my family. You're so antagonistic. You're making it difficult."

"I'm not antagonistic. I hardly know them."

"You're a hard person to get to know."

"I don't think I am."

"Are you sure about that? You told me yourself; you hide from conflict. And you seem really combative toward all of them. You hardly talked to Abigail at all."

"You were talking about work."

"Not the entire time."

"No, I guess not."

"You need to try harder," he said.

"You keep saying that. But so do they."

"I don't know why you're making this so difficult. I told you we're close, that it might be challenging. But I thought you were up to it. I didn't think you would be so critical of every little thing."

"I'm not."

He rolled onto his side. "Can you just try a little harder?"

"I am."

"I told you my father died when we were young. I told you the winemaking business is demanding and requires—"

"Okay. I'm sorry."

"Can you please just *try*?" he asked.

"Yes. Okay. I'll try harder."

"That's all I'm asking, babe. That's all." He leaned over and kissed me and then placed his hand over my breast. He gave me a gentle smile and kissed me again, longer this time.

But as I closed my eyes, all I could see was the horrified expression on Janice's face when she saw the results of my background check.

EIGHTEEN

CLAUDIA

When I greeted Janice as I walked into the entertainment room where they were all watching a baseball game, she gave me a cold glare and said nothing.

My stomach swam and I tasted a hint of bile in my throat. Had she managed to run the background check without the information Abigail said she needed? Had she poked into every dark corner of my life?

If she had, did this mean my engagement to Daniel would be over before dinner? Did he love me enough to stand up to his mother?

"It looks like they're doing well," I said, acknowledging her baseball team.

She turned her head away from me, shifting her position in her chair so her back was also facing me.

Usually, when Daniel was with me, she oozed charm and graciousness. He stood beside me, and she was acting as she had the day I'd arrived. But if she'd done the background check, wouldn't she say something instead of just turning away?

Daniel took my hand and pulled me toward the sofa. He sat down, tugging at my hand again in a suggestion that I should sit beside him. I was grateful for him holding on to my hand, stopping it from trembling. I shoved my other hand into my pocket.

Maybe it wasn't the background check. Not yet.

The others were talking about the game as it played out across the screen, so she couldn't be upset that I'd talked over the announcer. What was she angry about? What had I done now? I wanted to cry. I wanted to walk out of the house, leaving my clothes and belongings behind. I wanted to find a way to open those gates and walk out into the vineyards and just keep walking. I couldn't take this anymore. I had no idea what was going on with all of them and I was tired of trying to figure it out.

But then, I focused on the warmth of Daniel's hand, the press of his leg against mine, and I let myself relax. In less than four weeks, this would be over. I could do anything for four weeks. Maybe, after another week, if I stopped complaining about them, I'd be able to convince him we should leave. He would see that I'd spent enough time *getting to know them*. We were never going to click, and it was time to let things be.

Remembering my promise to Daniel that I was going to try harder, I let go of his hand and got up off the couch. I went to the chair where Janice was sitting. I pulled another footstool close to her chair and sat beside her.

"I don't know much about your team. Can you tell me about the players? Who are the—"

"I'm trying to watch. Will you stop talking, please."

"Everyone was talking so I thought—"

"I didn't hear that call!" Her voice was shrill. "What did he say, Elliot?"

"Strike," Elliot said.

"Does that pitcher throw a lot of—"

"I asked you to stop talking," she said.

Abigail was on her feet. "Where's the remote. I'll turn it up."

"If she wasn't asking idiotic questions, we wouldn't need it turned up."

"Sorry. I thought—"

"Claudia. Get a grip," Janice said.

Abigail sat on the footstool where her mother's feet were propped up and began massaging her left foot.

"Claudia," Daniel said.

I turned to look. He signaled for me to follow him out of the room. I was more than happy to get out of there. I couldn't win with these people.

In the hallway, he leaned close and spoke in a low voice. "She's upset."

"Obviously."

"Don't take it personally."

"Why wouldn't I?"

"Abigail said she was really hurt that we didn't invite her to go hiking with us."

"Are you serious?"

"She felt left out."

I stared at him. His expression was defeated, concerned.

Left out? Was she twelve years old? I wanted to laugh. Why would an adult woman feel left out because her grown children went hiking? It was the most ridiculous thing I'd heard. Although maybe not, with this family.

"I'll take her to lunch after the game is over," Daniel said. "She just needs some attention. She wants to feel included."

This woman was the owner of an incredibly successful winery. And she was snapping at me because I took her baby boy and little girl away for a few hours of hiking? And now he had to take her out for lunch to make up for it? Without me? What was I marrying into? Was I going to spend my entire life fighting with her over her son?

I gave him a grim smile. "I think I'll go for a swim," I said.

He put his arms around me and pulled me close. "That's a great idea."

Not only did Daniel and his mother go to lunch, Abigail and Elliot joined them. I watched from the second-floor landing as they went out the front door. I didn't think it was my imagination that Janice was beaming with victory.

After they left, I took a long walk around the property, following a path that wound through groups of palm trees, past several smaller houses that were more modern than the chateau, although they mimicked its architecture. They looked closed up and unused. I walked farther, down a slight incline and found the much talked about lake.

There was a small pier with a rowboat and a canoe tied to it and a ladder descending into the water. A small white gazebo stood on the shore. The lake looked about two hundred yards across and three hundred yards wide, although I wasn't a great judge of distance, so it was a bit of a guess.

The water was a deep, dark blue and so calm it reflected the two or three white puffy clouds overhead. It was so beautiful and serene, it struck me as strange that the chateau hadn't been built to look out over the water.

After a while, I returned to the main house. It was strangely silent. Greyson didn't seem to be anywhere around. Neither were the other staff members. Maybe when the family left, they took the opportunity to relax. I went to the second floor and walked down the hall to take a peek at the other bedrooms suites. The entire third floor belonged to Janice. I wasn't sure I had the courage to make my way up there, but I wanted to see what Elliot's and Abigail's rooms were like.

First, I checked out the guest rooms. There were three in the main part of the house. All three were quite large, with attached bathrooms, king-sized beds, small desks, large dressers, and walk-in closets that were stocked with bathrobes and swim towels, sun hats and jackets.

When I came to the next room that had double doors like Daniel's, telling me it might belong to one of his siblings, I half expected it to be locked, but when I turned the knob, the door opened.

The room clearly belonged to Abigail. It looked as if the décor hadn't changed since she was six years old. The bed had a ruffled pink spread embroidered with unicorns and the four posters supported an elaborate canopy. The wood was painted glossy white, as was the dresser. The prints on the walls were of fantastical creatures out of fairy tales—all princesses and good-looking princes, sprites, and charming animals.

The sitting room was more like a child's playroom. There was a desk with a sleek-looking computer on top, but in one corner was a large, four-story dollhouse filled with furniture and tiny dishes, lamps and books and miniature toys. There was a lounge chair piled with stuffed animals.

I left the room, puzzled by what I'd seen, wondering if she wanted her room to reflect her younger self, if it had never been redone, or if her mother insisted it be decorated that way.

When I entered the next room, which I assumed was Elliot's and now also Faith's, I found a similar atmosphere. Childhood prevailed. There were toys and shelves full of model airplanes and ships. There was a table with a game of checkers in progress, which didn't necessarily speak to a child playing, but at the same time, it didn't feel as if it belonged to a thirty-something-year-old man.

I knelt to look at the books on the shelves and saw rows of books for pre-teens.

"What are you doing?"

The sound of Greyson's voice, although it wasn't loud, hit me like a slap. I gasped and started to fall sideways, grabbing the shelf to keep from going over.

"Why are you in here?"

"I..."

"You don't belong here."

"I was just looking."

"This isn't your room."

"I know."

"You're in someone's private space."

I stood. "I'm sorry. I'm so sorry. I know I shouldn't, but I—"

"You need to leave. Right now."

"I wasn't prying. I just—"

"That's exactly what you were doing. Haven't you figured out that you need to watch what you do here?"

"What do you mean?"

He didn't answer. He simply gestured toward the door.

"I was only looking at the books."

I walked quickly to the door and out of the room, forced to squeeze past him because he was blocking most of the doorway.

"You need to be more careful," he said.

"Why?"

"Just stay where you belong."

"I don't know what you mean."

A moment later, he was gone. Almost as if a trap door had opened and swallowed him up.

I blinked. Where had he gone? Was there another staircase somewhere that I wasn't aware of? It made sense, given the age of the house, and its size. And the way the staff was always appearing at the right moment, seemingly from nowhere.

I hurried along the hallway to our rooms. I went inside and collapsed on the bed, breathing hard. Would he tell Janice? He hadn't said he would. If he did, what would happen? Would he tell Daniel? I put my hand on my heart, feeling it thump harder.

The things he'd said terrified me, if I thought about them too hard. Maybe he thought scaring me was enough. Maybe scaring me was enough for him.

NINETEEN
BEFORE: DANIEL

The yoga and meditation retreat was something I was doing for me. As expected, Elliot had rolled his eyes when I told him about it. Abigail had told me it was an excellent idea because I was so tightly wound, but then proceeded to make subtly disparaging comments about it, which was typical for her. Except when she was telling us how to live our lives, my mother liked to pretend she was encouraging us to fulfill our unique personalities, and so she pretended to support my two-week escape from the chateau and my family.

I knew each of them inside and out. At the same time, I didn't know them at all. I sat at the dining room table every night and looked at each of them in turn. They met my gaze, and I looked into their eyes. They smiled. But I couldn't guess what lay beneath those smiles. I tried, but I didn't really know.

Which was why I needed to get away for a while. My family was claustrophobic to the point that I couldn't breathe at times. Therefore, a two-week vacation focused on acquainting myself with my breath seemed like the perfect antidote.

Meeting a fascinating woman wasn't my objective, although it was definitely lurking in the back of my mind. The rules of the retreat forbade hookups, but that wasn't what I was after. If I was *after* anything, it was meeting someone outside the reach of my mother's influence. It was absurd that at the age of thirty-two, my mother was controlling my choice of a lifelong partner as rigidly as she controlled our family fortune along with the operations and branding of our winery. But that's how she was, and I'd grown up with it.

Only recently had I begun to question her view of the world. When you're effectively brainwashed, it takes a while to realize that's the case.

My mother had always had ideas—not just ideas, but iron-clad rules—about who her children should marry. She wanted our partners to fit into the family, although she never spelled out what that meant. Which left it to her *instinct*.

"We can't have outsiders tearing us apart," she told us. Often. It was something she started talking about when we were in high school, bringing our crushes to the house. "Families splinter when marriages aren't considered carefully. Outsiders come in with different ideas. They have traditions that don't align with ours. Other people who don't understand our family history disrupt our way of life. Everything will start to break. You don't notice the cracks at first, but when it crumbles to pieces, it's too late. We have to be careful. You have to trust me."

Always, we had to trust her. She had experience. She never said what that experience was, we needed to trust her. And because she'd been telling us that all our lives, from when we were small, from the day our father died, we did trust her. It's scary when the man who is the center of everything vanishes from your life. Of course, you trust the woman who's left holding you together, telling you that crying and indulging your feelings isn't going to change anything, therefore, it's best to keep them locked up.

I was in my thirties now. How long was this going to continue? I'd thought I had a good idea of the kind of woman she considered acceptable. Sweet was high on her list. And I knew how my mother defined sweet. Not overly ambitious. She wanted partners who could be absorbed into our family business. Partners who didn't have careers that would take them away from us or potentially threaten our business in any way. Her imagined threats were endless and sometimes far-fetched to the point of paranoia.

I'd known what she didn't like about Tina. I knew what bothered her about Faith, although she seemed to be coming around a little in her feelings.

So far, all of Abigail's relationships had burned hot and fast. None of the guys Abigail spent time with had even met my mother. I was fairly certain Abigail kept it that way on purpose. I wondered what she would do longer term. I wondered a lot about Abigail, but I didn't waste too much energy on it. I had enough problems of my own.

I shouldn't have allowed my mother to control who I chose to fall in love with and marry. I probably shouldn't have been living in her house at my age, but when you have an estate like ours, and a family business like ours, those strings aren't so easily severed. In fact, they aren't really strings. They're more like iron bars. You don't just snip them with a pair of pruning shears.

On the first day of the retreat, before it even began, I felt Claudia watching me while I mopped spilled smoothie off my jeans and shoes, thanks to the woman who toppled the pyramid of beverages. She looked cute, friendly, and approachable. She had long golden-brown hair woven into a loose braid and large hazel eyes. Her smile was wide and slightly crooked with a dimple on her left cheek. She was the personification of sweet.

But there was something about the way she stood, the wide stance of her muscular legs and the way her narrow hips were turned slightly toward the door, as if she were poised to run, that suggested she was wary. Behind that easy smile and those soft eyes was a calculating mind. She looked street-smart. It seems unbelievable to think I could assess all that just looking at a woman wearing yoga clothes, with bare feet, rings on two of her toes, but it was a feeling I got. Maybe it was her bare feet. Everyone else was wearing sandals.

Those bare feet seemed to say, I'm comfortable here. I own this place. I'm ready. Maybe they said nothing. Maybe I just wanted her because I sensed she was different from anyone I knew.

Maybe it was the rings on her toes, the rings in her ears, the tiny tattoo of a black rose that showed on her hip bone when she moved and her shirt lifted away from the waist of her pants.

It was unlikely she would fit my mother's definition of a partner who would blend seamlessly into our family. She was the very definition of an *outsider*. But when she smiled at me, I knew I had to meet her.

I crossed the room.

"Hi, I'm Daniel Keller. You look like a yoga expert. Can you give me the inside scoop?"

She laughed. "It's my first time." She extended her hand. Her grip was firm. "Claudia Gatlin."

We followed the rules of the retreat not to reveal anything about our careers or where we'd come from. We talked about why we were there, which didn't leave a lot of room for depth, since everyone was there to learn how to manage stress, to better understand their minds, to transcend the minutia and noise of daily life.

But even with that, after we talked, and her eyes locked onto mine, when I sensed the hint of rebellion in her tone and her demeanor, I knew I had to know her better.

Later, I wondered if I'd read her wrong.

TWENTY

CLAUDIA

Lying on the bed, brooding about what Greyson had said, trying to understand what he meant, became suddenly and almost violently intolerable. I bolted upright and out of the room. I would never figure out what his threatening words meant unless I asked him, and I was too scared to do that. I had no idea whether or not he was on my side, and I didn't want to say the wrong thing, something he might report to Janice.

While the family continued to spend the afternoon lunching in San Francisco, this was my chance to talk to Faith and find out what was going on with her. Maybe I could break through her ghostly shroud and get her to speak. If anyone in this house could understand what I was going through, it was Faith.

Maybe winning over Janice was hopeless. I'd made repeated vows to myself and broken them within hours. I'd promised Daniel I would try harder, but where was the effort on her part? Faith would be able to tell me if it was an impossible goal. She was the only one in this house with experience. She'd somehow made peace with the situation. Although she was also a woman who was capable of sitting silently while her boyfriend blatantly flirted with another woman, or whatever you wanted to call what Elliot had done. So maybe she had a high tolerance for bad behavior.

I found her lying beside the pool, as she often was when I looked out from our sitting room window. She seemed to have an endless supply of bikinis and one-piece swimsuits. She sometimes wore one in the morning and appeared in a different suit in the afternoon.

Now, she was wearing a hot pink string bikini. Her toenails were painted a matching pink. She had a thick, hammered gold ring on the middle finger of her left hand and three gold bracelets on her right wrist, one with a heart charm attached. It was engraved with the letters E and F entwined. Her face was covered with a white straw hat and her long blonde hair hung over the sides of the lounge chair, brushing the ground.

It felt intrusive to walk up to her and just start talking. It was possible she was in a deep sleep, and I would scare her to death. On the table beside her was a glass of white wine. The patio umbrella was angled so that most of her body was in the sun, but the wine and her bag on the ground beside her were in the shade.

I stood a few feet away, watching for any sign that she might be awake, possibly already aware of my presence, that she might have heard the door open when I came outside.

Everything was still, except her hair, drifting in the gentle breeze that moved through the garden and across the pool, rippling the surface of the water.

"Hi, Faith." I hoped my voice was loud enough to penetrate a light sleep, but not so loud it would frighten her.

She lifted her hand and moved her hat slightly, but didn't take it off her face or speak.

I walked to the foot of the chair. As my shadow fell over her, she lifted the hat off her face.

"Do you mind if I join you?" I wasn't sure what I was joining, making my question ridiculous. I wasn't wearing a swim-suit, so I wouldn't be lying in the sun. And I didn't have a glass of wine.

She pulled a tiny earbud out of her ear. "What?"

Now I understood why she seemed so disconnected at dinner, why her head swayed and she smiled at nothing when others talked. She must wear those earbuds all the time. Was that how she coped with all of them? "Do you mind if I join you?"

"It's your patio as much as it is mine."

I laughed. She had a sense of humor. That was good.

She didn't join my laughter. She still didn't sit up, but I took that as an invitation. I brought a chair from one of the tables over and placed it under the umbrella. I wished I had something to drink, but I hadn't planned any of this, and really, I didn't want to sit there for an hour. I had a few questions and that was it.

"We haven't had a chance to talk," I said.

"What's there to talk about?"

"I wanted to know if you have any suggestions for getting along with Janice." I needed to be bolder. Nothing would change if I wasn't. "I don't think she likes me... I *know* she doesn't like me." I laughed, hating that it sounded slightly unbalanced.

"So?"

"Well, I... I'm marrying her son. And I want to get along with her."

"Maybe don't try so hard. Just let her be. I don't get in her way and I'm pretty happy here."

"Are you involved in the winery?"

"Almost," she said.

"What does that mean?"

"I was almost going to work in the tasting room. That's how

I met Elliot. But then we got together, so I didn't end up working there."

"Oh. How is he doing?"

"What?"

"Everyone says he's fragile. And upset about—"

"Who's everyone?"

"Daniel. Abigail."

"I don't know anything about that."

"So, you don't think he's traumatized over whatever happened?" I asked.

"Whatever happened with what?"

"With his wife."

"What wife?" Faith asked.

"He... what?"

"I said, *what wife?*"

"He was married. You didn't know that?"

"I don't know anything about a wife."

"You didn't know he was married?" I asked.

"I said, I don't know anything about that."

"I guess something traumatic happened with his wife, but no one will say what. They won't even say if she's alive. Or dead. Daniel and Abigail act like he's too sensitive to talk about it. Does he seem really...?" I wanted to ask if he was unstable, but it seemed harsh. She might not like that.

"He has issues. But don't we all?" She laughed.

"Do you understand why they are how they are?"

"What do you mean? They just... are." She shrugged one shoulder

"They're so secretive. And cold." I'd wanted to ask if she'd heard the things Elliot had said to me, but now I knew she hadn't. "Did they do a background check on you?"

"Yes."

"Why?"

"They like to protect their assets. From gold diggers." She laughed. "I assume that's why. Does it matter?"

"Who does a background check on someone they love?"

"Why are you so worried? Is there something you don't want them to know?"

I took a few shallow breaths. I hardly knew her. I had no idea if I could trust her.

"It's not as bad as you think." She smiled, reaching out her hand to pat my knee, barely brushing it with her fingertips since she couldn't quite reach. "They don't dig up your whole life. I had something I was worried about too."

"Did they find it?"

She shook her head.

I took a breath and held it for a moment. "But this is... "

She pushed her sunglasses onto the top of her head, looking at me with kindness. "A dealbreaker, or something?"

"I don't know how Janice would take it."

"She's mostly concerned about their money. And their reputation, I think."

"That's why I'm worried. Please don't say anything." She was so much nicer than she'd seemed. The way she was looking at me made me feel that I'd completely misread her. It felt as if I'd found a friend after all.

"Of course not!"

"I was in a hospital. I mean a mental health place."

"Locked up?" Her voice was softer, sympathetic.

"Yes. When I was a teenager. I don't think Janice would—"

"That's supposed to be private. So, they probably wouldn't find out."

I felt the back of my neck relax. Maybe for the first time since Abigail had mentioned the background check. Of course. It was private. It wasn't as if the hospital had a list of graduates or something. I'd been a minor. It was supposed to be private.

Why was I worrying? I hadn't told Daniel. I would, I just hadn't, yet. It was a hard thing to bring up. But I would. Soon. After we left his family's house. I couldn't do it here. Not with the way they were treating me. Later. When I felt more myself again.

"I'm going to listen to my music now," Faith said. "If you don't have any more questions. Even if you do, I don't think I can answer them. 'K?"

"Sure." I stood. "It was nice talking to you."

She wiggled her fingers at me, then lowered her sunglasses and plugged the earbud back into her ear. It was the kind that was no larger than her fingernail, so it almost disappeared from sight.

I left the chair where it was and returned to the house. I went to the kitchen and poured myself half a glass of wine from the open bottle in the fridge. I stood at the counter and took a sip, my head spinning, unable to make sense of what she'd said. How could Faith not know that Elliot had been married? It didn't seem possible.

TWENTY-ONE
CLAUDIA

Daniel texted that they would be home shortly from their four-hour lunch. I took my glass of wine upstairs and went to the small, out of the way sitting room where I'd been able to hide out the last time. I needed to be alone, someplace where no one in this family would find me or even casually pass by. I needed to think, and I wanted to write to my sister and sort out my thoughts.

I tapped to open my email and began keying in words as fast as I could. My whole brain seemed to spill out, but I couldn't stop.

> You would tell me to leave. I know you would. But I love him so much. I'm so confused about how different Daniel seems. If I could get him away from here, I know we'd go back to normal. So here I am hiding out again, writing to you even though you can't answer. I know you'd tell me not to do that, also. To stop hiding from them.
>
> It's so creepy the way their moods keep changing. Elliot is a class A creep. I don't know why Daniel can't see that. It's not like he thinks it's okay, so don't start assuming he's a

creep too. It's just that he makes excuses because Elliot is wounded or sensitive or something.

They seem really damaged by their father's death. I guess that's what it is.

I tried talking to Elliot's new girlfriend and she didn't even know he was married. How can that happen? Maybe that's the only way you can get along in this family—you have to be completely clueless? But she's funny. A little, when she's not checked out. So, I don't think she's completely clueless.

I wish I could actually talk to you.

Although maybe I don't. LOL.

Because I absolutely know what you would say. You would say—get the hell out of there right now. Tell Daniel if he wants to be with me, he can do it on my terms. He can come back to Seattle and have a normal relationship.

You would tell me to cut his family out of my life.

But they run a family business. That's his career. So, it's not that easy.

And the funny thing is, I'm not sure it's that easy for me to leave. I can't just walk out. I'm a little bit trapped inside these walls. Ha, ha.

It's not really funny.

I'll write again soon.

Love, C. xx.

I hit send and put down my phone. I pulled my legs up and hugged them.

Now that I'd gotten all my feelings out, I felt a little guilty. I felt as if I'd betrayed Daniel. Just a little. This was his family. He loved them as much as I loved my sister. Probably. I couldn't imagine anyone loving anyone as much as I loved her, and they certainly weren't as lovable as my sister. Not even close. She deserved my love. But maybe he felt that way about them.

There were probably a million things I didn't know about

them, thousands of good times they'd shared, and so many nice things they'd done for him. Maybe I had it all wrong. Maybe they were protective of him, or something.

Just because Faith was slightly disconnected and didn't seem to know what was going on, that had nothing to do with me. She and Elliot weren't engaged. It was a different situation.

I would talk to Abigail. She knew her mother best. They were obviously close, and it was obvious she adored Janice. She loved her brothers. I'd assumed another outsider would understand, and now that my head was cleared from writing to my sister, I saw that was completely backward.

When I finally found Abigail, it was close to dinnertime. She was sitting in a tiny windowless room off the library. I hadn't realized it was there until I passed through the library for the third time and saw the recessed door between the bookcases.

There were two small, dark gray fabric-covered chairs, a low table between them, and walls that felt oppressive because they seemed very close due to the size of the room with the same twenty-foot ceilings as the library and the rest of the house, making the space feel disproportionate. A large, ornate mirror hung on one wall, reflecting the back of Abigail's head and shoulders. Old black-and-white photographs of the vineyards decorated the other walls.

I'd brought two glasses of red wine with me, carrying them carefully as I'd traipsed around the house, searching for her. Red was always her choice at dinner. I held one out to her. "Would you like a glass of wine?"

"Absolutely." She smiled and brushed an imaginary strand of hair off her face. She had it swept on top of her head again, her eyes heavily made up as they usually were. She took the glass, raised it toward mine in a wordless toast, and took a sip.

I took a seat beside her. "Did you have a good lunch?"

"We did, thank you."

"Janice is feeling better now that she had time with her children?" I asked.

She gave me look I couldn't interpret and took a sip of wine.

"I had a chance to talk to Faith while you were gone. It's surprising how little time we've had together even though we're living in the same house."

She smiled.

"It was a little shocking to find out she didn't realize Elliot had been married before."

"Did you just come here to gossip, Claudia?" Her voice had a teasing tone. "What a wicked girl."

"I don't think I'm gossiping. I was surprised, that's all."

"I told you we don't talk about Tina, for Elliot's sake."

"That seems like a pretty important thing to know about your boyfriend. That he was married."

"It's only important to you. Because you seem a little fixated on other peoples' business."

"No, I'm not."

"Then why do you keep asking about it?"

"Because everyone is making a secret of what happened to her."

"I already explained that."

"You did. It's just..." I took a sip of wine. It was impossible to explain to these people how strange they were. How abnormal their behavior was. Maybe it's impossible to explain to anyone when their behavior is outside the norm. We all think our idiosyncrasies and quirks are absolutely normal. "It's just strange that you wouldn't know that about your partner."

Abigail shrugged.

"Is that why your mother doesn't like me? Because she thinks I'm nosey?"

Abigail smirked. "My mother doesn't like you because you keep coming on to her son, when you're engaged to her other son."

"What?!"

"Your shameless flirting with Elliot. It's embarrassing." Abigail sipped her wine.

"I haven't flirted with Elliot. At all. Not ever."

"He's so vulnerable. That makes it worse," Abigail said.

"I'm not flirting with him."

"Flirting, coming on to him, whatever you want to call it."

"I'm not! I haven't!"

Abigail shrugged.

"Why would you say that? It's not true. Why would anyone think that? Why would your mother think that?"

"A sixth sense?"

"Well, her sixth sense is wrong. Because it's not true. He's been coming on to me. I told him to—"

"You asked why she doesn't like you, and I told you. Don't argue with me." Abigail took a long swallow of her wine and stood. She gave me a smile that seemed almost flirtatious and walked out of the room, her long, white dress trailing behind her.

TWENTY-TWO

CLAUDIA

I felt as if I was grinding my teeth all through dinner. The meal was an elaborate barbecue, cooked and served on the patio, with grilled prawns, sausages, and veggies, fresh watermelon so sweet it was like a dessert itself, and pasta salad. There was a selection of wines from their vineyard, all with little cards describing their profile, as if it were a formal tasting party.

Because I'd been raised by a mother who drank too much, I rarely drank more than a glass of wine or a single cocktail. My sister never touched alcohol at all. She was fanatical about it. Both of us knew it wasn't the alcohol itself that made my mother spew venom and do the things she did. Not everyone who drinks a few glasses of wine turns into a monster like she did, but for my sister, it didn't matter. The smell, even the sight of it, triggered her. It sent her spiraling into a place where she didn't want to exist.

I liked to have a glass of wine. I thought fancy cocktails with fruity flavors were fun.

But since arriving at the Keller estate, I'd found myself sipping more and more wine. I wasn't sure if it was because it flowed so frequently and freely, or because everyone else was doing it. Or, worst of all, because I was unbelievably tense, and I wanted to relax. Maybe it was a little bit of all those things.

That night, Daniel suggested we take a bottle of wine out to the gazebo for a romantic, moonlit date following the barbecue.

I should have been thrilled. It was a chance to be alone with him. But it meant drinking more wine, and I was painfully aware of my sister's voice in my head, telling me to be more careful.

"I don't know why I haven't shown you the lake," Daniel said. "It's amazing during the day, but under a full moon, it will take your breath away. Like you do mine." He kissed me.

I didn't tell him I'd already seen it. I didn't want to spoil his plans. Besides, I hadn't seen it under a full moon, or any moon.

So, with Daniel carrying an insulated canvas bag containing glasses and a bottle of wine in one hand, and holding my hand with the other, we walked slowly along the paved pathway, past the other seemingly unoccupied houses that no one had explained, headed toward the lake.

"Who lives in those houses?" I asked.

He squeezed my hand. "We can talk about that another time. Let's focus on what a beautiful night it is. Look up, the moon is already rising." He pointed through the palm trees.

It did look spectacular, glowing in the darkening sky, its soft white light making me feel peaceful and relaxed, but I wasn't sure why answering a simple question would detract from enjoying the night sky. So often, I asked a question and he changed the subject or refused to answer, making something unimportant seem almost sinister. For now, I didn't want to start another argument over unoccupied houses. Despite the romantic setting, I needed to tell him what his mother had said, that she believed I was flirting with Elliot. He had to set things right.

I admired the lake and the moonlight trailing across the lightly rippled water. We sat in the gazebo and Daniel filled our wineglasses. We toasted our love and kissed. We settled back and I asked Daniel if his mother had enjoyed having the attention of all her children at lunch. He said she had, but didn't provide any details.

We sat quietly for a while, sipping our wine and enjoying the quiet evening.

When Daniel refilled our glasses, I took a sip for courage and placed my hand on his leg. "I think I've really tried with your family, and I'm not saying I'm giving up, but I don't understand why they don't like me. No matter what I do, I feel so unwelcome. I don't even want to be here anymore." I told him what his mother had accused me of.

"Please stop doing this," he said softly. "Please, just stop."

"What am I doing?"

"You're being so dramatic. Misreading everything. Slandering them."

"Your mother is slandering *me*, if you want to use a word like that."

"Maybe Abigail got it wrong and—"

"I'm wondering if I should cut short my visit."

"You're not thinking about *their* feelings," he said. "Or mine. You came here to get to know them. To be introduced to our family business. We haven't even discussed that yet."

"Your mother said I came on to Elliot! I can't have her believing that. It was the exact opposite."

"Okay. Calm down. I don't know what happened." He put his head in his hands, resting his elbows on his knees. "I told you, my mother is overly protective of her children."

I shivered at the word, children. Yes, of course, they were her children. But somehow, he made it sound as if they were still small, wide-eyed, innocent children. In need of protection. I thought about Abigail's bedroom. And Elliot's. Only Daniel's looked as if it belonged to an adult.

"Because of my father dying when we were so young."

"I get that. I'm sure it was necessary, when you were young. But—"

"Elliot is wounded. She's especially watchful of him."

"You're not babies."

"You're acting like you don't love me anymore."

"Where did that come from? That has nothing—"

"If you love me, you'll accept my family. That's what people do when they love each other. They accept the difficult parts of the other person's life. It feels like all you want to do is stir things up. Half the time, I think you're imagining things."

"That's so unfair," I said.

He stood. "I need to clear my head. I'm going for a walk." He kissed the top of my head, stepped out of the gazebo, and disappeared into the night.

I sat there, stunned. I sipped my wine as my thoughts whirled around the conversation we'd just had. It felt as if our words had flown past each other, as if we hadn't even been talking about the same thing. Was he listening to me? What was going on with him? I felt as if he loved his mother, his entire family, more than me. He kept making excuses for them. No matter what they did or said, there was some crazy reason I should *understand* or *try harder* with them, or that I'd somehow *misinterpreted* what they meant.

When my wineglass was empty, I stood, slightly unsteady on my feet. I left the glasses and the half empty bottle in the gazebo and began walking back the way we'd come. It had promised to be such a romantic evening. I'd spoiled it by bringing up another complaint. But it needed talking about! I couldn't let that lie fester in Janice's mind. It was a horrible thing for her to think, much less say. She had no right to look at things from that distorted perspective. I didn't care how wounded her baby boy was. I'd done nothing to encourage him. He'd said awful things to me, and she'd been right there, listening to every word.

I saw the glow of the pool lights and the flames of the fire pit before I saw the water.

Daniel stood at the edge of the patio, facing his mother. Her hands were on his shoulders. They were having a conversation that appeared very intense, their faces as close to each other as his height would allow. She gazed up into his eyes, talking in a way that looked like she was comforting him, telling him something he desperately needed to hear, because he seemed to be drinking in her words as if they were life itself.

I watched for several long minutes.

She was doing most of the talking. He occasionally nodded. She paused and he spoke a word or two, then she would open her mouth for another flow of words.

Their voices were inaudible, but they filled the air around them.

Then, they moved closer. She put her arms around him. He bent over, holding her close and his body trembled, his back shaking as he sobbed into her arms.

TWENTY-THREE

CLAUDIA

I walked away from the pool area and entered the house through a side door. I didn't want to go up to our bedroom because I wasn't sure I was ready to see Daniel after he finished receiving comfort from his mother. It surely had something to do with me.

Had he told her I felt degraded and insulted? Had he done as I'd asked and confronted her about her slanderous comment? Given her comforting hug, it seemed unlikely. Or maybe he had, and that long flow of words was her defense, telling him more lies about me, things she'd dreamed up inside her own head.

I'd never seen my fiancé cry. I'd never even noticed tears in his eyes. What had she said to him that made him break down sobbing to the point that he'd fallen into her arms?

The pain in my heart was so sharp, I was having trouble breathing. What was I doing here, loving a man with my entire self while he poured out his soul to his mother, but walked away from me in the middle of a serious conversation because he had to *clear his head*?

Did he love me at all? He must. He did. I knew he did.

Until I'd arrived at this lavish, almost ominous-feeling house, he'd shown me his love in a hundred different ways. I was so confused I could hardly think. Every time I tried to tell him what I was feeling, he twisted it around so completely I wasn't sure if he'd heard me at all.

I returned to the sitting room where I'd been hiding out when I needed time to think. I curled up in the armchair, hugging my knees to my chest. I wished I had a blanket to pull over my head as I sometimes had when I was a child. I closed my eyes and let the tears pool behind my eyelids, hoping they didn't run down my cheeks. I couldn't bear the thought of one of them finding me crying.

After several minutes, I wiped my fingers across my bottom lashes and rearranged myself in the chair. I took out my phone and messaged two of my friends from work in our group chat.

Claudia:

> Hey, just checking in. Sorry I haven't been in touch. Too much vacationing, LOL. How are things?

I was thrilled to see both of them answer immediately.

Zoe:

> How are the wedding plans coming?

Shannon:

> Are you a wine connoisseur now? LOL.

I told them that, sadly, I'd done zero wedding planning, and I still couldn't tell a cab from a merlot unless someone told me beforehand what I was drinking. They were shocked at both answers. Of course, they wanted to know why.

I told them a bit about the quirks of the Keller family.

It was a mistake. As if they were tag-teaming, they started firing off comments about red flags.

> He should have your back in every single situation.

> His brother is creepy and if Daniel doesn't see that, it's a red flag.

> Why don't you know more about these meetings he goes to? Is the winery in trouble? If you marry him, will you be liable for debts or bankruptcy?

> Why are they all so secretive?

> What are they hiding?

> What is WRONG with Faith? She sounds like she's been silenced.

Before their suspicions could get darker than that, I told them that I might have given them the wrong impression. I was overreacting from the stress of meeting a very powerful family. It was nerves. They argued with me, telling me I definitely had not overreacted to Elliot's disgusting behavior. I told them I might have imagined that he was staring at me. I might have misheard.

The things I said to betray my own self sickened me, but I didn't like them attacking Daniel. They made the man I loved sound like a monster. They'd never met him, and they didn't know how amazing he was. They couldn't know how sweet and gentle and kind and funny he was. I'd done a terrible thing by dumping out all the toxic behavior of his family, while over the previous months, I hadn't said much about Daniel at all. I'd mentioned our dates and told them how much I loved him, but I hadn't talked about him as a person, as the incredible human being he was.

Now, they had a distorted picture of him. They would never see him the way I saw him. These were the friends I wanted in my wedding, alongside my sister, and I'd tarnished him in their eyes. I wanted to cry, wondering if I would be able to fix it now.

I found myself inventing lies about his family, trying to make them look good, trying to change Zoe's and Shannon's impression of them before it was too late, trying to find a way to make them see why Daniel was so protective of them, why he loved them and felt such loyalty to them. That was a good quality, a trait I admired and respected.

By the time I was finished whitewashing his family, it seemed as if they'd calmed down slightly, although I wasn't sure if they were having a private chat about me and how clueless I was. Maybe they were talking about what a mistake I was making. Maybe they were discussing an intervention. Or maybe I'd convinced them.

When I told them about the lovely meals in the elegant dining room, they asked for pictures. I sent a few of the ones I'd already taken. They were impressed and cooed over the luxury I was enjoying. I told them more about how Daniel and I saw the world in the same way, and they were charmed by that. I hoped they weren't lying to me, lying in the same way I was lying to myself about his family and all the things that were clearly wrong.

I stifled the whispers and ended the chat a few minutes later. I began a quick email to my sister.

Just saying a quick hi. I miss you. All I've done lately is complain and tell you scary things. I'm really sorry. Now, get ready for some gushing.

I don't know if I've told you how amazing my fiancé is. He's so smart. He knows an incredible amount about the history of California and the wine industry, and wine itself. He plays golf, and watches a lot of golf and knows all about the game and even manages to make it sound interesting. He's such a good listener. When we first got together, he wanted to know every detail about my work, and he would spend an hour or more every night asking me questions about my day. He's absolutely amazing, and I can't wait for you to meet him!

It made me feel better to tell her a few things I loved about Daniel.

In the end, I was tired of thinking about what anyone else might have to say about my situation. I just wanted to crawl into bed and cuddle up beside Daniel. I left my hideout and went to our bedroom. Daniel was waiting for me.

"Where were you?" Daniel asked.

"Checking in with friends from work."

"This late?"

"It's only ten-thirty." I put my phone on the charger and got ready for bed. When I slid in beside him, he pulled me close

"My family thinks you're isolating yourself."

"Is that what your mother said? I saw you crying."

He held me closer, pressing his face into my neck. "This is really hard. All I want is for you to care about each other. It shouldn't be so difficult."

I was exhausted. So exhausted I couldn't find the energy to say any more.

"I want all of you to feel connected."

It wasn't my fault there was no connection. I knew that for sure. But I was also too tired of it all to argue that point.

"Since you'll be working in the winery in some capacity, I thought that tomorrow we could meet with some of the team so you can get to know how things are structured."

"Okay."

"You don't sound excited," he said.

"I'm tired."

He stroked my hair, and we held each other, not talking. We fell asleep without making love.

In the morning, his alarm woke us at six. He was all business and efficiency. He had definite ideas about what I should wear for my introduction to the staff. It turned out to be the only slacks and business jacket I'd packed, paired with black high-heeled pumps, my hair pulled back into a low ponytail.

After a light breakfast, we drove out of the gates and half a mile up the road to the winery itself. It felt somehow entitled, or simply lazy, riding in a car for such a short distance, but there were no sidewalks out here in what was essentially agricultural space. The shoulders of the road were gravel and dirt, dipping into deep gullies at the edges of the vineyards.

The winery had a large iron arch with the name of Chateau Noir Winery across it. The drive to the main building that held the tasting room, a small store that sold cheeses, olives, and included a small deli, and a number of smaller rooms for private events stood at the end of a long driveway shaded by large oak trees on either side.

I was introduced to all their varieties of wine and given a tour of the wine-making facility where I learned about the process of bringing wine out of the round, plump grapes growing on vines stretched out for acres around us.

They took me to one of their wine caves. Daniel explained that they'd been introduced to the Napa Valley in the 1870s. According to the woman giving the tour, whose role wasn't clear to me, wine caves provided energy efficiency as well as efficient land use. "They're crucial for the proper storage and aging of wine." She tucked her long, magenta hair behind her ears and peered at me before leading us down the stone steps into the dimly lit cave.

The space made me feel smothered. I wasn't sure if it was because we were underground or because I'd been feeling smothered the entire time I'd been staying with Daniel, and this was just more of the same, but worse, as I imagined the door closing and the lights going out, leaving us trapped in the dark, silent, windowless space partially buried.

The hours after that were a whirlwind of handshaking and smiling, introductions of names and titles, marketing plans and meetings, most of which I forgot. Daniel assured me I would be given access to the organization chart and to the internal portal to help me sort it all out later.

On the drive back, Daniel announced that the entire staff loved me, as he'd known they would. He said I was so talented he had no doubt I would fit in perfectly. He made no mention of what my role would be, and I didn't ask. It was all too much. I was slightly confused by the purpose of the day. It seemed to be a series of meetings that I couldn't follow, with no real place for me, despite his enthusiasm.

It felt as if I'd been given a sales pitch, as if I was being roped into something I didn't want, and I couldn't figure out why I felt that way. But the impression was very strong, and the look on Daniel's face, as well as his attitude throughout the day, suggested that my only career option going forward was to work for his family.

It made me wonder if I would ever be allowed to leave Chateau Noir at all.

TWENTY-FOUR

CLAUDIA

After my meet-and-greet, I changed out of my business clothes and into cut-off shorts and loose white top to keep me cool in the late afternoon heat. I put on a sun hat and glasses, sunscreen and sneakers, and went out for a walk to explore the rest of the property that I hadn't had a chance to see. When we'd arrived home, Daniel had gone into the downstairs office to catch up on email.

Except for my two trips to the lake, I'd felt chained to the house and pool area. Maybe because I felt obligated to be social. But that wasn't working, so I was done making myself available.

Now, I wandered along the paths that went past the houses that hadn't been explained to me, through the stately palms that made me feel peaceful and reminded me of the yoga center where Daniel and I had met.

As I exited the grove of palm trees, I came to a garden that was an artistic arrangement of rocks, flowering shrubs, and succulents. Some of the rocks were simply large natural shapes that were placed in groups with gravelly sand around them. Others were flat stones stacked Zen-like, carefully balanced. I wondered if the gardener tended to them on a regular basis, if he had to re-build them after strong winds, or they were stable enough to maintain their presence even through winter storms.

At this time of year, I supposed they were mostly left alone. A narrow path of fine gravel bordered by more small stones wound through the garden. I walked slowly, my body feeling languid under the hot sun.

As I neared the wall that surrounded the property, there was an arched trellis. A vine grew over it with lush leaves and purple flowers, healthy and vibrant despite the direct sunlight. Under the trellis was a flat stone with the current year carved into it and the initials T.K.

I stared at the stone, lying in the small slice of shade created by the trellis.

Despite the heat, I felt something cold creeping up my body from the soles of my feet, winding through my legs, then racing faster to the top of my spine and across my scalp, making my hair follicles prickle as if someone was stabbing pins straight into my head.

I was absolutely certain I was looking at a very simple headstone for Tina Keller's grave.

TWENTY-FIVE

CLAUDIA

I shook my head as if I could make the thought go away.

My hat flipped off and fell on the ground. I picked it up and put it back on my head, tipping the brim so I could look more closely at the stone, although I didn't know what I expected to see. Either I was being overly dramatic, or I was absolutely correct. And I was inclined to follow my initial instinct and my body's echoing chills.

A date and a set of initials that were the same as those of Elliot's first wife. A trellis with flowers and a stone set in a secluded part of their property. One part of me couldn't imagine it being anything else but a grave. Another part of me couldn't comprehend it being her grave.

It was only a memorial spot. Of course, that's what it was. I was being dramatic. They wouldn't bury her on their own property! Was that even legal? It was simply a stone, something to remember her by. It was tucked away, far out of sight because of their obsession with protecting Elliot's sensitive feelings.

But something about it bothered me. The dirt around the area didn't have the same uniform feel as the rest of the garden. It was slightly uneven, slightly... something. Disturbed was too strong a word, but it was different in a way I couldn't quite describe, even to myself.

It felt like a grave. It did not *feel* like a memorial spot. And my first, immediate reaction had been, *This is Tina's grave.* Why would I think that? Something about that stone and the trellis and the entire area, the mood of the place, made every instinct deep in my nervous system scream silently in my head, *Don't take another step, you'll be walking on her grave.*

I took a few steps back, trying to get a better sense of what I was looking at, but my feelings didn't change.

After staring at it for another few minutes, trying to make myself believe it was simply a memorial stone, I turned and began walking as quickly as I could back toward the grove of palm trees. Once I reached them, I paused. I took off my hat and wiped my hand across my forehead. The palms offered minimal shade, although their gentle swaying presence felt cooling.

I replaced my hat and continued walking, my heart racing, my eyes gritty and dry from the heat. As I rounded the bend that led back toward the gardens surrounding the main house, I ran smack into Elliot.

"Whoa. Where are you going in such a hurry?" he asked.

"I need a drink of water."

"Okay, but why so upset? You look like you're having a panic attack." He took my upper arm.

"Let go of me."

He let go and I continued walking.

He hurried to keep up. "Is everything okay?"

"I don't know."

"You don't know?" He laughed.

"It's not funny. I think I saw..." I stopped walking. "Is your wife dead? Is she *buried* here?"

"Why do you want to know that?"

"Because I think I saw a grave."

"Why are you so obsessed with the past? It's not healthy."

"Is there a grave in your rock garden, or not?"

He moved closer to me, too close. I tried to step to the side, but a palm tree blocked my way.

He took another step closer. When he spoke, I could smell the mint of mouthwash on his breath. "Why are you trying to get away from me? You seem very afraid of me, and I don't understand why. It's insulting."

"I'm not afraid."

"I don't believe you."

"Why won't you answer my question?"

"Because it's morbid."

"It's not. I saw a stone with a date and your wife's initials. It looked like a grave marker."

"Did it?"

"It's a simple question. Is Tina buried out there or not?"

"Why are you so overly interested in what happened in the past? You weren't here. You didn't know her. You should be thinking about your future—as a bride."

"I'm not overly interested in the past."

"You need to leave my former wife alone. Let her rest in peace."

"So that is her grave?"

He shoved his hands into his pockets. He pulled out his phone, gave me a hard look, then turned and walked away.

I assumed that meant the answer was yes. I also realized they'd been talking about me. I shouldn't have been surprised. Any family would probably talk about a newcomer, about their sibling's fiancée. I wondered if Daniel had participated in those conversations. I wondered if they were discussing my failure to adapt to their expectations, whatever those might be. I wondered if they were rating me or trying to figure out how to get Daniel to break up with me.

I couldn't stop asking myself questions. I wondered if the

love Daniel and I felt for each other was strong enough to with-stand the animosity they felt toward me, or my own growing doubts about whether I wanted to put up with them.

A grave on their property? I shivered again, thinking about it.

I wondered if Daniel knew she was buried there.

TWENTY-SIX

CLAUDIA

I started running, taking a different path from the one I'd seen Elliot go down.

Sweat pooled at the base of my hairline and trickled down my back. Soon, my whole body was damp, my top clinging to my skin as if I'd just climbed out of the pool. I wasn't even sure why I was running. I wanted to find Daniel. I needed to talk to him. I needed to know if the marker I'd seen was a grave.

As I neared the garden at the back of the house, Janice appeared in front of me as if she'd blossomed out of the leafy plants surrounding us.

"Calm down, Claudia. There's no need to run."

I stopped.

"Elliot just texted me. He said you've worked yourself into a bit of a frenzy."

"I have not."

"Your face and all that sweat say otherwise."

"It's hot and I—"

"What's the problem?"

"Is Tina buried on your property?"

"Yes."

"Why wouldn't Elliot say?"

"It's been explained to you multiple times, Elliot is sensitive about his loss. And this family doesn't wallow in our grief. We don't obsess over the past like you seem to enjoy doing."

"That's not what I'm doing."

"Isn't it?"

"Why did you bury her here?"

"The Kellers take care of our family. It's always been that way. You can sit in judgment of us all you want, but we're loyal to each other and we love each other."

"Is it legal to bury someone in your yard?"

"Yes, as a matter of fact. Not that it's any of your business."

"What did her family think of that?"

"None of this has anything to do with you. It's concerning the way you keep poking around in Elliot's business."

I took off my hat and wiped my hand across my forehead, then across the back of my neck. "I'm not poking around in his business. I just wanted to know why everyone was acting like what happened to Tina was a big secret. Finding her buried here was a shock. I've never heard of something like that."

"A family like ours has to be more protective. I know Daniel has explained that to you. More than once."

So, he was telling his mother about our private conversations? I felt sick thinking about him repeating the things I'd said to her, sick knowing that she'd heard my private thoughts. What did she know about me that I wasn't aware of?

"It's a privilege to be a part of this family," she said.

I wanted to laugh. She was making them sound like royalty again. Who did this woman think she was? It was just a winery. They didn't own the Taj Mahal or a private island. She wasn't the ruler of a small country. She had a beautiful, historic estate in the Napa Valley. She owned a winery. It was unique, but it didn't mean she and her kids had liquid gold pumping through their veins. I bit the inside of my lip to keep from laughing.

"Did you have something you wanted to say?" Janice asked.

I shook my head.

"You don't seem like you want to blend in with this family. You don't seem like you value the same things we do."

"How would you know? You haven't spent any time with me. I'm trying to—"

"We don't know if we can trust you. I understand you have a secret of your own."

I stared at her. Did she know? Or was she trying to trap me? Had Faith broken my confidence? I couldn't believe... she'd promised.

Janice smiled with what looked like an attempt at sympathy. "And if we can't trust you, then you can't marry Daniel."

"Isn't that his choice?" I hadn't meant it as a question. It wasn't a question. Of course, it was his choice.

"No," Janice said. "It's not his choice." She looked at me as if this were a warning I should take seriously.

I stared at her, part of me wondering if she was teasing me. But she was not a woman who made teasing comments. A moment later, she was gone, as quickly as she'd appeared.

I continued along the path, more desperate than ever to talk to Daniel. Were they trying to chase me away? Maybe those strange encounters with each of them *had* all been tests and I'd failed every one.

TWENTY-SEVEN

CLAUDIA

Daniel didn't come out of his office until dinnertime. I sat beside him, my back rigid, and gobbled my food, eager to leave the table and get him alone. Although we'd had countless conversations about his family, and they'd all ended the same way, I was still foolishly hopeful that now, he would finally see things from my perspective.

From the moment we'd met, that was one of the things that made us click. We viewed other people and the world in the same way. It had been so unsettling, since I'd arrived at the estate, listening to him tell me he didn't hear the same words being spoken, didn't see the same looks, catch the same undertones. It made me feel as if we were existing in two different realities.

This time, I was the one to suggest a walk to the gazebo by the lake. He agreed.

We held hands as we strolled along the path. He told me again how much all the staff at the winery had loved me. "The next step is to figure out what position is a good fit for you."

"I love the job I have. I'm not sure—"

"I know you do, but Chateau Noir Winery is a family business."

"For your family."

"And soon, you'll be part of my family."

We hadn't discussed a date yet. When we were first engaged, we'd casually mentioned not wanting our engagement to last longer than a year. But that was the closest we'd come to making definite plans. Hearing him talk about me now as part of his family, which of course, he'd said many times, sent chills through my body. A month ago, those words gave me chills of excitement. Now, they were chills of fear running down my arms.

"Are you cold? I can't believe you're shivering in this heat," Daniel said.

"Just one of those random shivers."

He squeezed my hand.

We sat down in the gazebo, cuddling close to each other as the evening air drifting across the lake grew cooler.

After a few minutes of silence, I moved away and placed my hand on his leg. "I was walking around the rock garden today. It's really nice. But I... I guess you already knew Tina is *buried* here?"

He sighed. He put his hands over his face for a moment, then lowered them. "I should have told you."

"Yes. Finding her grave like that was awful."

"That's how Elliot wanted it."

"When I asked him about it, he seemed almost threatening."

"Threatening? About what?"

"I don't know. He seemed angry I knew about it, or that I was asking about her, about why you would bury someone on your own property. I'm not sure."

"He's—"

"Please don't give me that Elliot-is-sensitive story again."

"I doubt he meant to be threatening. I don't want to keep

telling you they aren't how you're perceiving them. It's starting to sound hollow, I realize that." He sighed again, more deeply this time.

"And then I talked to your mother. She said she didn't trust me. That none of you do. It sounded liked you've told her some of the things we talked about." I wondered if he would mention the fact that I was keeping a secret. I wondered if Janice knew what my secret was, if Daniel knew. How badly had Faith betrayed me?

"I mentioned you were upset."

He didn't know. It sounded as if he didn't know. "Please don't talk to her about the things I say."

He put his arm around my shoulders. "I'm sorry. I didn't tell her anything private, only that you were feeling uncomfortable. I'm really trying to make this work. I didn't expect it to be like this. I know she's... they're..." He squeezed my shoulder but didn't try to finish his thought.

"She told me it wasn't even your choice whether you married me."

He didn't respond. I waited, feeling more anxious the longer the silence stretched between us. Had he not heard me? I didn't think that was possible. We were sitting so close.

"It's my choice."

"You took a long time to answer. Why did she say that?"

"It's too hard to explain."

"You need to explain."

"You won't understand."

"Now, you definitely need to explain."

"It's my choice, okay. She just wants to be sure the people we fall in love with fit into our family. That they're not—"

"That's absurd."

"I knew you wouldn't understand. She's not picking our spouses. She just likes to offer her opinion."

"What is this, the eighteen hundreds?"

He laughed. He pulled me closer, maneuvering me onto his lap. He kissed my neck.

I giggled. "You aren't going to make me forget about the eighteen hundreds by doing that."

"I think I can."

"I'm serious. This is weird. It's all too weird. Burying her here! And deciding who you can marry. It's..." It was too much. There was too much to even talk anything through to its conclusion. Once again, we were leaving all these disturbing incidents hanging in the air around us, trailing after us, weighing us down, driving a wedge between us. I wondered if he felt it.

"Look..." His voice had taken a deeper tone. There was a finality to it. He laughed, and it sounded slightly uncomfortable. Or was I imagining that? "She's just protective, like I said. Can we leave it at that? And try again?"

So, he wanted me to overlook his brother treating me like a piece of meat. And his mother treating me like a gold digger. Everyone pretending his sister-in-law wasn't dead and then letting me find her body buried near their twelve-foot wall. Did he know how that sounded? But I didn't want to fight. I didn't want all of this to be so hard.

I was supposed to be looking at flowers and cake designs with his mother and sister. We were supposed to be picking a date and doing fun things together. I was on vacation, and I was supposed to be enjoying this luxurious estate and incredible food. What was I doing? But what were *they* doing? I wanted to leave. I wanted them to love me.

I was so confused I just wanted to go to sleep and wake up and find everything fixed.

A sudden wave of nausea washed over me. Had all this thinking affected my body so much that now it was going to suck all the thoughts from my head and expel them out of my stomach? I moved farther away from him, sliding along the bench and bending over slightly. I rested my hands on my belly. Another wave of nausea hit me.

"Are you okay?" Daniel moved closer. He placed his hand on my back.

I shifted away. "Don't touch me. I don't feel very good." Another wave overtook me. Was I going to be sick right here in the center of the gazebo? Right in front of Daniel? The thought was too awful, but I wasn't sure I could make it back to the house.

I stood slowly, one hand on my stomach, the other pressed hard against the wall of the gazebo to steady myself. I hoped the pressure of my hand against the wood might stabilize my body, might stop these waves crashing through me, stirring the contents of my stomach, pushing them up.

"I'm really not. I'm going back to the house." Thoughts of being sick on the path, beside the pool, somewhere inside that beautiful house overwhelmed me. "I don't feel well at all." I bolted out of the gazebo and began walking quickly back toward the house. Soon I was running, willing my stomach to maintain some control. My mind raced through the layout of the house, trying to recall the bathroom nearest to the back door.

There was a powder room in the wing where the offices were located. I ran faster. Fortunately, they'd left the doors open in the living room. I rushed through and around to the short hallway into the powder room, slamming the door closed behind me, and falling to my knees in front of the toilet.

When I came out of the powder room, Daniel was waiting for me. He helped me up the stairs. I didn't need help, but I appreciated his concern.

"This feels like food poisoning," I said. "I've had it twice before and the way it hit me feels the same." I spared him the details. "I wonder if the crab claws—"

"But we all had them, and I feel fine."

"Maybe because I'm smaller, it hit sooner."

He shrugged. He helped me undress and get into bed. After he'd supplied me with a glass of water, tissues, and a bowl, just in case, he got into bed beside me.

With my stomach settled for the moment, I was asleep before he'd finished checking his email and turned out the lights.

The first time I woke, feeling sick again, Daniel wasn't beside me. But I was in no condition to look for him. I was so miserable, even the thought of texting him to find out what he was up to wasn't worth the effort. I spent the rest of the night on the bathroom floor, sleeping on the small rug when I could.

I knew this was food poisoning. The symptoms were identical. The question that pressed into my head as hard as the tile floor beneath me was—why hadn't Daniel been sick?

TWENTY-EIGHT

DANIEL

Hearing Claudia being ill on the other side of the closed bathroom door was painful. I felt helpless. Useless. I suppose I wanted to be there for her, but at the same time, when I had a stomach upset, the last thing I wanted was someone breathing down my neck, asking how I felt, trying to *help*. It was an indignity best endured alone. So that's what I did.

When she first drifted to sleep, I'd poured myself a shot of whiskey, went to one of the guest rooms, and sat in bed to catch up on the news.

I needed time to think, although I knew thinking wasn't going to solve the issues between us. It was clear that Claudia didn't understand my family at all, and until I told her more about my history, she never would. I wasn't ready for that, and I knew my mother wasn't ready for that. No one was ready for that.

What I was asking of her was unfair, stepping into this mess without any guideposts. Expecting her to hold her own. It was impossible. But I'd believed she was up to it. And part of me still believed that. She was an amazing, savvy woman. I wasn't ready to let her go, and I couldn't tell her everything.

I understood why Claudia was losing her mind.

At the same time, anyone who hadn't been there couldn't understand. Not really. And part of the reason I didn't push back on my mother, insisting I had to tell her about our father, was because I wasn't sure Claudia would get it. I wasn't sure she would understand, even hearing the details, why things were the way they were.

My father had drowned in that lake.

When the four of us stood on the shore—my mother, with ten-year-old me, eight-year-old Elliot, and six-year-old Abigail huddled beside her—looking at my father's vacant face, we changed forever.

His skin was so white, his eyes closed, and yet it seemed as if they might open any minute. His lips were parted, and water spilled out in a continuous dribble. The way his arms floated beside him, the muscles looking as if they'd turned to pulp, was an image that cemented itself into our minds.

It never left. I still saw it in my dreams—mostly his face.

But Elliot was different. Elliot was haunted by my father's slack, empty face during his waking hours.

None of us could ever figure out if it was Elliot's age, or the way the events of that night unfolded, or his personality. We weren't making excuses for him when we said he was sensitive. He was, but also, horrifically insensitive. I'd been too optimistic. I'd believed the enigmatic woman I'd met would bring out a different side of Elliot. A different side in all of them.

So, I excused his *sensitivity* and his acting out, thinking it might change at any minute. Maybe being too sensitive causes some people to lash out? I don't know. Maybe they feel they have to protect themselves, or they want other people to feel as wounded and exposed and vulnerable as they feel? I'm not a psychiatrist. And maybe Elliot should have seen one. We all should have gone to therapy.

But that wasn't my mother's style. She gathered her chicks

around and told us how we would cope. We would stick together. We could take care of each other. We wouldn't wallow in our feelings, and above all, we would be loyal. To the death.

You can't force people not to wallow in their feelings. Elliot might have stopped wallowing on the surface, but he had a lot of feelings.

When Elliot saw his wife floating at the edge of the lake, those feelings rose to the surface like a creature coming back from the grave.

He went running into the water, falling on his face when it got too deep for him to maneuver with his shoes and jeans dragging him down. He grabbed Tina and picked her up. He tried breathing into her cold, lifeless lips that were already tinged blue. He howled like a badly wounded animal.

He was crying *Daddy! Baby!* Screaming for both of them over and over. *Come back! Don't leave me! I'm sorry!*

He fell into the water, holding her body.

It was the worst thing I'd ever experienced.

My mother had to drag him out. And we buried her on our property because he couldn't let her go.

He didn't ask how she'd ended up in the lake to begin with. He seemed resigned to the fact as if it were fate. Had he known how?

Remembering all of that, I downed my whiskey, poured two more shots, and downed those. It was something I didn't often recall in such vivid detail.

I couldn't tell Claudia. Not yet.

She was strong. She wanted me. She wanted respect. She wanted a family. She'd told me that. I brought her here to meet my family for a reason and I wasn't happy that it wasn't going at all the way I'd planned. In fact, it was the opposite, but I had to trust that she would show what she was made of.

TWENTY-NINE
CLAUDIA

I was showered and dressed, sitting in the armchair by the window sipping water from one of the bottles that Greyson stocked our room with every day. Daniel was nowhere in sight. I partially understood why he'd abandoned me in the middle of the night. But I'd also felt very alone, with half my body sprawled across the throw rug on the hard tile of the bathroom floor in a house where I was not only unwanted, but felt increasingly frightened.

Until my body was violently ridding itself of everything I'd eaten, I hadn't realized how scared I was. Between the unscalable walls with the secured gate, the decision to bury a woman in the back corner of their property along with the fact there was no obituary that I'd been able to locate, betrayal by a woman I'd thought might be on my side, and now the worst—as far as I knew, Daniel had not been sick.

I couldn't escape the thought that my food had been deliberately poisoned. It was a wild, paranoid thought, but it wouldn't leave me alone. I had no way of knowing if anyone else had been sick, but the fact that he wasn't, made me question what had happened. This was not a stomach virus.

The bedroom door opened, and Daniel stepped inside. "How are you feeling?"

"Weak. Still a little off, but better." I took a sip of water.

"You should stay in bed today."

"You're not sick? At all?"

"No." He laughed. "I probably shouldn't have come in here. I don't want to catch whatever it is."

"And what about the others?"

"Everyone's fine. Thanks for asking."

I hadn't asked because I was concerned. I'd asked because now my fear was deepening. If I told Daniel what I believed, he would not take it well. "I'm thinking it might be time for me to head back home," I said.

"You can recover here. I'm sure it's just a twenty-four-hour thing. You said you're already feeling better. By tomorrow—"

"It's not about being sick. I need to clear my head."

"Why? Is this you running away? Hiding, like you told me you've struggled with?"

"No."

"But you're here to—"

"I don't need to hear that again. It's not working. We were going to plan our wedding. Remember? Your mother and me? She doesn't even think I qualify to be in your family."

"Don't say it like that. Please." He came closer.

"You shouldn't get too close if you don't want to catch my *bug*."

He gave me a look that suggested he was slightly afraid of what I might say next, but I said nothing.

"I love you," he said.

"I know. And I love you."

"Then why can't you clear your head here?"

"Because I feel unwelcome. I feel trapped. I feel—"

"Trapped?"

"I can't even leave if I wanted to, without asking for your help. The gate is locked, and I have no idea how to open it."

He laughed. "You're joking, right? If you want to go somewhere, just ask."

"I shouldn't have to ask."

"Why do you want to leave me?"

"I'm not leaving *you*. I'm leaving this place. For now."

He flopped into the chair facing the bed. He stared at me, hardly blinking. "We need to talk this through."

"I don't know what else to say." I put the bottle to my lips and finished the rest of the water. I placed the bottle on the nightstand. I slid out of bed and stood, unsteady on my feet, and walked out of the room, closing the door softly behind me.

I shouldn't have rushed out so fast. As I walked along the hallway, I felt lightheaded and wobbly. I paused, placing my hand against the wall. To my left was the room where I'd gone to escape from his family before. I ducked inside and settled in the armchair, longing for another bottle of water, but too weak to get up.

I took my phone out of my pocket and opened an email to my sister.

I can't believe I'm writing this. I think someone here tried to poison me. I was really sick after dinner. I was the only one. I'm scared.

Staring at the words in black and white, the thing I feared still felt true. I hit send, then leaned my head back and closed my eyes, tucking the phone beside my hip. A moment later, I was asleep.

Voices in the hallway woke me. The voices were urgent whispers, Elliot and Faith, who sounded like they were having an argument.

"Why didn't you ever tell me?" Faith's voice was more like an angry hissing sound.

"It didn't seem importan'."

"Is that how you see me? Not important? You were married and you didn't think I was important enough to know about it?"

"Well, I'm not married anymore, riiight?"

He sounded drunk. I'd slept for a good length of time, I was sure, because I felt much less queasy, but I doubted it was past noon. How could he be this drunk so early in the day?

"I had a right to know."

"Now you know."

"Why didn't you tell me? Why did I have to find out from her?"

"What does it matter? We're together. Riiight?"

I heard a thud.

"Don't," Faith said. "I'm trying to talk to you."

"Nothin' to talk about."

"Why didn't you tell me you were married? Why didn't you tell me she was *dead*? How did she die?"

"I don't wanna talk about this."

"I do."

There was another thud.

"Elliot, stop. I'm not—"

"C'mon. You look so good."

"How did she die?"

"She drowned. Okay? Happy?"

"Of course, I'm not happy. I just wanted to know."

"A better question... a better quesh-un is why? Why did she die?" He laughed.

"What do you mean?"

"I'm not sure." He laughed again. "I shouldna said that. Forget it." There were several thuds, moving down the hall, as if he was stumbling away from her, banging against the wall, or possibly slamming his hand against it as he went.

This was followed by silence, so I assumed Faith had followed him, or left him alone. Either way, their words settled into my head like lead weights. What would Faith do with all of that? Would she go back to her detached state? Seeming not to care about anything? What did he mean? *Why did she die?*

His words suggested the *accident* might have been preventable.

THIRTY

CLAUDIA

Elliot's drunken words marched through my head, a drumbeat keeping time as they repeated themselves—*A better question is, why? Why did she die?*

I wanted to write what I'd heard to my sister, but I didn't want her to dig through my hundreds of emails when she came back online, reach the end, and decide I was ready to be re-committed to the psych ward. The drumbeat continued.

A better question is, why? Why did she die?
A better question is, why? Why did she die?
Why did she die?
Why did she die?
Why? Why? Why?

I felt like screaming. Why would he ask that, laughing as he posed the rhetorical-sounding question?

As my heart rate accelerated, keeping time with the drum-beat, I dug my phone out from the chair cushion and tapped out another email to my sister.

I know when you read these, everything will be fine. I hope.
Yes, I know it will. And I know I just sent you email a few

hours ago that might have sounded crazy, thinking someone is trying to poison me. But now, I just heard Elliot talking. He was drunk, but he made it sound like he might have killed his wife! I can't even. I don't know what to do! I wish you could read this. I'm glad you can't read it. I don't know.

I read what I'd written. I *did* believe it. There was no other way to interpret what he'd said, even drunk out of his mind. I tapped send.

Pushing myself out of the chair, I stood for a moment to get a sense of how I felt. Not too badly. I left the room and went looking for Daniel. I found him in one of the offices on the first floor, staring at an enormous computer screen filled with charts. He swiveled his chair the moment I spoke his name.

"Feeling better?" He stood and came toward me, reaching for my hand. He looked nervous.

"Quite a bit, thanks."

"Should we get you something to eat?"

"I'm not hungry."

"You need to replenish your strength."

"Not yet. Water is fine for now."

"What can I do for you?"

I took a step back from him, looking up to meet his gaze. "I think your brother killed Tina. Maybe it was an accident, a fight or a—"

"What the hell are you talking about?"

"I heard him and Faith arguing." I told him what I'd heard.

"And from that, you think he killed Tina?"

"Yes."

"That could mean anything. It could be an existential question."

"But it wasn't. And I think your mother's protecting him. Why is Tina's body buried here? Was there an autopsy? Does anyone outside your family even know she's dead?"

"Of course."

"Are you sure?"

"I don't know. I didn't ask."

"I'm asking questions you should have asked, that you should be asking right now. Or maybe you have and you're lying to me. I'm not really sure."

He was silent, staring at me, calculating his response.

"Why wasn't there an obituary?"

"You searched for her obituary? Why didn't you ask me?"

"Because you wouldn't even tell me if she was alive or dead. You keep telling me I'm overreacting. That I'm not giving your family a fair chance. I wanted to know for myself. And there isn't one."

"Maybe you just—"

"Maybe not. I don't know. I just think the whole situation is beyond strange. It gives me the creeps."

"Why do you think he killed her?"

"His behavior is not normal."

"I told you—"

"What he said really bothers me. I can't stop thinking about it."

He sighed. "But you said he was drunk, so—"

"It was still a really weird thing to say."

"You didn't hear the whole conversation. You don't know what else they said."

"No. But I think I heard enough," I said.

"You look really tired. Sleeping in a chair isn't the kind of rest you need. Why don't I get you comfortable in our bed? I can bring you some chicken broth, or a smoothie, if it's not too much for your stomach. And you can get some more sleep."

"I'm not staying in this house."

"You can't leave when you're weak and still feeling sick. Besides, I want to be with you. Don't you want to be with me?" He put his arms around me and pulled me against him. He pressed his forehead into the top of my head. "I need you here. I want to be with you. I know this has been almost unbearable, but I don't want you to leave. Can't you give them, *me*, another chance?"

I felt as if my heart was being slowly torn in half. I needed to get out of there. If not just for my sanity, possibly for my life. Was I overreacting? Had Daniel been right every time he said that? He wasn't saying it now, but he probably thought it would upset me. Maybe, inside, he was thinking I was still being dramatic. Thinking his brother was a killer, that someone had poisoned my food.

"Please don't leave. Please."

I decided to wait. Just for a little while. I wasn't sure how long, but for a while. The break in his voice, as if he might cry, the press of his body against mine. I knew he loved me. He would keep me safe. And maybe, if I stayed a little longer, when I was ready to leave, he would go with me. We could escape his family together.

Eating dinner that evening was nerve-wracking. If someone *had* put something in my food the night before to make me sick, to potentially kill me, would they do it again? I felt like I was a fool to be putting a single morsel of their food into my mouth. At the same time, I was hungry. With each bite, I chewed slowly and self-consciously, trying to make myself aware of the slightest hint of bitterness or any other flavor that didn't seem to fit with what we were being served.

I chastised myself for not filling up on fresh fruit before I'd sat down at the dinner table. I could have begged off, saying I was still not feeling well.

But would they, whoever *they* might be, do it twice? *Had* they done it? I still wasn't sure. It was so far outside anything in my experience. I must be imagining it, making up stories in my head. At the same time, it felt real. Maybe the trauma of being so violently ill, and the resulting dehydration, had affected my ability to think clearly. Maybe the horror of that grave and the outright hostility from his family was twisting my thoughts into strange, unrecognizable patterns.

As I cut a piece of perfectly cooked steak and placed it on my tongue, telling myself it was impossible to put poison in a piece of meat, chewing it carefully, I became aware of Abigail smiling at me.

She'd placed her utensils on her plate and pressed her hands together as if she were praying, or ready to clap. "Daniel! Have you shown Claudia her new home?"

I felt the fork drop from my fingers. It clattered on my plate, but no one looked at me. They all had their attention on Daniel, looking at him with eager anticipation. "New home?" I said, my voice sounding dull and robotic. "What new home?"

Daniel blushed slightly. He looked down at his plate, then turned his attention to me. He gave me a tender, almost bashful smile. "It's supposed to be a surprise. It was decorated for you, to your taste. Do you want to see it?"

See it? I wanted to run as fast as I could back to my apartment seven hundred miles away. I wanted to be inside my own home. I wanted Daniel there with me as it had been before I knew anything about this family. I didn't want a *new home*.

Immediately I knew what the new home must be—one of the houses I'd passed every time I walked to lake. The houses Daniel hadn't wanted to explain. They'd tried to make me feel I wasn't worthy of their family or Daniel, but that wasn't it at all. Their plan was to re-make me. They'd poisoned me, not to kill me, but to make me weak.

Now, my decision to stay a while longer so that Daniel and I could leave together didn't feel like my own decision at all. I was going to be kept here forever. I could feel it, I could see it in the way they were all smiling at me.

THIRTY-ONE
CLAUDIA

At first, Daniel wanted to take me to this *new home* immediately after dinner. I told him I wanted to talk to him first. Alone. I didn't want to ask questions about this home in front of his family.

We went up to our room. When Daniel closed the door, my first instinct was to look for a recording device. Abigail's suggestion that he show me this new home was too perfectly timed with my suggestion that I wanted to leave their estate. Either Daniel had told his family I'd said that, or they were listening to our conversations.

Was this another hint of paranoia in my mind, or were they actually doing that? It made sense to me that people were listening to us. I felt as if they always knew what I was doing, were always appearing when I least expected it. That they always knew where I was, or were one step ahead of me. It sometimes felt as if they knew what I was thinking. Did they? Or had the poison affected my mind? Was this a rational thought, or something slightly insane? I wasn't sure. It felt entirely sane.

I glanced at the corners of the ceiling, knowing as I did that any listening device would be so cleverly hidden there was no way I would see it with a casual look.

"What is she talking about?" I asked.

"The other houses on the property."

I nodded.

"They're for each of us, when we get married."

"Are you serious?"

"Yes. Why?"

"You plan to live with your mother for the rest of your life? All of you?"

"It's not how you're making it sound. I'm not living with my mother in that immature way you're saying it. We run a complex business. It's for convenience, really. We—"

"Come on, Daniel. Other families run complex business operations without living together."

"Do they? How do you know?"

I didn't, but I was sure it was true. This was weird and slightly pathetic. She didn't want to let go of her children. Ever. Maybe because her husband had died and left her alone, maybe for some other reason. I wasn't sure why, but this was too much. Far too much.

"I don't want to live here."

"You haven't even seen the house. You'll be amazed."

"I don't care how nice it is."

"I've explained that our business involves the entire family."

"You have. Several times."

"So, this is important. Don't you even want to see it? You're not giving it a chance. You're not giving *me* a chance."

When he said things like that, his words hit me in my core. It was too hard to fight him. I didn't want to fight him. I didn't want any of this. I didn't want these thoughts of murder and poison and a woman trying to keep me from marrying her son, while at the same time wanting to hold me captive inside a twelve-foot wall with a security gate I couldn't operate.

I let him hold me for a few minutes. After a while, I felt as if he was propping me up. My legs were limp, and I wasn't sure if it was the lingering effects of my poisoning, my weakening resolve, or my need for him. My desire for him. Maybe it was pure exhaustion.

"May I show it to you?" he asked.

"I don't know." I moved away from him. "Maybe. I guess." I felt my pocket, checking for my phone. I wasn't sure why. Habit, I suppose. It wasn't as if I would hear from my sister. And my friends from work had gone dark, mostly because my replies to them had been so few and far between.

"Let me show it to you. Please?"

"Okay. But I need to find my phone."

"Why do you need it now?"

"I don't know. Habit."

"Where did you last see it?"

"I think when I was in that sitting room with the huge, cozy armchair and the jigsaw puzzle."

We walked down the hall. We entered the room where I'd napped and woken to overhear Elliot and Faith. I shoved my hand between the chair cushion and the arm, feeling around for my phone. It wasn't there. I lifted the cushion. No phone.

I knelt down and looked under the chair. I sat back on my heels. "I can't believe I left it in here, but I was upset—"

"Maybe Greyson picked it up."

Daniel and I went downstairs. His family was in the entertainment room watching a movie.

"Hey, has anyone seen Claudia's phone?" Daniel asked.

Without turning their attention from the screen, they all gave quick shakes of their heads to indicate they hadn't. I wasn't convinced they'd even heard him, the movements were so slight, but Daniel seemed to accept their responses.

Greyson was sitting at the kitchen bar, a mug of tea on the counter in front of him.

"Haven't seen it," he said, in answer to Daniel's question. "But it can't have gone far."

"I think it was in the room with the jigsaw puzzle," I said.

"He said he hasn't seen it," Daniel said, moving toward the back door.

When Daniel turned away, Greyson gave me a sympathetic look. "It's isolated enough here, not having a phone would be—"

"Let's go look at the house," Daniel said. "You don't need your phone."

I felt exactly the opposite. Greyson read my mind. I couldn't leave this place. My phone was the only thing connecting me to the rest of my life, the last thing tying me to the outside world. To reality.

I dragged Daniel back to the sitting room where I'd napped. "Call it," I said.

He pulled out his phone and tapped my number. I always kept my phone on silent, but as we stood there, not speaking, we should have heard it vibrating. There was nothing.

THIRTY-TWO

CLAUDIA

I collapsed into the armchair. Without my phone, I was completely cut off from my sister. It was a ridiculous way to feel, because I'd been cut off from her for months. My emails were nothing but an electronic diary that she would read at some imagined future point in time. Most of the stories would be old news by the time she saw them. Some of them, not news at all.

For my entire life my sister had been my protector. I knew it was childish of me to think of her that way, but it was how we'd grown up. Knowing I couldn't instantly tap out a message to her made me feel unbearably anxious.

Worse, was the knowledge that someone in this house had taken it. And worse still, was the awareness that sharing that thought with Daniel would open yet another round of him begging me not to accuse his family of doing bad things, making excuses for them, telling me I was taking it the wrong way.

"I don't understand why you think you need your phone right this minute," Daniel said. "I'm here. Who do you need to text or call?"

"I just want to know where it is. It bothers me that someone took it."

I waited for him to say he felt the same. Instead, he glared at me, then tried to soften his expression. He moved closer until his legs were touching mine. "Let's go see the house. Your phone will turn up. They always do."

"This house came at me out of nowhere. The timing seems a little..."

"A little, what?"

"A little convenient. Like it's a distraction. Did you tell your mother what I said? That I want to leave?"

"I haven't even talked to her. When would I have done that? I've been with you."

I didn't know. But he could send a quick text as easily as I could. "Did you say something to Abigail? No one mentioned this house for a week and a half. The minute I find out your brother might have killed his wife, that your mother is probably protecting him from being found out, and I tell you I want to leave, suddenly everyone is excited for me to see some house I'm supposed to fall in love with. Two days ago, they didn't think I was worthy of marrying you."

"No one said that. Ever."

"Hmm."

"Why can't you see what's going on here? I don't think your family is simply loyal and close, I think—"

"Stop. Just stop."

"I'm scared. Can't you understand that? It looks like someone tried to poison me."

"No one poisoned you. No one killed Elliot's wife. It was a horrible accident."

"How? How did she drown? Didn't she know how to swim?"

"Do we have to get into that? Why can't you trust me?"

"Because I keep finding out things you never told me."

He was silent. He took a step back from the chair, so our legs were no longer touching. I missed the feel of him against me. I wanted to leave this place. I wanted to leave more than almost anything I'd ever wanted. My body was screaming at me, every cell was crying out that I needed to escape. But I missed the feel of his legs against mine. I loved him so much, I wasn't sure I could leave *him*.

I was so confused. How could I love him so deeply and be so afraid of his family? How could I love him but continuously feel he wasn't listening to anything I said? How could he not *see* what I was seeing?

"Let's go back to your room," I said. "My phone must be there. Maybe I left it on the closet shelf when I was changing clothes. Or something." I couldn't think where I might have left it. The more I thought about it, the more certain I was that I'd put it in my pocket after I'd emailed my sister when I was sitting in this very chair. And then we'd gone to dinner. But I hadn't been feeling well. Maybe my memory was blurry.

When we stepped into the bedroom, Daniel hit my number again on his phone.

The answering vibration of my phone rattling and buzzing against wood were distinct, coming from inside the cabinet at the top of his dresser. I went to the cabinet and pulled the handle. It was locked.

"Why is it locked?" I asked.

"I don't know."

"Why is my phone in there?"

"I don't know."

"What kind of answer is that? It's your dresser. And it's locked. Is that how you plan to keep me here? In your little house that was decorated just for me?"

"I didn't put it there."

"Well, someone did. Who else has a key?"

"I'm sure there's an explanation."

"So, you have the only key?"

"I thought so, but..."

"Unlock it."

He went to the nightstand and got his keys. "I didn't take your phone. I swear I didn't. And I didn't lock it in the cabinet. I didn't do this."

"Then who did?"

"I don't know. I can't explain it. Maybe you... you've been weak. Delirious? You haven't eaten."

"Do not blame this on me."

"No. I shouldn't have said that. I'm sorry. I'm just trying to make sense of it." He pulled out his keys and stood staring at them, not speaking, his back turned toward me so I couldn't read his expression.

THIRTY-THREE

CLAUDIA

As Daniel turned, I saw a brief look of fear flicker across his face. It was so quick, I wondered whether I'd imagined it.

"The key isn't here," he said.

"You think someone stole my phone, took your key, and locked my phone in your dresser?"

He stared at me. He didn't nod; he didn't look away.

I wasn't sure if I should be scared of him. Was he telling me the truth about the key? About my phone? About anything? Without my phone, there was no way to get someone to pick me up. Even if I had my phone, that gate with its mysterious lock had simmered at the back of my mind since it closed behind me the day I arrived.

Maybe they were holding me captive now that they knew about my past. They knew I wasn't fit for their family, but because I knew about Tina's death, they couldn't let me leave. They couldn't let me communicate with anyone. Faith had betrayed me. She was worse than all of them! The one person, aside from Daniel, who I thought might keep me safe here, had told them I was in a mental health facility.

"Please believe me. I'm on your team, babe." He came toward me.

For the first time ever, my first instinct was to shrink away from him. The size of him compared to my five-foot-five frame was intimidating. Until that moment, he'd made me feel safe. "If you're on my team, leave with me," I said.

"I can't abandon my family. Running the winery is my career, my livelihood. What would I even do? Okay, maybe someone took your phone. But it's still likely there's a reasonable explanation. Maybe the housekeeper put it away and someone locked the cabinet."

"And took your key?"

"I don't know. Sometimes things look one way and there's a completely logical explanation."

"If you say so. But I'm not staying here."

"Just see our house. And then I'll go. We can stay at a B&B in Calistoga and work through all of this."

"I won't be living in the house, so I don't see the point in having a tour."

"It's not going to be like this."

"Like what?"

"We'll work it out." He tried to put his arms around me.

"How we can *work out* the fact that your brother killed his wife? Or watched her die and did nothing? Whatever happened to make your mother decide to bury her in your own backyard so no one would find out she was dead." I'd wondered about Tina's family, but since their wedding announcement said her parents were deceased, maybe her extended family wasn't close. Her social media had that comment about going *off-grid*, so it was possible no one at all had put much effort, if any, into looking for her. Maybe they assumed she was too good for them now, living a wildly lavish life on a beautiful, historic estate with a household staff to meet all her needs.

Daniel took my hand. "Let's go see it."

"And then you're leaving with me?"

He sighed.

"You said—"

"Yes. I said we can stay at a B&B."

"Anywhere. I just need to get out of here."

"I want you to feel comfortable. I want you to know how much I love you, that I'm taking care of you. That my family respects you. No matter what impression you have."

I didn't have an impression. I had facts. Was he gaslighting me again? Or was he truly that blind to how awful they were? I kept flipping back and forth, and it was making it hard for me to stick with my decision to leave. I knew what my friends had been trying to say, until I cut them off. I absolutely knew what my sister would say, no matter how much I pretended otherwise, writing to her in silence.

We walked down the stairs. No one was in the living room as we passed through and out to the back patio where the waterfalls splashed in the warm evening air, the soft lights giving the impression that life was tranquil.

Walking past the pool, I looked into the water, wondering why I was wasting my time with this. I supposed it was genuine curiosity. I couldn't understand why this house had never been mentioned until this evening. He was acting as if he'd been planning this all along.

I wouldn't have wanted this even before I learned about how controlling and creepy they were. There was no way I would ever live in a house on his mother's property.

As we passed the outdoor kitchen area, I was startled to see Greyson sitting at a small table, gazing at the pool. He had a whiskey glass in front of him and was smoking a cigarette. Daniel went ahead of me. As I slowed my steps to smile at Greyson, he mumbled something. I stopped.

I looked at him. "What?"

He put the cigarette to his lips. The tip glowed for a moment, then he took it away and blew out a stream of smoke.

"It might not be wise to live in one of those houses. Elliot's wife did that. The main house is safer. More people around."

"Why?"

He put the cigarette to his lips again.

"Why do you say that?"

"What's wrong?" Daniel called back to me.

"Nothing," I said.

"It's not *safe*?" I asked in a low voice.

He took a sip from his drink. His gaze met mine.

"Why isn't it safe?"

"The last one..." He put the cigarette to his lips.

"The last one, what?"

"Daniel is waiting." He picked up his drink and finished it. He stood, put out his cigarette in the ashtray, then took his glass and went into the house.

THIRTY-FOUR

CLAUDIA

Catching up to Daniel, I took his hand. "Did Tina and Elliot live in one of these houses?"

"Yes, why?"

"It's just so strange. Everyone living together. And the other one is for Abigail?"

"Of course." He squeezed my hand.

"I don't get it. Why would all of you want to live on the same property as your mother? Don't you want some independence? It's bad enough working together. You're going to eat dinner together every night for the rest of your lives? What about when we have kids?"

"They can grow up with their cousins. How great is that?"

"This isn't a safe place for children, with all the unfenced water."

He laughed. "I'm glad you're thinking about children instead of running away from here. But that's a long way away. We'll figure out something."

I wasn't thinking about children at all. I was trying to understand what he was thinking. I wanted him to explain why he accepted this situation as if it were normal. I wanted to know if he'd ever given any thought at all to having a normal, independent life outside the direct line of sight of his mother and his siblings.

"Did Tina like the house?"

"Let's talk about that later. I want to show you the house."

He sounded excited. He seemed to think I would lose my will to leave the moment I'd had a tour of a house I'd never asked for and didn't want.

He put his key in the front door lock. I didn't understand why he needed a key, since it was sitting on their own property that was locked down like a military base, but I said nothing.

We went inside and until my brain caught up with my senses, I had a quick intake of breath, half a heartbeat of falling in love. From what I could see in the entryway, the house was nothing like the main house. There was none of the lavish, overdone, too-formal décor. It was open and light. Even at night, I could imagine what it would be like in the daytime.

The walls were pale peach, and the furniture was modern and simple. The carpets were soft colors, and the wood floors were ash. The artwork was modern and peaceful. There were no statues, no chandeliers, and no heavy antiques, velvet, or mahogany anywhere in sight.

He walked me around, showing me a good-sized house with a living room, family room, and a formal dining room that looked out on a garden with a pond. There was a library and a small TV room on the first floor. Between the library and TV room was a separate climate-controlled wine storage room. He opened the door briefly to let me peek inside.

The bedrooms on the second floor all had large windows with simple coverings rather than the heavy brocade draperies that were featured in many of the rooms in his mother's chateau.

I loved it. But I would never live there.

"What do you think?"

"It's very nice," I said.

"I know what you like." He pulled me close and gave me a long, deep kiss, to which I yielded.

We walked down the stairs, pausing on the landing where a small collection of family photographs and a few empty frames hung on the wall. "These are waiting for us to fill them," Daniel said.

"Mm."

He started down the second set of stairs.

"This is you and your dad, when you were nine, or ten?"

"Yeah. Let's go."

"How did your father die? You've never said."

"I don't want to talk about it."

"Are you serious? Daniel. Maybe that's what's wrong with your family. You don't talk about *anything*. You bury it all, and then it erupts in this bizarre behavior."

"Not true. And our behavior isn't bizarre."

"Yes, it is."

"We're in constant communication. A business of this size and complexity requires—"

"Your father died twenty years ago. At least. Why can't you tell me how he died? A heart attack? Cancer?"

"Stop."

"No, you stop." He turned and looked up at me. "Why can't you tell me how your father died? We're engaged. Married people share all the parts of their lives, they understand the past so they know who the other person is."

"He drowned, okay? It was awful, and we don't talk about it. A lot of years have passed and—"

"I'm not asking for gory details. I asked a simple question. You, and your whole family, make things seem creepy and weird by refusing to answer the simplest questions. When you refuse, it gives the impression you're hiding something. Don't you see that?"

"I see that you want to dig into every painful thing you can find. You want to rip us apart."

"I don't. I love you. But I want to know about you, and I want to understand the crazy people you love so much, the people you're so utterly loyal to."

"They aren't crazy."

"I'm sorry I said that."

"Okay. Do you like the house?"

I wanted to know if his father had drowned in the lake, but I could imagine how that question would go over. Pain was etched across his face. Why was it still so painful after all this time? I still felt pain over the way my mother had treated me, and the horrible thing that had happened to her, but it wasn't so raw. I didn't lash out if someone asked me about her. I suppose I still lashed out, but I had things under control more than this family did. I was able to interact like a normal human being. My secrets weren't buried so deep I didn't know they were there, unlike the Keller family secrets seemed to be.

"Do you? Like the house?"

"It's very nice."

"That's all you can say?"

I walked down the stairs to meet him. "I thought we agreed to leave. To get some perspective." He looked so vulnerable, I didn't have the heart to tell him I would never live in this house. I couldn't tell him that right now. Maybe later. Maybe a long time later. But not now.

THIRTY-FIVE

CLAUDIA

We stood on the front porch of the house that would never be lived in, unless Daniel married a woman who wasn't me. I put my arm around his waist, maybe to make up for my own feelings of sadness, knowing I would be letting him down. He'd clearly spent time thinking about what I liked and arranged to have the house decorated with me in mind. He'd dreamed of us living there together. No matter how strange it was that he wanted to remain so close to his mother, it was sweet that he'd had daydreams of living in such a beautiful home with me. Maybe that's why he couldn't hear what I was saying.

I stroked his arm. "Why is it so hard for you to talk about his death, even after all these years? Why was it so terrible? Why can't you tell me?"

"What would that accomplish?"

"It would help me know you better. Maybe it would help me understand your family. You're shutting me out of some-thing important. I've told you about the traumas from my life. Hiding from my mother so she wouldn't drag me across the kitchen floor and shove my hands into her vomit until I cleaned it up." I shuddered. Except for my sister, no one else knew that story. I hated telling him something so shameful when he wouldn't tell me a thing about the pain in his life.

"I've never talked about it," he said.

"If you can't talk about it, maybe you should have had therapy. All of you."

"Elliot took it a lot harder than I did. He blames me. That's another reason I don't want to talk about it."

"What *happened*?"

He leaned against the door. After a moment, he turned, pressing his forehead against the wood.

At first, I thought he was crying, but his body stiffened, then he turned back to me. His face looked drawn in the dim light over the door.

"My mother doesn't swim."

I looked at him, waiting for more. It was a confusing way to start, but I wasn't going to speak and interrupt the flow before it started.

"My father was canoeing. It was night. Elliot and I were already in bed, but for whatever reason, Abigail was still awake. She'd demanded my father take her out in the canoe. My mother was on the pier, I think, telling him to come back. I don't know. It wasn't a great idea to go canoeing at night." He was quiet for a few seconds, breathing hard. "The canoe capsized."

His voice broke. He put his hand over his face for a moment, then continued. "Abigail was only six, but because she was wearing a life vest, and the canoe turned back onto its side, she managed to hang on, or something. I was never sure of all the details. I wasn't there, so I don't really know."

He gasped as if he couldn't get enough air. "My mother was screaming. She ran to the house and woke Elliot and me. We came out and she was screaming at us to go get them while she called for emergency help, but we're a long way from emergency help. Right?

"Elliot got there first. He pulled Abigail out of the water.

And then we looked for my father. There are a lot of vines and grasses growing on the bottom on the lake, and somehow, my father got tangled in them... and..." He shrugged. "Now you know. Let's go back to the house." He started walking.

"Wait," I said.

He walked faster.

"Daniel, wait. We should talk about it."

"What the hell is wrong with you? There's nothing to *talk* about."

"But I can tell you feel—"

"It doesn't matter how I feel. It happened and it can't be changed. We survived. We don't need to discuss it. We don't need to second-guess it. We don't need to mope around about what could have or should have or might have been different or who should have or could have done this, that, or the other thing."

"That's not what I mean. It's obvious you feel—"

"I feel because you made me describe the whole thing. We should be thinking about our future, not some terrible thing that happened a long time ago and can't be changed. Not ever. It's over. It is what it is, right?"

"You can't just brush off your father's tragic, traumatizing death with a quip."

"You asked me to tell you, and I told you. What do you want from me?"

I wasn't sure what I wanted. The story sounded confusing. I didn't understand why a little girl would be canoeing with her father at night. A child that age wouldn't even be able to paddle a canoe. But he clearly didn't need me questioning the circumstances. He was right about that part. It was also clear that he hadn't dealt with it at all.

Why hadn't they had therapy? Why had Janice let them down like that?

I probably wasn't one to talk. At the same time, I knew a lot about traumatic death. More than most. And the Keller children had watched their father die right before their eyes.

Shouldn't they have talked to a professional when they were small? And Janice herself, unable to swim, standing there while her husband was trapped at the bottom of a pristine but deadly lake?

And now they lived with that lake, and enjoyed it as a tranquil, inspirational retreat on their property? I shivered thinking about it. If it were me, I would have drained it and planted a field of wildflowers or something. How could they sit in that gazebo and look at that sapphire water and feel any sort of peace?

Clearly, Daniel felt no peace at all. I didn't understand why he'd taken me out there for a romantic evening, sharing a bottle of wine, to watch the moonlight on the water, gazing out at the spot where he'd watched his father lose his life.

THIRTY-SIX

TWENTY YEARS AGO: ELLIOT

I was dreaming about playing with my black lab and the kid next door. Except, there were no kids next door. There was no one next door because there was no next door. There was no one living around us for miles. As far as we could see from the second-floor windows that looked over the walls surrounding our property, all we saw were endless rolling hills and valleys of grapevines, stretched on wooden arms that turned to monsters in the shadows before dark. I didn't have a dog either.

But in my dream, I had a dog. And kids next door. So, I was pretty happy, and I didn't like hearing my mother screaming at me. At first, I thought it was because I'd let the dog into the house. Then I realized the dream was over and my mother was yanking the blankets off my bed, crying that I had to help.

"Get up! Run!" She grabbed my ankles, dragging me off my bed as she shouted to my brother across the hall, "Daniel! Are you *up*? Your father's in the lake. You need to find him. Hurry! Before it's too late!" She was sobbing, slapping at me, pulling me toward the door.

I was out of bed, stumbling across the room in my pajama pants, no shirt because it was a hot summer evening.

Lunging out of the room into the hallway, I was met with bright lights and a clear view of my mother's panicked face.

"Hurry! You have to *run*! He's under the water. I think he's trapped. Hurry *up*!" She ran back to Daniel's room. I heard the smack of her hand on bare skin. "Get *up*!"

I didn't wait to hear more. I ran down the stairs, almost falling on my face as I skipped steps. I raced through the living room, across the patio, and along the edge of the pool. There were lights along the sides of the pathway leading toward the lake. I could see the lights in the gazebo and the fairy lights strung above the pier.

Gasping for air, running as fast as I could, I tore through the night, my bare feet hitting the path, hardly noticing stray pebbles that pierced my skin.

The water was so dark. I sloshed into the lake while my mother screamed, trying to yell at me where my sister and father were, where the capsized canoe was. I swam out and found my sister. Her tiny hands gripped the edge of the canoe. Her entire body was shivering. Not from cold, but because she was scared. She could swim a little, she was six, but not in deep water like that. Not at night, alone. I dragged her, holding her up out of the water with the help of her life vest until we reached shallow water, and I could put my feet on the muddy bottom of the lake.

By then I was crying so hard I could hardly see. I didn't know where Daniel was. My mother screamed hysterically. I couldn't even understand what she was saying.

I went back into the water, feeling sick to my stomach and so tired, thinking how long it had been since the canoe went over and my mother ran all the way to house and up to our rooms and all the way back and I swam to my sister and carried her to the shore.

All that time, all that *time*, my father had been under the water. Somewhere. I didn't even know where.

I swam out to the canoe. It was drifting, moving in circles, a big hollow thing like a dark red log, turning slowly in the water. I was screaming and crying, "Daddy! Daddy! Dad! Where are you?!"

I dove under but I couldn't see at all. It was so dark. I was crying so hard I couldn't hold my breath for more than a few seconds. I came up and dove so many times I didn't even know where I was. I wasn't sure anymore where the canoe was.

Then I saw his face, and I swam toward him. His eyes were closed, and his mouth was partially open, and I knew he wasn't holding his breath. I screamed, sucking in buckets of water, so I had to shoot up to the surface. I howled up to the sky, but I had to get him. And then Daniel was beside me, and we went down together.

My father was wearing these boots that had hooks that the leather laces wrapped around. The underwater vines had caught on those hooks. We had to tear at the vines. They were thin, but really strong and hard to break. We had to keep going up for air and diving down. Finally, we tore them off. We each took one of his arms and tried to hold him up and we swam with him to the shallow water.

By the time we got there, my mother had taken my sister to the house.

The paramedics were there. They took him out of the water, and we collapsed on the ground. They took care of us, and him, and... it's all a blur.

We didn't leave the lake until the sun was starting to come up.

He shouldn't have taken the canoe out at night.

But Abigail.

She always had to have her way. She cried and threw a fit. She wanted to go for a boat ride. She always did that. She was always throwing fits and getting her way. He always gave her what she wanted. My mother didn't, but he did. Anything she wanted, she got it. She wanted to chase the moon across the water. So, he took her out in the canoe.

My mother was on the pier, upset that he'd given in to her again.

Mommy begged me to save him, and I couldn't. It was my fault I didn't save him in time. Daniel said it wasn't, but if I'd run faster, if I'd let Abigail hang onto the canoe in her life vest for a while, if I'd turned the canoe over and put her inside, I could have saved him. I *would* have saved him.

If Daniel hadn't stayed in bed so long. If he got up when my mother told him to, and helped me, Daddy wouldn't have drowned.

THIRTY-SEVEN
NOW: CLAUDIA

I didn't sleep all night. Or maybe I did because I was in a weird dream-state that involved running up and down the stairs of the house I'd been given or would be given when I married Daniel. Except they didn't want me to marry him.

I was so confused.

Greyson said the house wasn't safe. He almost implied that Tina died because she'd moved into one of these houses with Elliot.

They said the house was decorated specially for me. Maybe that meant it was my tomb. Did it?

Faith told them I'd been confined to the mental health facility. Why had she done that? I thought I could trust her. I thought she was like me! She was funny and she pretended she was nice and easygoing and she understood why I was worried, and then the first thing she did was run to my worst enemy and tell her something horrible that made my future mother-in-law decide I wasn't worthy of being in their family. Now that Janice knew about the mental health facility, what if she dug deeper in the background check and found out what I did to get placed there?

Did I still want to be in their family?

I still loved Daniel. But I hated them. They were horrible, awful people.

Janice was like my mother—cruel. Hateful. The only difference was, she hid it. Or she tried to. She kept her claws retracted. She sliced you open with her words instead of with the daggers on the ends of her fingers and the ones in the wood block on the kitchen counter.

Sleeping was hard because my stomach felt like there was a knife buried deep in my stomach, piercing every part of my belly. Searing pain that made me curl into a ball.

I was crying silently, trying to hold the pain inside. I'd learned how to do that when I was a tiny little girl. I knew how to keep pain to myself. I couldn't let Daniel hear me. I wasn't sure why. I just knew I couldn't.

Someone had poisoned me, and he didn't believe me. He didn't believe they'd stolen my phone. He didn't even believe his mother treated me like a stray cat the day I arrived.

He wouldn't believe me now.

Why did I still love him? I suppose because I remembered how he used to be, before he brought me here.

I remembered the first time he smiled at me. I remembered him staring at me, and how his eyes looked deep into mine and it felt as if we understood each other.

He understood who I was, and I understood who he was. Maybe we were just two damaged people searching for something we shouldn't have been asking of the other.

I felt another stabbing pain and bit down hard on my tongue. I had to do something to make this pain stop. I got out of bed and crept quietly across the room. I opened the door and went into the hallway.

Someone else was awake.

Something had woken me. Music maybe? A very soft sound of music, but I couldn't tell where it was coming from.

I crept through the house. I could hear them, but I couldn't see anyone. And I could still hear the music, so soft I couldn't say what the song was, or if there were words. After I'd walked along the hallways on the second floor, and then slowly down the massive staircase and through the rooms on the first floor, I paused in the living room. I still felt their presence, but I couldn't see anyone.

Opening the door, I stepped outside. The only sound was the splashing of the waterfalls. It was too late, even for the chirping of crickets. Then, I heard the music again. Was it louder? I didn't think so, because I still couldn't quite hear it. The softness of it was starting to make me feel crazy, tickling at my brain, but not able to decipher the notes.

I wandered around for a long time, not sure where I was going, twinkling lights burning into my eyes in some areas, then plunged into total darkness as I wandered off the paths in others. I felt as if all the bad memories of my time at Chateau Noir unraveled in my mind, pummeling my body. I wasn't sure if I was awake or dreaming. I wrestled with people I couldn't see, shoving them away from me.

After a while, my head felt clear again.

I started walking along the path to the lake. I wasn't sure why, maybe I wanted to see where Daniel's father had lost his life. Maybe I could understand why he would sit in that gazebo and look out at the water and feel calm. It made no sense. Or was the music coming from that direction?

The lights along the sides of the path led the way. I saw the gazebo in the distance. The fairy lights were turned on. Someone was sitting inside.

Feeling as if I was in a dream as I stepped into the gazebo, still slightly unwell and feverish, barely aware of who was sitting there, I drank the wine that was offered. It wasn't long before I realized my mistake. It too was laced with something meant to weaken my body, and worse, my mind.

The fairy lights became one large glittering blur. I heard the lapping sound of the water on the shore, overtaking the music that had now died out. My fingers were numb and a similar numbness spread through my toes and was slowly moving to my ankles. If I didn't run now, I would end up in that lake. Just like Daniel's father. Just like Tina.

Floating with blank eyes, staring up at the sky until they pulled me out and placed me in a forgotten grave.

As I felt myself being dragged toward the water, I clawed at the hands gripping my wrists. I broke free, not knowing how, fighting like a wild animal, knowing I had nothing to lose and only my life to save.

And then I ran. I ran faster than I ever had, along the path. Despite the numbness, I ran, breathing hard, hearing footsteps behind me, faster and faster. I raced to the door of the house where I was meant to live with Daniel. Maybe I could find a place to hide, if it wasn't too late.

PART TWO

THIRTY-EIGHT

PRESENT DAY, THREE MONTHS LATER: RENEE

I climbed out of the car and looked at the stunning ivy-covered chateau with the long pool of water and refreshing fountains in front, flanked by large, tree-shaded lawns.

Daniel stood just outside of the oversized arched doors, waiting to invite me into that beautiful home that provided sanctuary to monsters.

I returned his smile as he walked toward me and kissed me on the lips. He whispered into my ear as he swept me toward the massive front doors. "You look gorgeous. My mother can't wait to meet you. She'll absolutely love you. She'll see how perfect you are for me. My other half." He kissed me again before ushering me inside, leaving me alone for a moment while he went to get his mother.

I stood in the entryway, feeling demure and unlike my usual self in a pink cotton dress with matching pink flip-flops, my hair pulled back, my eyes wide with wonder. Of course, I would appear to be his perfectly fitted other half. I'd studied him. I knew everything he liked. I knew his quirks and dislikes. I knew the kind of woman who would fit into this family. I'd made myself into the perfect woman for him.

I moved my hair in front of my shoulder, so the soft curls fell over my collarbone and down across the top of my breast. The low voices of Daniel and his mother traveled into the entryway.

I knew about this house as well. Voices carried. How this family lived here without being more aware of that, I wasn't sure. Maybe they were too self-absorbed to notice. Maybe they were so used to being here alone, to living with their secrets, they'd never had to keep their voices down until recently, and so they'd never noticed.

Now, I heard his mother. Her rich, warm tones making her sound welcoming, but her words, bitter and cold. "It's too soon for you to get engaged again. I promise you, that girl is a viper."

"You can't do this to me. You have to give her a chance." Daniel's voice was an urgent, childish whisper. Pleading and meek.

I might have been a viper. A treacherous snake entering their home. Ready to betray them. But this was a pit of vipers. I knew that for a fact. Someone here had murdered my sister—Claudia.

THIRTY-NINE

RENEE

Janice swept around the corner and into the entryway.

"Renee. How lovely to meet you." She took my hand. "What a beautiful ring." She let go of my hand just as quickly, as if she'd burned herself. "Such a quick engagement. You're not..." She looked pointedly at my abdomen, then returned her attention to my face with a grim smile. "Are you?"

"Am I, what?"

"Don't be naïve, Renee. You and Daniel have only known each other, what? Two months? And you're already engaged? I'm asking if you're pregnant."

I laughed. "Oh! No, I'm not. But thanks for asking."

She gave me a tight-lipped smile. Still holding my gaze, she said, "This one has a sharp tongue."

"*This* one? Am I auditioning for a harem?"

Her mouth opened and she stared at me. She closed it firmly.

"Renee." Daniel said. "That's not—"

"Why don't you get dressed for our cocktail party," Janice said. "I'm sure you want a shower after your flight. I'll see you on the patio at five." With that, she turned and walked down the hallway, her high heels clicking on the tile, echoing into the living room with its cavernous ceiling.

"Why did you say that?" Daniel whispered, guiding me toward the stairs.

"Say what?"

"All of it, actually."

"She was rude."

"She wasn't—"

"She was." I kissed his cheek.

"You need to—" he said.

"Yes. Okay." I gave him another kiss, but I was here for one reason only—to find out who had murdered my sister and where they'd buried her body. Janice was in for quite a few surprises. A viper indeed.

In one of her emails, Claudia had told me that Janice was cold and dismissive to her when they were alone, but gushing and warm when Daniel was around. With me just now, that hadn't been the case. I wondered why she'd allowed her claws to come out when he was present. It was possible I'd pushed too fast. Two months was a rapid progression from setting up a slim but believable background as Renee Harris to conceal my identity as Riley Gatlin, the sister of Daniel's previous fiancée. From first meeting him during a tasting and tour of the Chateau Noir Winery to a one and a half carat diamond on my left finger. But I had no time to waste.

The police had done next to nothing when I returned from my trip to find hundreds of emails from my sister, but no sign of her. I'd immediately reported her missing. The Napa police had contacted the Keller family, even paid them a visit, but they hadn't gotten a warrant to search their property. There was *no probable cause*. Her phone had last pinged from San Francisco. Multiple times.

The last thing she'd posted on social media stated she was going *off-grid*, whatever the hell that meant. The police had contacted her friends from work a few weeks prior to that. They'd reported that she seemed happy here, only slightly uneasy about fitting into a wealthy, prominent family whose lifestyle was so different from Claudia's. They said they'd warned her of a few potential red flags in the relationship with her fiancé, but there was nothing that they would call *threatening*. It was simply that Daniel seemed to put his family first, not her. That was no reason to suspect the man or his family of causing his fiancée's disappearance!

The police agreed there was great cause for concern, but no one had seen her, so there was no real starting place. The family said she'd left their estate suddenly and without giving any explanation.

The police were *looking*. I'd given them a photo, but that was it.

Young women go missing every day. They *take off*, I was told. Law enforcement couldn't *do much* if no one had seen her. It was true there hadn't been any activity on her credit cards. She'd sublet her apartment before leaving for her stay with Daniel's family. The family was upstanding and respected and just because she'd stayed with them and left without providing a reason, vanishing after that, did not cause them to assume murder. They told me to calm down.

I was not going to calm down. But I decided then I would absolutely channel my lack of calm into something proactive. So here I was, pretending I was wildly in love with Daniel Keller.

This family had no idea how much I knew about him. Claudia had been very detailed in her emails. She shared all her secrets with me. We'd always done that. We had to do that in order to survive our childhood. I knew this family as well as she had after living with them for weeks. I knew them even better, because I had the perspective of distance.

In Claudia's emails, I read the story of her relationship with

Daniel, their engagement, and the increasingly frantic accounts of her time spent with the Keller family.

The emails stopped abruptly. I'd texted her as soon as I was back online. She hadn't responded. I'd seen her weird post about going *off-grid* but had assumed it had nothing to do with me. I'd texted a few more times and called repeatedly, but my calls went right to voice mail.

After a day and a half trying to reach her, I called the police. Their first words were to calm down.

I was certain that if her phone pinged in San Francisco, it was not pinging from her hand. She'd described the Kellers' electronic gate and twelve-foot walls. She'd never mentioned any plans to leave the estate. And now, there'd been no communication from her for several weeks, after a year of almost daily emails. Someone else had her phone.

I hadn't turned her emails over to the police. Maybe I should have, but when they opened the conversation with a directive to *calm down*, I had a feeling where it was going to go, and that feeling turned out to be accurate.

So, I gave them an overview of her experiences, leaving out the creepiest, because I didn't want them distracted by a body buried on the property. I wanted them looking for Claudia. But their efforts on that front had been half-hearted, at best.

My efforts would be whole-hearted. I would not leave this house without finding out what they'd done to her. I had a sick, horrible feeling that vow might mean I would be leaving with her body. I tried not to think about that, but if that turned out to be the case, I was prepared.

They were going to face my wrath. I'd protected Claudia all my life and I was not stopping now.

FORTY

RENEE

The cocktail party turned out to be a *party* of three, just as Claudia had described from her arrival day. Janice asked questions about my life and career. She wanted to know about my family and how Daniel and I had met. She seemed pleased that I'd worked as a caregiver to the elderly.

She was not pleased that I didn't want a cocktail.

"Not even a gin and tonic?"

"No, thank you."

"A glass of our reserve Chardonnay? You can't say no to that." She gave me an insistent smile.

"No, thank you. Do you have sparkling water?"

"This is a cocktail party, Renee."

"I don't drink alcohol."

"Why not? We own a winery!"

That wasn't any of her business.

"Mom," Daniel said.

"It's a legitimate question," Janice said. "Are you an alcoholic?"

"Mom! She doesn't have to—"

"I can speak for myself. I don't want a cocktail or wine. I

asked for sparkling water. May I have some?" I looked up at Greyson who was hovering slightly behind Janice's left elbow. It looked as if he might be hiding a smirk.

"Yes, certainly," Greyson said. "Would you like a slice of lemon or lime with that?"

"Lemon sounds nice." I gave him a glowing smile.

After the drinks were served, Janice raised her martini. "Welcome to our family, Renee. We look forward to getting to know you."

We all sipped our drinks, silent for a moment or two.

When I asked where the rest of the family was, Janice took another sip of her martini and asked whether Daniel had given me a tour of the house. I told her he hadn't. She offered to do that herself, after she finished her cocktail.

The tour was informative and told me Janice was all about going over the top, with lighting, with art, with dramatic style, with authentic period pieces of furniture to fit the chateau that had been built in the late eighteen hundreds.

I was introduced to Daniel's brother when we entered the dining room. He greeted me with a cool smile, then turned his attention to Janice.

Dinner was filet mignon and whipped potatoes with buttered baby carrots. There was a lot of wine, and neither Elliot nor his mother liked it that I refused even a sip. There was a long discussion about the quality of their wine, the pleasures of wine, the ages of their wine, the history of their wine cellar, and how wine was meant to enhance the food that had been so expertly prepared. The subtext suggested I was not enjoying my food to its fullest without dribbling alcohol across my palate before and after each bite.

It tasted quite nice to me.

When the meal was over, they went into the entertainment room and turned on a baseball game. They watched the game in silence except when they complained about calls they disagreed with or let out the occasional cheer or groan. Janice was the most engaged. Elliot and Daniel seemed to be there for her enjoyment, but maybe I was reading into it.

I was suddenly aware of how much I was going to have to endure to find out what happened to my sister.

Later, we entered Daniel's bedroom, but I remained near the door. "Is there another room where I can sleep?"

"Why?" He looked concerned.

"I'm not feeling well." It wasn't the best excuse, and I should have thought of a more solid reason, especially remembering Claudia's belief that she'd been poisoned, but it was the only thing I could think of without causing a major disruption.

"Do you have a headache or something?"

I gave him a limp smile. "My stomach is..." I placed my hand on my abdomen. "I just, I would feel better in a bed by myself."

"Why aren't you feeling well?"

"I'm not sure." I laughed softly, trying to keep my laughter limp and weak to maintain the lie, something I was fairly good at when it was absolutely necessary. A matter of life and death. "Maybe the flight?" I didn't want to venture into the food poisoning or he might wonder, remembering Claudia.

"Let me get you some water. Change your clothes, go lie down, and you'll feel better."

"I really don't—"

"You'll be fine."

"There are so many bedrooms. Surely there's somewhere else?"

His expression softened. He came toward me and touched my cheek. "It's safer if you sleep with me," he said.

"Safer? That's not very comforting. *Safer?*"

He laughed. "I shouldn't have said that." He laughed again. "I don't know why I said that. But yes, safer because you don't know the layout of the house. If you get up in the middle of the night, you might get lost, or—"

"That's crazy."

"I'd just feel better if you were with me."

"I feel better sleeping by myself when I don't feel well. Can't you understand that?"

He shook his head.

He wasn't going to offer another bedroom. I could gather up my PJs and toothbrush and wander the halls looking for a room, or I could climb into that absurdly high bed with its fur throw and keep to the plan.

I'd already slept beside him. I wasn't sure why it was bothering me now. Maybe because I was on his turf. Now, I was locked inside the walls that Claudia had mentioned repeatedly. I could disappear as completely as she had. There was no escape. I was now completely in the hands of this disturbing family, and I had to perform twenty-four-seven.

The only one who could save me was myself.

FORTY-ONE

RENEE

When Daniel turned off the bedside light, his hand slithered across the mattress and found mine. He patted it gently.

"I hope you feel better." His voice was low.

I imagined him speaking in that gentle voice to my sister. Night after night. I imagined him holding her hand when she was ill, holding her close when she wasn't. And then, someone in this house doing something unspeakable to her. Now, she'd vanished. Had she been strangled? Stabbed? Where was she? Had one of them taken her to the lake and held her under the water while she thrashed and fought for her life, and then buried her somewhere on this vast property? Which one?

If I was the kind of woman who cried easily, I would be crying now. I'd cried plenty of tears for her when I realized she wasn't going to answer my messages or calls. But now, my heart was a cold, solid stone, filled with determination. Behind my eyes were burning flames that would destroy this family.

I lay awake most of the night. I knew I needed to sleep. I couldn't spend days, or more likely, weeks in this house staring into the darkness, alert to every sound, every shift in temperature. But this first night, my mind was not going to allow me to let down my guard, even for a moment. I couldn't sleep. I could only think about my sister.

I didn't toss and turn with restlessness and frustration at my inability to fall asleep. I lay still on my back, staring into the darkness, remembering Claudia's emails.

In the morning, I was beyond tired, but still very much alert. Daniel's side of the bed was empty, so I must have fallen asleep at some point.

I showered, dressed, and went downstairs. Janice and Daniel were in the kitchen. They were sitting at the bar, sipping espresso.

"How did you sleep?" Janice asked.

"Not well, to be honest." I went to the espresso machine.

"Don't touch that. Greyson will make whatever you'd like," Janice said.

Hearing his name, Greyson was suddenly in the room. He listed the coffee drinks he could make for me. I chose a cappuccino.

"I'm sorry you didn't sleep well," Janice said. "The mattress, our pillows are top—"

"I doubt it was the mattress," I said.

"What was it?" She sounded only mildly concerned, not bothering to make eye contact with me.

"Probably just an unfamiliar place."

"I have some lorazepam. I don't use them regularly, but the prescription is up to date. I'm happy to—"

"I don't need a sleeping pill," I said.

"I feel terrible that you were lying there all night, Renee. We don't want that."

"I'm fine now."

"What about tonight?"

"I'm sure I'll sleep tonight."

"I don't want you to be uncomfortable. Please take one. I'll get the bottle for you. So, you have them handy." She slid off the bar stool.

"Please don't," I said. "I don't want them."

"Daniel said you weren't feeling well."

I shot Daniel a look, but he avoided my gaze.

"Maybe I sensed something after all," Janice said. She smiled. "You're sure you're not pregnant? Is that why you're refusing to take something to help you sleep?"

"I'm not. I wasn't feeling well. Let's not go imagining things."

"I'm very intuitive. Maybe you are and you don't even know it." She gave me a teasing smile. "It would be fine with us, don't worry about the wedding, or the timing of—"

"I'm not pregnant! So please stop."

She glared at me as if I'd told her the wedding was off.

"I know my own body. I don't appreciate other people thinking they can figure it out better than I can."

"Then let me get the lorazepam. I don't want you feeling uncomfortable."

"No, thank you."

"One or two won't hurt. You won't get addicted after a few nights, if that's what you're worried about," she said.

"I'm sure I'll sleep well tonight. One bout of insomnia doesn't require medication." I gave her a reassuring smile.

I needed to keep better control of our conversation if I was going to stay focused on finding out what happened to Claudia. Talking about pregnancy and sleeping pills was going in the wrong direction. "Let me have my coffee and breakfast and I'm sure I'll feel much better."

Janice left the room while Greyson made me an omelet and toast. He placed the cloth napkin on my lap and put out a selection of condiments to season my omelet. I gave him a grateful smile. He responded with a friendly wink. I had to look away to keep from laughing. He seemed to be almost entertained by this creepy family. How did he manage it?

I was nearly finished eating when Janice returned. She handed me a clear glass vial with a black plastic cap. Inside were six white tablets. I handed the vial back to her. "I said, I don't need sleeping pills."

"I'm concerned. I feel terrible that you didn't sleep well."

I laughed. "It was one night."

"I'll ask Greyson to put them in your nightstand in case you change your mind." She put her hand on my shoulder and rubbed it gently. "No one will think less of you for taking them, if that's what you're worried about."

"Please don't. I can take care of my health. And I prefer not to use drugs for sleeping, or staying awake, for that matter."

She glanced at my cappuccino, but said nothing.

"Fine. I've allowed one, mostly innocuous drug, that's also a delicious beverage, into my life. But I'm not taking a sleeping pill, and I don't want to talk about it anymore and I don't want those left in my nightstand. We can forget all about one sleepless night."

Janice left the room again, leaving the pills on the breakfast bar in front of me.

While I finished eating, I stared at the vial of pills. Why was the first thing that happened to me here a suggestion that she wanted to put me into a deep sleep that might incapacitate me?

FORTY-TWO

RENEE

That afternoon, I met Daniel's sister, Abigail. She pounced on me as I was coming out of the kitchen with what I now viewed as my drug of choice—an iced latte. I'd almost had to sneak into the kitchen in order to avoid having Greyson make it for me. He wanted to do everything for me, including opening water bottles. A housekeeper, a woman I mostly saw from the back as she disappeared around corners, did all the things he didn't, everything from making our bed, to replacing my damp bath towel with a clean one, to moving my PJs from the bathroom hook where I'd left them to a hanger in the closet.

Abigail smiled at me, her full lips heavily glossed with a color that was similar to my coffee drink. She extended her hand. "Hi, Renee. I'm Abigail, Daniel's sister."

I shook her hand.

"I'm so excited he's getting married. Let me see your ring."

I moved my coffee to my right hand and held out my left.

"So beautiful. You must be so proud."

It wasn't the word I would have chosen for being in love and getting married. It caught me by surprise. I wasn't sure how to respond. "He's an amazing man," I said.

She smiled. "I want to make an amazing dinner to celebrate your happiness."

"How thoughtful," I said.

"Tonight."

"That's—"

"You have to tell me all your favorite foods."

"Okay. Let me give it some thought. Have you asked Daniel?"

"I know what he likes."

"Why don't you tell me, and I can suggest a few things that are compatible."

"Don't worry about that. Just tell me what you like. All the faves."

I sighed. "There's not a lot I don't like."

"I want your favorites. Not just the everyday likes."

"Veggies—green beans. Grilled peppers are always good."

"What kind of meat?"

"I don't know. I really... you've put me on the spot. How are you going to get all this in time?"

"We can order and have it delivered. It's no problem. Just tell me what you love."

"I love clams. Crab. Snapper."

"My mother hates clams."

I laughed. "Okay. Oysters."

She nodded. "I'm not sure Elliot—"

"You know, Daniel is your brother. Maybe you should focus on what he likes. If he's happy, I'll be thrilled." I patted her arm.

She seemed to recoil slightly.

We finally settled the favorite foods, with a compromise between what Daniel liked, and my absolute favorite dessert— fresh peach pie.

"Can I help you get it ready?" I asked.

"You're the guest of honor," Abigail said.

I'd hoped to find out more about her, dig into their family, but maybe she sensed that I was over-eager.

I left her to her dinner preparations. Then, forty-five minutes before she'd told us to make our appearance in the dining room, I showed up in the kitchen, already dressed in a black dress and black shoes with high silver heels, ready to offer help, and get her talking.

"You look amazing," Abigail said.

"Thank you. I wanted to see if I could help."

"I already told you—you're the guest of honor."

"I'm just drifting around with nothing to do. Please let me at least put out napkins, or water glasses."

"Greyson will take care of that."

I leaned against the counter. "Did you make a dinner like this for Daniel and his former fiancée?"

Abigail's smile stiffened, then disappeared entirely. "How do you know about her?"

"Daniel told me. Obviously. We talked about our other relationships. Doesn't everyone?"

She grunted softly and drove her knife through the red snapper she was cutting.

"What was she like?" I asked.

"Why do you care?"

I laughed. "Just curious."

"That's a weird thing to talk about right before your engagement dinner."

"She's just a bit of a ghost. Daniel didn't want to talk about her. And I'm just curious if I'm anything like her." I laughed softly. "Since he and I got together so soon after he split with her. That's all."

"You're nothing like her," Abigail said. "And good riddance."

"Why—"

"Let me see some pictures of you and Daniel."

"You're cutting the fish."

"I can take a short break." She turned and began washing her hands, chattering nonstop about how photogenic Daniel was, and she was sure I was too because my dark hair and blue eyes were such a stunning contrast.

It was what set my sister and I apart—her light brown hair with blonde streaks, my dark hair, taking after our mysterious, never seen father. Her hazel eyes and my bright blue. People hadn't believed we were sisters when we were young. That was to my advantage now. Our smiles were identical, but a smile wasn't something people tended to focus on or remember.

"And your face is so perfectly shaped," Abigail said. "Your wedding photos are going to be breathtaking."

I pulled out my phone, playing along with her game. I would get back to my questions in a moment when her guard was lowered again. I showed her a few selfies in restaurants and bars.

"Oh, so cute." She swiped her finger back and forth across my screen.

I didn't like her touching my phone, I didn't like her swiping around as if she had a right to explore my phone. It wasn't as if there were a lot of incriminating things on there. I'd bought a burner phone before I started my relationship with Daniel, so there were no pictures of Claudia and me. Our text and email histories weren't present. That phone was powered down, tucked into an interior pocket of one of my bags. But still, I didn't like her presumption she could put her fish-scale-encrusted fingers all over the screen.

I took a step away from her.

Abigail picked up the boning knife and resumed cutting the fish. Then, she paused again. "Actually, I could use your help. Would you get the large salad bowl out of the lower left cabinet in that room?" She pointed the knife across the island toward a good-sized storage room that housed the pantry as well.

"Leave your phone there so I can see more pics."

"There aren't—"

"I might want to use one of those for the company newsletter. To announce your engagement. I need to see them again before I choose."

I sighed and left my phone on the counter. I went into the storage room, calling back to ask which bowl she wanted.

"The large glass one. You can't miss it."

I returned with the bowl and placed it on the counter. She then sent me to the fridge for salad ingredients. Once I was busy chopping veggies and tearing butter lettuce, I figured she'd had time to cool down over my earlier interrogation.

"Why did you say good riddance to Daniel's former fiancée? I had the impression from what he said that she was kind of a sweet, easygoing—"

"She didn't belong here."

"What happened? You're scaring me a little." I laughed, with what I hoped was a nervous edge. It wasn't difficult.

"It's nothing scary. He just needed to get that girl out of his life. It was a good thing. The best choice."

"I thought she took off. That she kind of disappeared, or something. That's what Daniel made it sound like. You're making it sound like he broke up with her."

"And she took off."

Her words were disconnected from what I'd said. As if she hadn't been fully listening. "That's why she disappeared? Because he broke up with her?"

"My mother did not care for her. Not at *all*." She laughed. Her laughter swelled until it seemed to fill the entire kitchen, which was no small feat.

It sounded like a cackle. I wasn't sure if I was imagining it, or it was the flow of the whole conversation that made me feel very unsettled, and more than a little frightened. I'd come here so confident that because I knew what I was getting into, I would be in control. I could figure out what happened to Claudia. But that laugh was downright terrifying.

Maybe it was only my lack of sleep, the pressure to take sleeping pills, her clear disdain for Claudia. All of it.

FORTY-THREE

ABIGAIL

Talking to Renee made me think about my mother.

And my brothers' parade of women through this house.

I'd had a few relationships, but nothing serious yet. Because I knew exactly the kind of man I wanted, and the kind of man who would make the perfect partner for me. My brothers seemed to be practicing the scattershot approach.

My brothers were both a little unstable, through no fault of their own. They'd been traumatized by our father's death. Not that I wasn't. I was right there, but my trauma was different from theirs. No one had expected me to save his life. No one woke me in the middle of the night and sent me diving under the surface of a dark, cold lake, trying to see where he might be.

Of course, they blamed themselves for his death.

Maybe they were also more traumatized because they were boys. They kept their feelings inside instead of expressing them. Although my mother insisted we all keep our feelings inside, so that's probably not it. She called it wallowing when we talked about our feelings, when we cried or moped. But she certainly found ways to express hers. She indulged the expression of her emotions—by demanding we stay close to her every second of our lives. By making sure we were only equipped to work in the family business so we could never leave. We were tied to her emotionally and financially. Socially, too, in many ways. And of course, careerwise, which wasn't just a financial handcuff, but also our sense of satisfaction, our place in the world.

As a little girl, my emotions weren't as squashed as my brothers'. Maybe.

Or maybe they had issues because they thought our mother blamed them. I honestly don't know. It wasn't as if we were allowed to talk about it. Most healthy adult siblings would have found a way to talk about things among themselves, to work out the kinks in the shared, and unshared, aspects of their upbringing. I suppose that speaks to how unhealthy we were.

For whatever reason, maybe because they were blinded by the feelings of blame, by the fear of wallowing which led to an extreme lack of self-insight, my brothers did not seem to understand my mother's power. As a result, they didn't listen to her. They were always fighting her. Overtly, and passively. They'd done it since they were young.

My mother was a force to be reckoned with, as the cliché notes. She had a multi-million-dollar winery to run after my father's death. She had three young children to raise by herself.

My brothers didn't respect the strength required to do that.

She knew what she was doing. She had to figure things out. She had to be smart and tough. They thought they knew better. Despite not having a father around after the ages of eight and ten to feed them a diet of male entitlement, they still grew up thinking they were smarter and more competent and savvier than my mother. Maybe it wasn't about being male at all. Maybe it was about being a Keller. I should know. But for me, it didn't manifest as underestimation of my mother.

My mother knew what kind of partner would suit each of us. She knew us better than anyone. Why couldn't they see that? She'd given birth to them, raised them with my father.

Watched them suffer the loss of their father. She stood as a guardian over their guilt and shame for failing to save his life.

She knew the responsibility each one carried for that failure. She knew Elliot's guilt, and she knew Daniel's shame, buried so deep he didn't even know it was there. She knew everything about those men. And she knew the type of woman who would fit each of them. She knew the traits that would blend into our family. Also critically important, she knew what kind of women she would get along with and the personalities that would mesh with mine.

My mother had so much wisdom. It was awe-inspiring.

I couldn't understand why Daniel and Elliot didn't trust that. Why they *refused* to trust that wisdom and insight. It wasn't that difficult! They acted as if it was some badge of honor to choose a woman themselves. Who cared? It wasn't as if my mother was going to choose someone unattractive or uninteresting.

What did they think the benefit was of running into a stranger and finding out about another person in bits and pieces, asking a million questions, trying to figure out if this person would be a good fit? They tried to force their chosen female partners into the family after they'd fallen in love.

It was backward.

My mother knew what kind of women were suited to our family business. My brothers were making life difficult for her. They didn't even understand their own nature. They thought they were normal men. They thought meeting a woman and carrying on a typical relationship could work out with a charming happily ever after, that those women wouldn't start to wonder about them.

FORTY-FOUR

RENEE

Our engagement dinner was boisterous, but not because of me.

Daniel and his siblings laughed and talked as if I wasn't there. They told stories about the winery and the people who worked there. They recalled events from their childhood, teasing each other when their memories didn't line up, arguing playfully about who was remembering correctly and who was willfully altering the story to make himself or herself come out looking better.

The food was delicious, but no one seemed interested in my opinion, even Abigail, for all her insistence on knowing the specifics of my favorites.

When the meal was over, I told Daniel I needed some time alone. I wanted to go for a walk around their property. I needed to be outdoors. I needed to escape their braying laughter. The stories and jokes had felt like a deliberate attempt to make me feel like an outsider. Had they been? I had no interest in being part of this dark, murderous group, so it wasn't as if I was feeling insecure or lonely. Rather, I had a detached view of the situation. Which made me believe they were absolutely going out of their way to highlight the fact I didn't belong and I never would. A wedding and a gold band on my finger wouldn't change that. I would never share their history, and they wanted to be sure I understood that, celebratory dinner or not.

Why?

Was all of that engineered by the matriarch? They seemed determined to please her in every little thing. It felt as if none of them had developed beyond the emotional ages they'd been when their father died. Was that the truth? Or was I over-analyzing them?

"I'll go with you," Daniel said.

"I need time alone."

"Why?"

"I just do. It's a beautiful evening and I want to enjoy the quiet."

"We don't have to talk."

I placed my hand gently on his chest. "I need a few minutes."

"You don't know your way around."

I laughed. "It's not that complicated. There are paths, and walls. I doubt I'll get lost."

"I don't know if—"

"I just want to go for a fifteen-minute walk by myself. Okay?"

He nodded, but he looked concerned, as if there were something deeply unsettling about a simple request to spend a few minutes alone. I kissed his cheek and walked quickly through the living room, trailing my hand across the skirt of the statue that stood near the doors as I went out.

I walked along the edge of the pool, calmed already by the splashing of the waterfalls and the silence of the surrounding night, the fading of the voices inside the house.

I knew where I was going. I had my phone as a flashlight, but for now, the paths were lit by small lights, and the sun had just disappeared behind the mountains, leaving a deep purplish-blue color across the sky.

I was on my way to see Tina Keller's grave that Claudia had written about.

Seeing it for myself seemed important. The need to find it, to see that flat stone with her initials and a vague date, a marker that barely indicated it was a grave at all, had burned inside me since I arrived. Part of me was terrified I would find another stone nearby with Claudia's initials scraped into the surface above the year.

I didn't truly think they would be audacious enough to bury my sister and mark her grave. Not when the police had been here asking about her. But the police hadn't come onto the property. And that had been two months ago. Did they think they were safe now? Or maybe there would be a suggestion of a grave without a marker, waiting for time to pass.

I walked quickly along the path, trying not to look over my shoulder to check that Daniel wasn't following me. I didn't think he was, but he'd been so reluctant to let me go, I could imagine his curiosity getting the best of him.

When I came to the rock garden that had been mentioned in Claudia's email, I slowed my pace. I also indulged in a quick peek over my shoulder. No one was behind me. No one I could see in the growing darkness. If he had followed, it probably didn't matter, although I wanted time to clear my thoughts. I wanted to think about what Abigail had said. The chatter over dinner had filled my head with so much noise, I felt the need to sweep it clean.

What did those words mean—that Daniel's fiancée needed to be *out of his life*?

In the shadowy light, I saw the trellis and a few artistically designed rock towers, but nothing else. I moved more slowly now, careful to be sure I didn't veer off the path where it was more difficult to see, even with my unnaturally bright light.

As I approached the trellis, I felt an unexpected surge of emotion. It was a fear that Claudia's fate was even worse than Tina's, if that were possible. Tina's death had been described as a tragic accident, her body buried, weird though it was to choose a spot on their property, in plain sight. No one was hiding anything. They knew how she died, and although they'd been absurdly reluctant and secretive about it at first, they had finally told Claudia about her death.

My sister's fate was a complete mystery.

I stared at the smooth flat stone with Tina's initials and the year of her death. There was nothing to suggest another body had been buried here. Still, my throat felt swollen, my head spinning with the anxious, imagined worst-case scenarios that come when there are no answers.

The only relief I felt was the relief that there wasn't an unmarked grave, waiting for a stone with my sister's initials. All the tension in my body, all the knots that had formed during my conversation with Abigail and throughout the surreal dinner party unwound themselves. I found myself standing straighter, turning away, and walking with slightly more ease.

For now, my curiosity turned to the rest of the walled property that I hadn't yet explored.

While the winery itself with its tasting room, fermentation and bottling facility, wine caves, and over fifteen hundred acres of vineyards, was a few miles down the road from the estate where the chateau was situated, there was a single wine cave on the property.

I'd learned from one of Claudia's emails that originally the chateau and surrounding property, including the lake, were part of the winery. I supposed it was before Janice and her husband became so insular and decided they needed to wall themselves and their children off from their employees and customers.

They'd left the single wine cave on their property as a storage place for their private collection. After each year's wines were released, a portion were taken to their wine cave for easy access before they were moved to the wine storage room inside the chateau to provide a selection for meals.

It wasn't that I thought I would find Claudia there, although the horrifying thought had crossed my mind because the caves I'd seen when I toured the winery with Daniel were only partially above ground, covered with earth and grasses and greenery, the entrances dark and hidden, almost as if they could be easily repurposed as tombs.

During our tour, he'd rushed me past them, and I wanted to see what it looked like inside. Until that tour, I'd never heard of storing wine in caves.

I walked to the far side of the property, following a section of the path where the small lights along the edge stopped and I had to rely on my phone's light to lead the way. Walking down a gentle slope, I found the wooden doors with the iron bands that held the slats in place, almost as if they were wine barrels themselves. I pressed down on the large iron handle and pulled open the door.

It moved with surprising ease. I stepped inside. Instead of the aroma of wine that I'd expected, I was assaulted by a foul odor. I pressed my hand over my nose, taking thin breaths through my mouth.

Aiming the light toward the ground I saw there were stone steps leading deeper underground. I glanced behind me at the door. A chill ran through me, wondering if I'd been followed. This time, it turned to fear. If I had been followed, would someone lock me inside and leave me for weeks on end, letting me waste away and die? Was my curiosity too risky?

I took a few steps toward the stairs that were carved out of the stone. I shone my light down.

I gasped softly, recoiling. Something... not something, someone lay at the bottom of the steps.

FORTY-FIVE

RENEE

I hurried down a few steps, no longer caring about the door behind me. I held up my light, letting it cast a wide circle around the space in front of me.

Her body lay on the ground at the bottom of the stone staircase.

At first glance, she looked serene, as if she were sleeping there. Her pale blue dress spread around her, shimmering in the ghostly light of the wine cave. The fabric looked so soft, as if it were made of expensive silk, but the design was simple and casual—a sundress for a summer picnic. The strands of her hair were equally silky, light brown with streaks of blonde. Her arm, resting on the bottom step, was relaxed, with three gold bracelets dangling from her wrist, one with a heart charm attached.

But when I took another step down, her face was all wrong. It wasn't filled with pain or torment, but at the same time, it didn't have a look of rest about it, like it should if she were peacefully dreaming. It was blank and cold. Her skin was too white with a sickly gray shadow. Her lips were too dark, parted slightly with a stiff quality to them. Her eyes were closed but they appeared sunken and almost glued shut.

Her toes were pointed in a way that didn't look natural. Her chest was motionless.

The air caught in my own chest and for several seconds, I couldn't breathe. I didn't scream or gasp or cry. I stared, the edges of my vision growing dark.

Looking at her was the second most horrifying experience of my life. And gazing at her lifeless face, I knew that if I didn't uncover the secrets this family was hiding, it was only a matter of time before someone looked with horror on my own lifeless body.

It took only seconds, less than seconds, for the airless, frozen shock to leave my body. I screamed, a long, wailing sound. The woman lying at my feet like a soft, discarded pile of clothing, her eyes permanently closed, was a stranger to me.

But the entwined E and F engraved on the heart charm attached to her bracelet was something I knew about. Claudia had told me about that charm. It had led her to believe that Faith and Elliot were more closely connected than the image they projected, where they seemed to drift about, hardly noticing the other.

The woman lying on the floor must be Faith Beckett. The woman Claudia had mentioned often in her emails, but who had been nowhere in sight since I'd arrived, whose name hadn't been mentioned once.

How had she ended up dead in the wine cave? How long had she been lying there? When was the last time Greyson had restocked the wine? It might have been months. She looked as if she'd been there for a while. I wasn't sure how I knew that. I just felt it. Something about the look of her skin. As if the cool, underground room had preserved her body, but wouldn't do so for much longer.

I pressed my hand over my mouth to stop the screams,

trying to calm myself so I could think. I turned and ran up the stairs, racing toward the house.

As I ran, I had a terrifying thought—what if she wasn't really dead? Only unconscious. What if she'd been held captive down there all this time?

I stopped, breathing hard. I should go back. Maybe I'd panicked and overreacted. Could she only be unconscious? I started to turn. No. No, she was dead. I knew she was dead. No one's face looked like that. I took a slow, deep breath. I needed to calm myself. I couldn't let on that I knew who she was. My heart thudded so hard I could hardly think. It felt impossible to carry on lying right now, but I had no choice. I began running again, pushing myself faster. I wrenched open one of the French doors and stumbled into the living room.

The faint aroma of fish wafted into the room from the nearby kitchen. Greyson was picking up two empty wine glasses that had been left on the end tables.

"Someone's dead! There's a woman's body—" My voice broke.

Greyson set a glass down hard on the marble-topped table. "What? Are you… what woman?"

"In the wine cave. She's dead! At the bottom of the steps. We need to call the paramedics or police. Someone!"

He stepped away from the table. "Show me." As he walked toward the doors, he pulled his phone out of his pocket, texting as he walked.

"I need to get Daniel." I turned away from Greyson and hurried into the entryway, climbing the staircase two steps at a time. I found Daniel sitting up in bed, looking at his phone. He startled when he saw me.

"Someone's dead! She—" My voice caught, and a sob came out of me. I didn't even know this woman. I wasn't crying out of grief, but the horror of it. The terror of what it meant. For my sister, for me.

Or maybe it was grief, in part. For a woman staying with a man she didn't quite seem to trust, for reasons Claudia hadn't been able to comprehend and that I would now never understand. No one would.

I sensed movement behind me. I turned.

Abigail stood in the doorway. "What's going on?"

Daniel threw back the covers. "Dead? How do you know—"

"She fell down the stairs! Or she was... she's in the wine cave. She looks so, so awful."

"How do you know?"

"I saw her!"

"When?"

"Just now. On my walk."

"Are you sure?" Abigail asked. "How do you know she's dead?"

Daniel was pulling on jeans and a T-shirt, shoving his feet into sneakers.

I turned slightly. "Yes, I'm sure. We need to call—"

"Slow down. Show us. We'll decide what we should do."

"*Decide?*" I said.

"Show me," Abigail said.

The three of us hurried down the stairs and outside. Daniel began a slow jog toward the wine cave. I followed, kicking off my flip-flops and carrying them so I could run more easily.

When we reached the cave, Janice was already there, holding a large portable all-weather lamp. Greyson was nowhere in sight.

"Oh, God." Daniel grabbed my arm.

"It's Faith." Janice kept her back to us, the lamp and her attention on Faith's body at the bottom of the stone stairs. "That poor girl."

Abigail put her arm around her mother's waist and pulled her close.

"Who is she?" I asked.

"Elliot's girlfriend. We thought she'd... Well, never mind. There's no need to talk about it now," Janice said.

"Where's Elliot?" Daniel asked.

"You need to tell him," Abigail said.

"Greyson's getting a tarp, and help. To remove her body." Janice still hadn't turned. Her voice was calm and low. If the night air hadn't been unusually silent, it would have been difficult to hear.

"You shouldn't move her," I said. "The police will want to see how we found her."

Janice turned slowly, pushing her daughter's arm away from her waist. "We don't need to bother the police. It's clearly a suicide."

"How do you know that?" I asked. "Did she leave a note?"

"Her mood. Her behavior. I just know."

"We still need to call them. Because—"

"We do not need to call anyone. You're not in charge here, Renee. So please keep your thoughts to yourself."

"I didn't say I was in charge. But when someone dies under unusual circumstances, you call the police. That's how it's done."

"Daniel, will you take her back to the house, please? And when you find Elliot, make sure he doesn't come out here."

"This is wrong," I said. "You can't—"

"Daniel!"

Daniel took my hand and tugged gently. I yanked it away from him. "What's going on here? Daniel told me Elliot's wife is buried here. So, are you planning to take Faith out and bury her right beside his *wife*? Just drop her in the ground like she never existed? The police need to find out how she died. They need to—"

"She threw herself down the stairs," Janice said. "It's obvious. We thought she'd run off. Just like... Will you please leave so we can take care of this without a lot of drama and arguing?"

"You have no proof that she threw herself down the stairs. She might have—"

"She's dead at the bottom of a stone staircase."

"It could have been drugs, she might have been drunk, she could have been hit over the head, she could have—"

"What are you trying to say?" Janice gave me a cold look that appeared to be a warning, even in the shadowy light.

Daniel grabbed my hand again. "Don't answer that. Please, let's go. My mother can handle this. It doesn't have anything to do with us."

"It? She isn't a dead rodent! She's a woman who was supposedly loved by your brother. She disappeared, or something. I don't even know. And now she turns up dead, weeks later? Months? I don't know. I thought she was someone you cared about. What about her family? Her friends? You don't just bury someone in your yard. The police need to—"

"That's enough," Janice said. "Daniel, I asked you to take her back to the house."

"Good idea," I said. "I can call the police." I turned and started walking back toward the house. I hadn't reached the palm trees when I saw Elliot hurrying along the path, breathing hard.

"What happened? Oh my God. She didn't. Please tell me this isn't... She isn't...?" His voice broke.

I stopped and reached for him. He moved out of my way, but Daniel was right behind me, sent by his mother, no doubt, to prevent me from calling the police. Daniel put a hand on Elliot's shoulder. "Don't go over there."

Elliot turned away, letting out a loud, painful cry.

The sound he made hit my stomach like a dull knife, driving its way into my gut. I doubled over, knowing his pain was real, tearing him apart. At the same time, I couldn't help wondering if both these men were killers—raised in such an oppressive environment, that something had snapped inside, something turning them into monsters who, for some deep psychological reason, hated the women who loved them.

It strained credibility to imagine two brothers becoming cold-blooded killers, but I didn't know what else to think. I felt the dull knife dragging through my heart, digging out fears that my sister might be buried on this property after all, her grave unmarked forever.

FORTY-SIX

RENEE

Elliott broke away from Daniel. He lunged forward, starting to run. Daniel went after him, grabbing at his shirt. Elliot jumped to the side, taking hold of his brother's wrist and twisting it until Daniel cried out and released his grip. Elliot kicked Daniel's shin, and as Daniel stumbled slightly, Elliot backed away, turned, and took off at a full sprint.

I continued toward the house.

I heard Daniel behind me, walking quickly, then Abigail's voice, telling him to slow down.

"Wait," Abigail said. A moment later, they were both beside me. Daniel took hold of my upper arm.

"Let go," I said.

He let go.

"We need to talk," Abigail said, pulling him away from me. "This is all happening too fast. Can you calm down for a minute?"

"I'm calm," I said.

"Let's just stop and talk," she said.

"There's no time. They're going to drag her body out of the cave and dump her in the ground. I need to call the police. I'm not even sure they can get here before they move her. And once that happens, I think it's more difficult for the coroner to—"

"Please wait. Please listen to me." She tried to grab my hand.

I moved away from her grasping fingers. "Her family needs to be notified too."

"My mother will take care of that," Abigail said.

"Will she?" I asked. "It looks to me like your mother wants to get her in the ground as fast as she can. Pretend she never existed."

"Don't say that," Daniel said. "Why are you saying that?"

"Because it's messed up. A woman's body has been entombed in your wine cave! The woman your brother loved. A woman who no one has mentioned since I arrived. Who hasn't been seen anywhere around here, as far as I know, and they're acting like it's nothing but an inconvenience. Your mother isn't a forensic specialist. She has no idea how she died."

"She knows people," Abigail said.

"Do you hear the words coming out of your mouth?"

"We'll notify her family." Abigail looked confident, as if she absolutely believed this. "If they're concerned, they can do an autopsy, or whatever. But if my mother thinks she killed herself, she's probably right. I don't see the point of getting the police involved in something so painful and personal."

"That is not how things work. Maybe you live in a world where you make up your own laws, but I don't." I cut myself off before I said more.

"What?"

"Nothing. I just don't understand how you think." We were at the back of the house now. I stepped inside and hurried to the stairs, running up two at a time, with Abigail and Daniel both at my heels.

"Please don't call the police. My mother won't take it well," Abigail said.

I laughed. Then I felt slightly ill. Was this going to make it more difficult for me to find out what had happened to my sister? Or would the police dig more deeply into her disappearance once they were here trying to find out what had happened to Faith? I wasn't sure. Part of me was wildly optimistic that this meant I no longer had to keep up this charade, that I no longer had to continue with the lies to deal with this deeply disturbing family. But another part of me was scared. Would they get lawyers, and secure their fortress even more tightly against the outside world? Was I closing the doors over my sister's grave forever?

I had to cling to the first thought. I had to hope this would open things up.

I charged into the bedroom and went to the nightstand where I'd left my phone. I grabbed it off the charging pad. Instead of opening as my face encountered the screen, the keypad appeared, requiring me to enter my passcode. Thinking it must have had a software update overnight, I tapped in my passcode.

It reset, wanting me to re-enter the passcode.

I tapped it in again. The phone remained locked. I stared at it helplessly. After a few seconds, my brain clicked into gear. Of course, I could still call 9-1-1 without the passcode. I swiped up to access the emergency feature. I tapped the numbers, but nothing happened. I moved the phone away from my ear.

"Can you please calm down," Abigail said. "You don't need to call right this minute."

I looked at the top of the screen. There was no cell service. I swiped down to check if airplane mode was enabled. The icon to turn it on and off was missing from the screen.

What was going on? I kept trying until it locked me out, suggesting I try later.

"Something's wrong," I said.

"What?" Daniel asked.

"My phone won't let me in. And someone turned off my cell access!"

"Can we please talk about this?" Abigail asked.

"Now it's locked me out."

"You're anxious, you probably entered it wrong," Abigail said.

"I didn't enter it wrong. And I sure didn't remove the airplane mode access. Give me one of your phones so I can call."

"We're not calling the police," Abigail said.

"That's a crime," I said. "Do you realize that?"

She closed her eyes and tipped her head back for a moment. She looked at me again. "Can we please talk about this?"

Daniel looked at Abigail, then me, but said nothing.

"I wonder how long I have to wait before it will let me try my passcode again," I said.

"Renee, we need to talk and you're not focused on what's important right now," Abigail said.

"I am. Someone changed the passcode on my phone."

"How is that possible?" Daniel asked.

"I don't know, but it's locked, and I know I entered it correctly. Even if I made a mistake the first time, which I'm sure I didn't, I was very careful the other times. There's no way I entered it wrong."

"You must have," Abigail said.

I threw my phone on the bed. "Did you reset it?"

"I don't know your passcode," she said. "How would I even do that?"

I glared at Daniel. He looked worried, slightly trapped

"I don't know," I said. "You saw me unlock it or something."

"Are you accusing me of blocking your access to your phone?" Abigail asked.

"You don't want me to call the police. So yes, I am."

"I didn't even know she was dead when I left the house. I couldn't have done that."

"Someone messed with my phone. That's all I know." I wasn't a technical person. There were probably lots of ways someone could access my phone and change the passcode. For all I knew, there were remote ways to reset it. Maybe someone had hacked my account. Maybe someone had called my provider. I didn't know how it had happened, but I did know I'd entered the code correctly and now, I couldn't get into the phone.

Later, when I was alone, I would get my other phone, my real phone. But for now, I was helpless.

FORTY-SEVEN

RENEE

Daniel insisted I needed some tea. Janice and Elliot were seated at the kitchen bar, sipping red wine so dark, I couldn't look at it. The color made me think of blood.

There hadn't been any visible blood around Faith's body. But as images of the horrifying sight flashed through my memory, I kept seeing the angle of her neck, distorted in a way that caused waves of nausea to pass over me.

No one at the bar was talking. Elliot was teary-eyed, gripping the edge of the counter for support. Janice was calm. Until she saw me, that is. Then, she looked concerned. She turned her attention immediately to Abigail and Daniel. "Where have you been?"

I spoke before either one could answer. "I was trying to call the police, which needs to be done right away. Is anyone going to do that?"

She ignored me, still looking directly at Daniel. Elliot stared into his wineglass, then took a long swallow. He reached for the bottle and refilled his glass.

"Do you want tea?" Daniel asked. "Or something else?"

When I didn't respond, he proceeded to fill the kettle with water.

"Who changed the passcode on my phone? I can't unlock it," I said.

No one answered.

"My passcode doesn't work. Someone was—"

"No one touched your phone," Janice said.

"You're wrong, because the passcode doesn't work."

"I told you, I think you entered it wrong," Abigail said.

"I didn't."

"You're upset," Abigail said. "I've done it so many times. Have a glass of wine."

"Faith's body is lying in your wine cave, and no one is doing anything about it!"

"Calm down," Janice said. "Greyson is taking care of it as we speak."

"Digging a hole in the ground like you would for a pet cat is not how you handle a woman's unexplained death. Her body should be taken by a coroner, then given a proper burial or cremation. The police need to investigate how she died. And I need a phone so I can notify—"

"You sound hysterical," Janice said.

"I'm the only rational person here," I said.

"Are you sure you don't want a small glass of wine?" Abigail asked. "It would help you relax a little."

"You know I don't drink. And I don't need to relax! I need you to—"

"I think she needs a sedative," Janice said.

"I'm not taking anything. Is someone going to give me a phone, or not?"

"We're not," Janice said. "We told you how this will be taken care of. We'll give Faith a beautiful burial. I'll take care of notifying her family. And you'll learn to adapt to how we do things." She took a sip of her wine.

I grabbed the mug Daniel had placed in front of me, in desperate need of some soothing, calming tea. I took a few sips, then carried it out of the room. I would get my other phone and call the police. It would expose the fact that I had two phones, but at this point, that was an insignificant issue.

More than anything, I wanted to grab all my bags, use that phone to order an Uber, and get out of this place. But escaping meant leaving my sister behind. Forever. And right now, I was gripped with a certainty that was more painful and more deeply rooted than ever, a certainty that I wouldn't be able to save her. Instead, her body was buried somewhere on this property.

I climbed the stairs slowly, sipping my tea as I went. I'd expected Daniel to follow me and was surprised, but relieved, that he'd left me alone.

As I closed the door to his room, I turned the lock.

I placed the tea on the nightstand, opened the closet, and pulled out my bag with the concealed interior pocket. I unzipped it and shoved my hand inside. My phone wasn't there. I didn't have to feel around. The pocket was small, and the phone was the only thing that had been stored there.

I sat down hard on the floor and put my face in my hands. Maybe I wouldn't be leaving this place either. Claudia and I would both end up here, our bodies hidden until the end of time. The thought was too much. I took my hands away from my face, stood, and shoved my bag into the closet.

The door handle rattled, followed by a knock.

"Renee. Why did you lock the door? Let me in. Please." Daniel's tone was quiet, gentle.

I went to the door and unlocked it, deciding in the few steps it took me to get there that I still wouldn't tell him about the second phone.

"Why did you lock me out?"

"I needed a minute."

"For what?"

"Your family is breaking the law."

"I—"

"They don't know how Faith died. And I don't trust your mother to notify her family. Her friends. Not to mention—"

"Faith didn't have any family. Her mother died when she was twenty. She never knew her father. But the thing is, if we call the police, there's no evidence anyone killed her. And—"

"That's their job to determine. To find evidence."

Was that the deal with these guys? Did they look for women who didn't have much family so that no one noticed when they went missing? That was the case with my sister and me. All we had was each other. And all she had now was me. If I pushed too hard to call the police, I would lose all hope of finding her body, or that slim, still lingering, desperate hope that she might still be alive.

If I found my sister, or found out who killed her, I would find who had killed Faith as well. And there was no doubt in my mind she had been killed. She didn't just *throw herself down* those stairs.

As my thoughts whirled, I continued talking. "It's creepy to bury people on your property. Even if it's legal. And I'm sure you still have to notify the authorities of a death. It makes me think she absolutely did not kill herself. Don't you realize how..." I needed to stop talking. I shouldn't be sharing my fearful thoughts. My shock at finding her body, at experiencing their reaction, was spilling out of me and causing me to talk without thinking.

He collapsed onto the bed. "I know we're not like other families. My father died when we were young and—"

"I know that. It doesn't mean you can use it as an excuse to do whatever you want. Your mother doesn't get to break the law. Your family can't blame every weird thing they feel like doing on losing your father, or husband, too soon. Millions of people lose a parent or their spouse when they're young."

"I wasn't finished."

I folded my arms and waited.

"My mother wanted to grieve alone. She wanted us all to stay close."

I stared at him, watching the contortions of his face. I didn't understand what this had to do with Faith's death and their refusal to report it. If he thought I was going to excuse what they were doing because they'd experienced trauma, he was wrong.

"We buried my father here."

"You just stuck him in the ground? Without a coffin?"

"We used a, uhm. My mother constructed a box."

"Oh my God."

"It's not what it sounds like."

"It's exactly what it sounds like."

"That's not how it felt at the time. Or now. It was sacred. It was meaningful."

"It's disgusting."

Tears filled his eyes. He shook his head gently. "It wasn't like that. The four of us said goodbye without all kinds of paperwork and officials and medical people. We kept him with us."

"Didn't anyone wonder what happened to him? He owned one of the largest wineries in—"

"Not really. You'd be surprised how little curiosity and interest people have in the lives of others, if their focus and expectations are managed."

"Didn't your mother need a death certificate to take full ownership of the winery?"

"We have good lawyers. And the people who work for us are loyal. My parents treat our employees really well, pay them generously." He shrugged.

Paying good lawyers well and getting a death certificate when there was no body to be processed through normal channels didn't quite add up in my mind, but the loyalty part... I could imagine what might fall under that umbrella.

"It felt really good having my father here with us." Daniel looked at me as if hearing those words would easily shift my feelings in the opposite direction.

"He was dead!"

He continued as if he hadn't heard me. "It's become what we do. We want to keep the people who are part of our lives close. Even in death. You can judge us. You can refuse to understand. But I hope you'll try to." He stood. "Until you live through it, maybe you can't understand." It almost sounded as if he were delivering a speech, playing a part, expecting that someone might be listening. Maybe someone was.

He walked to the door, opened it slowly, and left the room.

I didn't understand at all. What they'd done was demented. I was risking my life to find my sister as I clung to the irrational hope she might be alive. If she was dead, I would take her body with me and give her a proper burial. And then, I would make these people pay for what they'd done.

FORTY-EIGHT
RENEE

By morning, I was exhausted from a mostly sleepless night spent turning over the macabre and deeply disturbing behavior of Daniel's family. I vowed to keep my restlessness to myself so there would be no more discussion of sleeping pills.

I checked my phone, but was still locked out. I showered, dressed, and went downstairs to find the family gathered in the living room. Plans were being made to bury Faith's body that day.

As I listened to the chilling sound of their voices discussing the logistics as if this were nothing more than a rearrangement of the rock garden, my mind began to twist itself into knots again, wondering if I'd made the wrong choice in deciding not to continue fighting Daniel for access to a phone to contact emergency services. In letting them carry out their plan— putting my desire to find out what had happened to my sister above doing the right thing for Faith.

Or was that a dead end no matter how hard I fought? Did Janice with her *loyal* employees and *good* lawyers also have *supportive* connections in the local police department? How much of the security staff at the winery were former police who had buddies and relatives still on active duty?

I felt as if my morals were dissolving as the voices of the Keller family swirled around me, seeping into my brain, infecting me like some kind of virus. I was here to find out about Claudia. Maybe I was rationalizing, but I had to believe that finding out what had happened to her would provide answers to the questions around Tina and Faith.

They could bury Faith while I kept my attention on my sister.

Janice was standing near the doorway. She turned and started walking across the patio. Her offspring followed her like ducklings, as if they were small children, scurrying behind, anxious that they might lose sight of her if they weren't careful to keep up.

Once they were past the pool area, I stepped outside, following them at a distance to the wine cave.

Greyson and Daniel were carrying Faith's body up the stairs.

Elliot stood with his back to the entrance, looking up at the sky. Janice and Abigail watched with detached interest.

When her body was out of the cave, they wrapped it in white linen fabric, then placed it in a wood box. I watched in horror, wondering if the box had already been stored in one of the sheds, or hastily made during the few short hours we'd slept.

Then, they loaded the box onto the back of a truck and Greyson drove to the area in the rock garden where Tina was buried. The family walked there. When we arrived, Daniel and Greyson dragged Faith's makeshift coffin out of the truck bed. A grave had already been dug. I was sickened and stunned by their efficiency. It was starting to seem as if they'd been prepared for this. As if it were some kind of routine they'd practiced before.

But if that was the case, where was Claudia? Why wasn't she also buried here?

I felt a sob rise up in me. I clapped my hand over my mouth. Daniel put his arm around my shoulders, and I let him keep it there, feeling the need of someone to keep me upright.

He pulled me closer, and I leaned into him, strangely comforted, startled by a pleasant feeling of warmth as I felt my heart crack. What had they done with my sister?!

He thought I was weeping for Faith. If I was, I was almost alone in my grief. The only other person showing even a hint of sadness was Elliot, and all I saw from him was a drawn expression that made him look twenty years older. Was it grief, or guilt?

Once Faith's body had been lowered into her grave, Janice spoke the most bizarre eulogy I'd ever witnessed. "Rest in peace, Faith. We hope you find what you're looking for."

Then, everyone turned and started walking back toward the house.

Inside, they went their separate ways.

It wasn't even noon, but I felt as if I'd been awake for a day and a half. I went into one of the unused guest rooms, closed and locked the door, climbed onto the bed, and slid under the covers. Despite my churning thoughts, I fell asleep within seconds. I didn't wake until dinnertime.

I returned to Daniel's room. The moment I stepped inside, he appeared in the doorway from the adjoining sitting room. "Where were you? I was worried."

"I took a nap."

"Where?"

"In one of the guest rooms."

"Are you okay?"

"Not at all."

"We're having a dinner to remember Faith."

"That seems absurd."

He gave me a puzzled look. "You should wear a dress."

I wanted to laugh. I'd reached the point of feeling I was living in a lucid dream—aware that I was dreaming, unable to escape, confused and uncertain because all the people around me were acting as if they knew things I didn't, and lived by a different set of rules and beliefs than I did. They acted as if they were completely sane and normal, that there was something wrong with me.

I changed into a black sleeveless dress and black high-heeled shoes, and we went downstairs for another family meal that was sure to be even more bizarre than the others.

The meal was roasted quail stuffed with risotto and grilled peppers. I managed to choke down a few bites, trying to keep my attention on my plate. Elliot was across from me, and every time I glanced up, he was staring at me. Each time I cut a piece of meat or placed a forkful of risotto in my mouth, he asked whether I was enjoying my food. He wanted to know if it was seasoned correctly, if it was cooked to my liking, if the temperature was right.

His questions made my skin crawl. The others carried on a separate conversation, not seeming to notice Elliot was occasionally talking over them, oblivious to my discomfort. They were eating their food with gusto. Only Elliot seemed to be struggling to eat the way I was.

Finally, I couldn't take it anymore. My appetite was nonexistent, even though I'd eaten nothing but an apple for breakfast and no lunch at all.

I pushed my chair away from the table. "I'm going to lie down."

"Are you okay?" Daniel asked.

Elliot was halfway out of his chair. "Is the food making you—"

"It's not the food." I walked out of the room as quickly as my high heels would allow. I didn't want to go to the rooms Daniel and I shared. He would follow me the moment he had a chance to escape from his mother's attention.

Once I was past the doorway, out of their sight, I turned left. I paused and slipped off my shoes so they wouldn't hear my footsteps. Holding my shoes by the heels, like the stems of wine-glasses, I hurried along the hallway to the wing where the offices were located. There was another door out to the grassy area of the garden.

Leaving my shoes by one of the armchairs in Daniel's office, I slipped out the door. I walked onto the lawn and let my bare feet sink into the cool, soft blades of grass.

When I'd devised my plan to make myself into the woman this family would welcome with open arms, I hadn't given a lot of thought to exactly how I was going to find out what had happened to Claudia. I was scared she was dead, but at the same time, I was aware that deep inside, I was filled with hope that my fears would be proven wrong.

Since I'd been here, I'd learned nothing about what had happened to her. All I'd accomplished was to alienate every single one of them. I was fairly sure I was further away from finding out what had happened to Claudia than I'd been when I arrived.

There was no one I could ask directly. There didn't seem to be any chance of getting a truthful answer from any of them on any topic. I'd walked around most of the property and hadn't seen any other graves.

I crossed the grass and began walking toward the lake. It was already dark, so I moved slowly, watching the ground that was illuminated by the lamps lining the path. When I reached the gazebo, I went inside. I was surprised, given what had happened that morning, that someone had turned on the fairy lights strung around the gazebo.

I sat on the bench and looked out at the dark water in front of me. If Claudia was in there, like Tina had been, I would never find her on my own. But wouldn't I feel something if she was? Wouldn't I sense her presence in some way, feel some awareness that her life had ended here?

I tucked my feet back under the bench, leaning forward to hug my knees, trying to find some comfort in squeezing my body into a tight ball. As my bare feet scraped the ground, my toe caught on something cool and metallic. I stood and bent down, feeling under the bench, trying to see in the near darkness, with only the tiny lights to help me.

The fine gravel rubbed across my fingertips until I felt the chain. I pulled it out, letting it dangle across three of my fingers.

The tiny lights weren't necessary for me to know what it was. The broken chain, missing its butterfly charm, was identical to the bracelet hidden inside my suitcase where no one would see it and recognize it. Claudia and I had worn those matching bracelets every day. I'd bought them when I graduated from high school. They had been my promise to her that even though I was starting a new phase in my life, I wouldn't leave her behind.

A sob caught in my throat, then spilled out. She never would have left her bracelet here. She would have searched the entire gazebo, she would have crawled on her hands and knees in the dark to find it. Something had happened to her here. Something violent that broke the chain and forced her to leave without it.

FORTY-NINE

RENEE

As I curled my fingers around Claudia's bracelet, holding it close to my heart. I sat down on the bench and let the tears come hard and fast. More than I'd realized, I'd hoped Claudia was alive. I'd *believed* she was alive. The fact that there wasn't a grave had convinced me she hadn't been murdered.

But finding her bracelet like this—the chain snapped—was proof someone had been violent with her.

I sobbed harder, thinking of how it must have been for her, mistreated and assaulted without me there to help. What had they done? Was she tied up? Were weights attached to her body that caused her to sink to the bottom of the lake? Was that why I hadn't discovered a gravesite?

I was crying so hard it felt as if knives were tearing across my throat and lungs. My nails dug into the palm of my hand as I clung to the bracelet, wanting to keep this last piece of her close to me.

Every woman who came to this house died. But I wasn't entirely sure that Elliot had killed his wife and now his girlfriend. And Claudia had never mentioned Daniel being physically abusive. So, to suddenly escalate to murder didn't fit.

Something different was going on.

Was Janice killing every woman who dared to take her sons away from her?

Did she want them to remain celibate their entire lives? Or did she have an image in her mind of the kind of woman she wanted for them, women she could control and manipulate like she did her daughter and sons? The women they chose on their own weren't easily managed, so she got rid of them?

It was too bizarre to even think about. Between my broken sobs, I felt hysterical, maniacal laughter rising up inside me. It didn't seem real. Could this be happening? Did someone with such a distorted view of the world actually exist? It was both impossible to believe and the only explanation that seemed to make sense.

But it still didn't answer the question—where was my sister?

As my sobs grew softer, more rational thoughts taking over my despair, I heard Daniel calling my name as he approached the gazebo.

I tried to steady my voice but failed. "In here," I said.

He strode toward the gazebo and stepped inside. He crossed the small space and put his hands on my shoulders, pulling me up into his arms. "What happened?"

I leaned into him, crying softly. "Every woman who marries into this family dies."

He rubbed my back. "That's not true. Faith and Elliot weren't engaged."

"That's what you're focusing on? Whether or not she had a ring?"

"Well, I—"

"His wife drowned. His girlfriend was pushed down the stairs, or something. And—"

"I know it feels that way right now, because you found her body. But it's just a coincidence. The situations are different."

"I was locked out of my phone, and the women who come here die!"

He looked around, peering through the open sides of the gazebo. "Shh. Do you know how crazy you sound?"

"Do I?"

"Yes."

"I feel trapped."

"Let's go relax. I'll give you a massage. You can take a bath. We can get a good night's sleep. That's what both of us need."

I needed to figure out a way to find my sister's body. That's what this had come to. I needed to face that cold reality. I certainly couldn't drain the lake or go diving into twelve to fifteen feet of water across all that distance. Maybe she wasn't in the lake at all. Like Faith, maybe she too was in a dark tomb. Were there other wine caves I didn't know about? Was it possible she was somewhere outside the estate? In one of the caves at the winery itself?

What I needed to do was to get a grip. I was letting him see too much of me. I was letting all of them see too much of me. The shock of finding Faith's body, their behavior after, and now this, was all too much. I was losing sight of my goal. I was forgetting the role I needed to play.

Living a lie wasn't difficult for me. I've always been a person who will do absolutely anything for someone she loves. And I loved my sister with every cell in my body, with all my heart. I've always done whatever was necessary for her when she needed me.

I lied about what happened with Claudia and my mother, to make sure Claudia got the help she needed instead of prison time. I lied once to get on a jury when they asked me if I knew anyone who had committed a serious crime.

Hell, I even lied in my travel journal because I left out the parts about when I got sick and the time I was mugged. I left out some of the really stupid things I did that an experienced trav-

WELCOME TO THE FAMILY   235

eler should not have done. They were only lies of omission, but I know those are still considered lies. Still, I wanted to remember the good times. Doesn't everyone?

"You're absolutely right," I said. "I need to relax. A massage and a good night's sleep are all that's necessary." I let him put his arm around me and lead me back to the chateau.

FIFTY

RENEE

At three in the morning, we were woken by the frantic vibrating of Daniel's phone on the nightstand. I heard him fumble, knock it to the floor, then felt him lean over the side of the bed to pick it up.

"Yeah?" His voice was thick with sleep.

"Huh? Oh. Uh-huh." He was sitting up now, swinging his legs over the side of the bed, walking toward the closet. He opened it and grabbed his jeans and a T-shirt off the shelf. "Yeah. On my way."

"What's wrong?"

"A fire at one of our vineyards. It's small. Under control already, but I need to check it out."

"Now?"

"Yes." He went into the bathroom and closed the door. When he came out, he shoved his feet into shoes and was gone before I could ask any more.

I collapsed back onto the pillow and after a while, I drifted into a state where I felt I was still awake, but at the same time, surreal dreams played through my mind. Senseless stories blending events of the past few days and other random parts of my life.

At six, I woke fully alert. I took a leisurely shower, wondering how long it would take Daniel to assess the fire damage.

When I came out of the bathroom, Elliot was standing in the doorway of our room. He was holding a breakfast tray, complete with a metal cover on a large plate, a small pot of coffee, two mugs, and a bowl of strawberries with a small pitcher of cream beside it.

"Daniel asked me to look after you." He walked into the room without an invitation. He crossed the bedroom and went into the sitting room, placing the tray on the table between the two armchairs.

"I'm sure he didn't mean—"

"I knew you'd be hungry. You haven't been eating enough."

The way he said it made me think immediately of the lorazepam his mother had been trying to shove down my throat. Was it possible he'd laced my food with it? I thought of Claudia's email outlining the description of her bout with food poisoning.

I glanced at my phone on the nightstand. Still locked and unusable.

"I need to borrow your phone," I said.

"Why?"

"Because mine's locked."

He gave me a look as if to say he didn't believe me.

I held out my hand. "I need to call to get my passcode reset."

"If you say so."

I didn't want him to know I wasn't calling my regular provider, that this was a burner phone. I took his phone that he handed over reluctantly and went into the bathroom.

"What's the big secret?" he asked.

I closed the door without answering. It only took ten minutes for me to reach a human who said she could easily reset the passcode. It would take thirty to sixty minutes for the default to take effect.

After I hung up, I came out of the bathroom. I handed the phone back to Elliot. He grunted and shoved it into his pocket. I put my phone on the charger.

"Shall I pour us some coffee?" he asked.

"Us?"

"I brought two mugs. I thought I'd keep you company." He grinned. "Looking after you."

"No thanks."

"No coffee?"

"No need to look after me. I'd rather enjoy breakfast by myself."

"That's not very familial of you."

I grimaced. "I didn't sleep well. Maybe we can catch up later."

He heaved a deep, put-upon sigh. A moment later he was gone.

I slurped down two mugs of coffee and ate the strawberries and bacon, leaving the scrambled egg and toast. I took a few more sips of coffee and hurried out of the room. The hallway was empty. I ran down the staircase and was out the front door without seeing anyone.

It was highly likely this was a waste of time, but I needed to get a closer look at the front gate. I had to see if there was a way to open it from the inside. Maybe I wasn't as locked in as I believed I was. Maybe the stately opening and closing of the gates every time a car entered or left was simply for show and I'd taken it to mean more than it did.

I hurried past the rectangular pool of water and the violently splashing fountains that speckled my arms with cold water. I crossed the drive, the twelve-foot walls looking much higher as I drew closer. The latch where the gates met was inside a black box that prevented me from seeing how they connected. The bars on the gates themselves were narrowly spaced, impossible to squeeze through and impossible to scale because the crossbar was easily eleven feet off the ground. The gates were installed into concrete walls on either side.

The hinges looked typical and told me nothing about how it functioned. There was nothing on the wall on either side to hold a keypad or anything to operate the gates without the remote control I'd seen the drivers and Daniel use.

The box at the center of the gates was just above eye level. I reached up and ran my fingers along the edge. It was tightly sealed. There didn't appear to be any way to open it. If there was a keypad inside, I had no way to access it. There didn't appear to be a lock allowing access to the box.

I turned to face the house. It was a beautiful structure—old and stately. There was nothing threatening about it, but still, looking at the dark windows and all the ivy covering the exterior, it felt unwelcoming. Maybe that was inside my head, my knowledge of the people who lived within its walls.

Slowly, I walked back toward the large arched doors. As I walked, I had the sensation I was being watched. Because of the dark windows, it was impossible to see inside.

Was someone watching me? It didn't matter. I had a right to walk to the gate and check for a way to open it. There was nothing wrong with that. Or was there? It was possible all of them felt threatened by my mere presence. By any outsider's presence. I wondered, for the first time, if Abigail had ever tried to bring home a man she wanted to be in a relationship with or marry. Had he been treated the same way? Was he also lying at the bottom of the lake or in an unmarked grave?

An icy chill ran down my arms. I wondered if my slight shiver had also been observed.

I opened the door and stepped inside.

Climbing the stairs, I gripped the railing, feeling somewhat lightheaded. I wasn't sure if it was the overdose of sunlight followed by the relative darkness inside and moving too quickly up the stairs, or too much coffee and not enough food. When I reached the top of the stairs, I paused, waiting for my heart rate to slow.

I opened the bedroom door and came face-to-face with Elliot, as if he'd been ready to open it himself. "I came to get the tray, and you were gone." His tone was accusing and petulant.

"I just…" I couldn't think of a plausible reason why I'd left. Why didn't I tell him the truth? I'd never been shown how the gate worked. I had a right to know. And he had no right to be in my room.

"You just what?"

"I went out."

"Out, where?"

"What does it matter to you? I went out. Thanks for getting the tray."

"Where did you go?"

"I don't have to account to you for how I spend my time."

"You're acting a little off-balance and I'm worried about you."

"No need to worry." I moved around him, glad to put space between us. I walked past the bed and went to the nightstand on my side. "Where's my phone?"

"Your phone?"

"I left it charging. They reset the passcode, but it had died, so I left it charging here. It's gone."

"I haven't seen it."

"It was right here. Has anyone else been in the room?"

"How would I know? I wasn't here."

He was making it sound as if the phone wouldn't have gone missing if I'd stayed in the room where I belonged. I felt an irrational rage simmering in my chest. I wanted to scream at him that no one should be in this room. That if someone from the household staff came in for a legitimate reason, they should not be touching my phone. And what legitimate reason was there at this time of day? The room was spotless. I'd made the bed myself, despite Daniel's constant reminders it wasn't necessary.

"Someone took my phone." I kept my tone steady, quieter than usual so the rage didn't spill out. The rage wasn't about the phone, but at the same time, it felt like it was. The phone stolen from my suitcase. The altered passcode, my missing, probably dead sister. The other dead women. The sealed front gates. Was it rage, or terror?

"Calm down," Elliot said.

"I'm calm. I want my phone."

"I don't know where it is. Look under the bed."

I knelt on the floor and peered under the bed. There wasn't a dust bunny or a stray thread anywhere. There was certainly no phone. I stood, glaring at him.

"I don't know what to tell you. Maybe you for—"

"You can stop right there. I did not forget." I turned my back on him and went to the sitting room. I grabbed a strawberry and ate it. I picked up a slice of toast and ate that, not bothering to sit down, refilling my coffee mug as I ate. They'd turned me into a prisoner. I had no idea how I was going to find my sister's body, or escape.

FIFTY-ONE

RENEE

He followed me into the sitting room. He went to the breakfast tray and poured himself a cup of coffee.

"If you didn't take my phone," I said, "someone else in your family, or someone on the staff did."

He sighed and placed his mug on the tray with a loud, decisive thunk. "You act as if this family is trying to take you prisoner. Why are you doing that?"

"Am I?"

"We're all a little concerned that you're having a breakdown. Are you having trouble dealing with a close-knit family because your childhood was so difficult?"

I laughed bitterly. Had Daniel made up stories about me, or laced his stories with the bits of truth he possessed, trying to make them feel some compassion for me? "No."

"All we've done is try to get to know you, to welcome you. The things you're saying and doing are breaking our hearts. Do you realize that?"

He had no clue what a broken heart felt like. I didn't think anyone who lived under this roof possessed a heart, but I kept that thought to myself.

"We could arrange for you to go horseback riding while Daniel is tied up. Or are you going to spend all day obsessing over your missing phone?"

"It's not missing. It was stolen."

He sighed again. "Is that a no, or a yes?"

"Are you going to ask the others about my phone?"

"No. I'm not accusing my family of being thieves. They'd be insulted and hurt."

I thought about searching the room while he watched, but I knew it wasn't there. If Elliot had taken it, he would have removed it from the room while I was gone.

Riding a horse would clear my head. It would keep my mind focused on the animal and what I was doing. I'd only gone riding twice before in my life. I could breathe fresh air and lose myself under the open sky. I wouldn't have to see or talk to anyone in the Keller family.

"Horseback riding sounds like a good idea," I said. "But it's been years. And even then, I was a beginner."

"Don't worry. We have experts in our stables. At the winery." He gave me a glowing smile. "I'll drive you over. I'll ask Abigail to join you, so the two of you can spend some time together."

I felt the small, short burst of joy pop as if he'd stabbed it with a pin.

An hour later, as Elliot pulled his car close to the gates and touched the remote, I tried to keep my attention on the black box fixed to the gate, ignoring Abigail's chatter in the backseat. It did me no good. There was no visible change in the box to give any suggestion of what was going on inside. It made me wonder what would happen in an emergency.

What if there was a fire? Could emergency vehicles get inside if no one from the family was reachable to open the gates? What about a terrible storm? Although I couldn't imagine how that might impact them because their power lines were underground, and there were no trees large enough to cause catastrophic damage if they fell on the chateau. Maybe there were rescue plans in place. Their money probably took care of a lot of things that regular people needed to concern themselves with.

We passed through the gates, and they closed behind us.

The riding experience was spectacular, despite Abigail's presence. Elliot waited in the car, keeping himself busy on his phone. Whether he was working, or playing games, or simply emailing friends, it was impossible to say.

The stablehand who helped us clearly loved the regal animals. She chose a sweet white mare for me to ride. Abigail, it turned out, had her own horse, as did her siblings. It shouldn't have surprised me, but it did, because Daniel had never said a word about it.

After some instructions about mounting, dismounting, using the reins and the pressure of my legs for guidance, as well as voice commands, we set off.

We spent nearly three hours traveling on dirt roads through the vineyard, beneath pristine blue sky, headed toward a seemingly endless horizon. Hawks drifted on the breeze as we passed majestic oak trees, endless acres of vines sprouting plump grapes, and heard nothing but the sounds of the horse hooves clopping on the hard-packed dirt. Surprisingly, Abigail didn't keep up her usual stream of chatter. It was the most peaceful I'd felt in a very long time.

All that open space, being outside the enclosure, even though I didn't always see the walls surrounding the property, I felt them, completely cleared my mind. It reset my determination, reminding me again that I was never going to find out what happened to Claudia if I kept slipping back into my increasingly hostile attitude toward this family.

My whole purpose in coming had been to endear myself to them. From the moment I arrived, I'd done the opposite, letting my feelings for my sister, and fears for my own safety override the one thing I wanted. The only thing that mattered. I needed to get a grip on my emotions. I needed to swallow the rage and plaster a constant smile on my face. I needed to creep back inside the skin of the woman I'd invented and remain there.

As we rode slowly back to the stables, feeling the solid body of the mare beneath me, I wondered about Abigail's silence during our ride. It was almost as if she wanted to give me space to think and settle back into the false persona I'd created for myself.

She was equally quiet during the short drive back to the chateau.

The only sound I heard as the gates opened before us was the unnaturally loud thudding of my pulse against my eardrums. My animal instinct was screaming at me that I should open the car door and fling myself out onto the palm-lined drive. I should run now while I had the chance. I should have whispered into the horse's ear and told her to run, to carry me as far as she could away from these murderous people.

Inside the house, Elliot hurried up the stairs. I turned, thinking Abigail was behind me, but she'd disappeared. I went to the kitchen to get something cold to drink.

Greyson stepped out of the pantry as if he'd been waiting for me. "What can I get you?"

"I was just going to grab a bottle of sparkling water. And maybe—"

"Have a seat on the patio. I'll take care of everything."

"But I just want—"

He smiled. "I'm here to take care of everything. You must know that. Please go outside and relax."

"But I—"

"Please, Renee."

I trudged out of the kitchen. I wasn't used to feeling

defeated by the simple act of trying to fill a glass with water or figure out what I wanted for my own snack.

As I passed through the living room, Abigail reappeared, coming from the direction of the offices. She grabbed my wrist and pulled me close to her side. She put her face close to my ear, and whispered, "I need to talk to you." She continued tugging gently on my arm, leading me toward the massive, silent library.

She pushed me gently into one of the dark green leather wing chairs and sat in another chair, facing me. "You really need to try harder with my mother."

"What?"

"She thinks you're ungrateful. That you don't want to be part of this family. She thinks you're not interested in the family business."

"Ungrateful? How have I been ungrateful?"

"It's an impression."

"What does that mean? What have I been ungrateful for?"

"It's an honor to be part of this family. And you're very critical."

"I'm not critical."

"We can see it in your eyes, the way you twist your lips—your distaste for our decorating style, our food. Our lifestyle."

I assumed she meant not approving of their secretive, unceremonious burial of women who died in unexplained ways on their property, dumping them into the ground as if they couldn't wait to be rid of them. "I don't think I twist my lips."

"You're critical."

"I don't—"

"If you don't respect our winery, if you're not interested and supportive of it, how can you marry Daniel? I know our family might seem different, and maybe a little... well, it doesn't matter. We're very close. We stick together. And we want you to be part of us. But my mother needs to feel that you *love* us. That you accept us as we are."

"I want that too." I felt a wave of nausea as I told this shameful lie. I was glad I didn't have to elaborate. Not yet anyway.

"I'm not sure you're getting what I'm saying." Abigail's large eyes with their thick, dark outlines bored into mine. "She needs to feel that you love her like a mother, like you loved your own mother. She needs to see, and feel, in her *gut*, that you're one hundred percent devoted to her son. And that you're loyal to all of us."

"That sounds..." I caught myself short. My *own* mother?

The first time I'd seen Janice smile at me and I'd looked into her eyes, I'd seen my own mother lurking inside, like a monster resurrected from her grave. There was a woman who saw her children not as vital human beings in their own right, but as her possessions, existing only as an elixir to soothe and satisfy her own demons.

Don't argue. Be the woman they want, the woman they can trust.

"Yes?" Abigail asked. "Is that too difficult? Are you incapable of that?"

"No, it's not too difficult. It sounds like you really want me to be part of your family. It makes me feel really good." The lie caused a feeling of vertigo to wash over me, turning the edges of my vision dark, even though I was sitting down.

Abigail smiled. I couldn't help thinking her smile looked like that of a carnivore ready to devour its prey. Maybe because I'd made myself into a weak, compliant creature.

FIFTY-TWO

JANICE

No one can comprehend the damage that was done to my children that dreadful night. Watching their father drown while they stood helplessly by, arriving too late to save him, and perhaps too young to accomplish the job. But I didn't know that at the time.

The cries that came from them were sounds that no mother should ever have to hear. They were the sounds you might expect if your small children had flames licking at their skin, trapped in a building engulfed by fire. Their sweet little faces were marred forever. The scars on their hearts were invisible to me, but I could feel them as if my own heart had been carefully cut by a scalpel and pieces lifted out while I lay awake on a cold metal table.

I wrapped my arms around them. I turned their heads away from the remains of their father.

After, I devoted myself to them day and night. I sat by their beds when they had nightmares, holding their hands, whispering soothing words. I read stories to make them stronger. I gave them my own words of wisdom to make them tough and resilient.

At the same time, I became a fierce executive at the top of the winemaking world. I made Chateau Noir into a world-class winery with award-winning wines. I made it even more successful than it had been when Sam and I were working side by side.

At home and with our family business, I protected my children. They would never suffer again like they had that night. They needed protecting. They deserved it. I'd let them down once, and it would never happen again. I protected our finances and our property. I protected the winery from the relentless threat of outside forces and corruption. Most of all, I protected my children from their worst memories, from each other, from outsiders. I protected them from experiencing any more pain.

When he was alive, Sam had protected our family. He'd built a compound of sorts for us on a large piece of property, secured from any kind of predator or disaster. He'd built our financial empire from the ground up. He was a man who knew that families thrived when they protected themselves from outside forces intent on destruction. Unfortunately, the world is a cruel place, with threats coming from every direction. Those who don't take precautions often live their lives in fear. Some of them suffer horribly. We never lived in fear.

Yes, a single tragedy invaded our safe enclosure despite our best efforts, but it would never happen again. Never. It was unforeseen, although it shouldn't have been. After that night, I had the painful wisdom of experience.

I knew from the time my children reached their teens, even before, that the spouses they chose needed to understand all of that, without being fed the lurid details of it all. The women and man my children were bound to for life needed to love us and become part of our family. They could not stand outside in judgment.

Women and men like that are difficult, almost impossible, to find. Even when their own family is flawed, most people tend to think the way they do things is the way things *should* be done. Finding adaptable mates is challenging. And my children were not always willing participants in the process.

Some people, most people, I suppose, think adult children don't need protecting. If they do, the parents have failed to do their job.

But they do need protecting. Sometimes, from their own worst impulses.

FIFTY-THREE

RENEE

After dinner and a dessert hour that stretched into two hours while Daniel told his family, in agonizing detail, about the damage from the fire at the vineyard, I was ready to climb the long flight of stairs and collapse into bed.

Although it didn't appear on the surface to require a lot of physical exertion, riding a horse for three hours, an activity my body wasn't accustomed to, had left me sore and exhausted.

Daniel and I excused ourselves together. As we walked through the living room toward the entryway, I looked up the staircase, wondering if I had it in me to climb those aging but elegant stairs that looked so grand, but sometimes felt absolutely treacherous.

Pausing, I put my one hand on the newel post and the other on Daniel's arm. "I'm trying really hard with your family."

"I can see that."

"But Abigail gave me a little talking to. She—"

"Not here. We shouldn't…" He looked around. "That's great that you're getting closer to her. She's hard to get to know, so it's good you're making an effort."

"It wasn't like that. She was lecturing me."

"How?"

I told him what his sister had said, her voice low and urgent, almost threatening. As if this family had very dark secrets I needed to vow I would keep before I was allowed to get any closer. Not that I had any desire whatsoever to do that. And of course, I was certain that one of their secrets was the murder of my sister.

"I don't think that's anything I haven't already told you," Daniel said. "We—"

"It absolutely is. Janice wants to be my *mother*? I owe one hundred percent loyalty? What's she talking about? Why am I starting to feel like a prisoner here? No phone, no way to get out of the gates unless I ask a family member to open them."

"Do you want to leave?" He moved away from me. "You can leave any time you want."

"I should be able to come and go when I want to, without asking for help, but it feels like that's not possible."

"You're being ridiculous. I don't understand why you think you can't come and go."

"The gates are locked, and I have no idea how to open them."

He groaned. "Can we go upstairs? We shouldn't be having this conversation here." He curled his hands into fists. "The gates are a security feature. The locking mechanism is to prevent intruders from easily getting in. We don't just hand remote devices out to everyone who visits. Do you hear how you sound?"

"What about my phone?"

"What about it? I don't know where your phone is."

"What about the passcode getting reset?"

He folded his arms across his chest. "We were talking about Abigail telling you how to make my mother happy, and now you're acting like they've kidnapped you."

"I didn't misplace my phone. And I didn't enter the passcode incorrectly. I'm not stupid. Someone in this house knows where it is."

Like a small dog, eager to be taken on an evening walk, Elliot scampered around the corner into the entryway. "Are you still upset about your phone?" he asked.

Since he'd already heard what I'd said, I suddenly no longer cared what else Elliot heard. "I haven't messaged my friends in days. I haven't posted on social media. They're going to wonder what's going on. They're going to worry about me."

"Are they?" Elliot asked. "Friends come and go. Family is forever. Your friends will forget all about you."

It felt as if my heart stopped beating for half a second. I looked at him, but he wouldn't meet my gaze.

"You're assuming my friends will forget me?"

Daniel was silent.

Elliot shrugged. "It happens."

"You said they *will* forget, as if it's a done deal. You didn't say they might, or they could. Or that's what often happens. You said, *will*. As if I'm going to disappear. As if you already know they'll never hear from me again."

"I think you're hearing things that aren't being said." Elliot sauntered toward the front doors. He opened the left-hand door and stepped outside, closing it behind him.

I looked at Daniel.

"I think he's right," Daniel said. "You might be reading into things. Maybe take a step back."

"But—"

"I'm not sure about the phone. It's upsetting. But I—you're not a prisoner here. You can leave whenever you want. Just say the word."

FIFTY-FOUR

RENEE

I'd done a miserable job remaining compliant and accepting. My desire for my phone, for some connection to the outside world was eating me alive and I'd let that overwhelm my devotion to Claudia. I wanted my phone. I needed my phone! Not for an urgent call, just for the sense that I had an escape route. Despite Daniel's words, that somehow failed to penetrate to my core, I felt as if I could die in this place, just as the others had, and no one would know.

Both phones might already be in a dumpster in San Francisco or even buried beneath spoiled garbage back in Seattle. When the police finally did go looking for me, they would think I'd been at the chateau for a brief stay, weeks earlier. Even now, was anyone curious that they hadn't heard from me? I had no way of knowing.

No matter how much I needed to endear myself to this disturbing family in order to find Claudia, surely it wouldn't permanently damage my effort if I pushed them harder to tell me what they'd done with my phone. Maybe there was a reasonable explanation.

. . .

In the morning, after my shower and breakfast, I found Abigail in the workout room located in the same wing as the offices. She was using three-pound dumbbells to perform curls. The rounded curves and visibility of her biceps looked more distinct than I would have expected from a three-pound weight, but maybe this was a rest day during which she followed a lighter routine.

She wore hot pink Capri leggings, athletic shoes, and a white leotard that was cut up over her hip bones. Her hair was slicked up into a tight bun that was perched on top of her head. She was in full makeup, but there wasn't a drop of perspiration on her face.

"If you're here to work out, you're not dressed properly." She eyed my cutoff jeans and T-shirt.

"I'm not planning to work out."

"I'd rather not have an audience."

"I just wanted to ask you a question, if you have time for a short break."

"I'm in the middle of a set."

"I can wait."

"I already told you, I don't want an audience."

"I won't watch."

She heaved a dramatic sigh, bent over slightly, and let the weights fall to the mat. "What do you need?"

"I guess you heard I was looking for my phone."

"I heard you locked yourself out of it."

I decided not to argue that point, as I'd also decided not to mention my real phone. I needed to get the burner back. That was all. "Have you seen it anywhere?"

"No."

"Did anyone mention finding it? Greyson or the house-keeper, or—"

"If they had, they would have given it to you."

"If someone on the staff found it, would they—"

"I don't know anything about your phone."

"Okay. It's really weird that it just vanished."

She bent over and picked up the weights. "Is that all?"

"Do you think someone took it?"

"Why would anyone want your phone?"

I was moving into dangerous territory, but I was desperate. Pretending this was a casual request wasn't getting me anywhere. "You said Janice doesn't trust me. Do you think she might have taken it, if she was worried I would report Faith's death to the police?"

She laughed sharply. "My mother would not *steal* your phone."

"You said—"

"Are you accusing her of being a thief?"

"You said she doesn't trust me. Hearing you say that shocked me. And it's obvious she doesn't like me."

"You misunderstand her. She cares about you. Needing your loyalty and wanting your love doesn't mean she doesn't like you. Those are different things. She wants to feel assured that you're connected to this family. Is that too difficult for you to understand?"

"I understand that. I'm asking if she might have taken my phone so I couldn't report Faith's death."

"You'd have to ask her. But it's probably not a good idea to accuse her of being a thief."

"I'm not. I'm asking if she was determined to make sure I didn't call the police."

Abigail curled the weights, bringing them up toward her shoulders. She gave me a triumphant smile, as if she'd just performed a Herculean task with the three pounds in each of her hands. Her eyes were wide, the whites showing around the edges of the iris, staring at me with such intensity I wondered if it had been strenuous after all.

"Thanks." I left the room and went to the kitchen. I drank a glass of water. I grabbed a chocolate chip cookie off a plate on the counter and walked back toward the living room, nibbling it. I wandered around the entire ground floor, hoping to find Janice. All the rooms were empty, even the workout room by the time I passed by it again. I went out to the patio, walking through the various garden areas, but those were also devoid of human life.

Returning to the house, I assumed they were all upstairs, working on laptops in their bedrooms, or perhaps they were having a conference in one of Janice's private rooms on the third floor—an entire apartment I'd never seen.

I settled in the living room and picked up a book off the coffee table. If she went anywhere on the first floor, she would have to pass this way.

The book was about the history of the Napa Valley. Within a few minutes, I was engrossed. When Janice entered the room an hour later, I was surprised that so much time had passed. I quickly placed the book on the table, regretting that I'd lost my place.

"Janice." I stood.

"Are you enjoying that book?" she asked.

"Yes."

"You can borrow it."

"Thank you."

She picked it up and handed it to me.

"I wanted to ask if you've seen my cell phone."

"No."

"Are you sure? I wondered because—"

"Am I *sure*? Why wouldn't I be *sure* of my answer to a simple question?"

"I... well, I know you were really upset that I wanted to call the police. Right after that, it went missing, so I—"

"You think I took your phone?"

I held her gaze. I didn't have to answer.

"You don't need your phone, Renee. Once you're working for the winery, we'll provide a phone for you. But for now, why would you need a phone? You're part of our family. We're all here with you." She smiled.

"I want to stay in touch with my friends. With my work—"

"I thought you quit your job?"

"Yes, but I still keep in touch. And my friends are going to worry about me. And I want to speak to them. They're my friends!"

"Friends forget you so easily. You're young, so maybe you haven't learned that yet. Family is forever."

I wondered if she'd brainwashed her children with that belief. I was beginning to wonder if any of these people had friends. They seemed to spend all their time with each other and their absurdly loyal employees.

"Don't worry about your phone. No one is looking for you. It would have been posted on your social media that you're going off the grid." She smiled. "But you're not on social media. Daniel reminded me. Enjoy the book."

She turned and walked quickly out of the room.

I hadn't used social media on my burner phone, with the identity I was using to hide my relationship to Claudia, but I remembered Claudia's last social media post—*Going off-grid.* Such a ridiculous statement. At the same time, such a horrifying statement. I felt my bones turn to ice. The book started to slide out of my hands as I lost the feeling in my fingertips. I regained my grip just before it fell to the floor.

FIFTY-FIVE

RENEE

Greyson left a note on my pillow that Daniel had taken an unexpected flight to Portland, Oregon. He was visiting the famous Willamette Valley wine region to consult with some experts on a new variety the Chateau Noir Winery was exploring. He would miss me terribly but see me when he returned. I wasn't sure if I felt abandoned, frightened, or pleased that I had two entire days to myself. Except for his family.

Mostly, I felt angry that he couldn't text me this information because I didn't have a phone! It seemed callous on his part that he'd asked Greyson to leave the note without considering how that highlighted my inability to communicate.

While he was gone, I would be eating dinner alone with his monstrous family. Although, that might be easier, in some ways. I could relax and not feel I had to maintain the performance of being wildly in love with the man seated beside me at the table.

I might also have more freedom to search the property for something I still, despite my rational mind, despite all odds, hoped I wouldn't find—a barely marked grave belonging to my sister. I still didn't want to believe they'd simply left her to rot at the bottom of the lake. I didn't want to believe she was dead at all. But every time I looked at those gates and saw that inaccessible black box and the unscalable walls, I found it almost impossible to imagine anything else.

Dinner was uneventful. I felt slightly more welcomed than usual and I wondered if Daniel had instructed them to put forth extra effort while he was gone. They asked about my childhood and how Daniel and I had met. I was well-prepared with a few brief, but fully detailed stories of my background, stories that didn't include my sister or the violence of our upbringing so there was no risk that they might recognize any similarities.

I embellished the story of how I'd met Daniel, and was pleased that they seemed to lap it up like puppies served their first plate of leftovers.

After the meal, I excused myself and went to bed with the Napa Valley history book Janice had lent me. I read until midnight, then turned out the light, thinking I would fall easily to sleep. I'd relaxed my mind with distracting historical events that were far-removed from my life. I'd sipped from a mug of tea that was supposed to calm me. I had the massive bed all to myself.

Instead, the moment the bedside light was out, my eyelids opened wide as I remembered Abigail's words from earlier that day. It felt as if my eyelids were stuck to the inside of my skull. Even when I tried forcing them closed, they sprang open, my eyes determined to peer into the darkness.

My mind began racing through all the things that had happened since my arrival, and before. I thought about Claudia's emails, chastising myself for not being available when she'd needed me so desperately.

I twisted in the sheets, hugging the pillow. What had happened to her? Where was she?

If she was dead, wouldn't I feel a clear sense that she was no longer inhabiting the planet? I hoped I would, but I wasn't sure.

Would I sense her presence if she was breathing, if her heart was beating somewhere on this property?

If she had somehow managed to escape through those iron gates, if she'd persuaded someone on the staff to help her slip out unnoticed, she would have contacted me. That meant, if she was alive, she was locked up, and without her phone. A prisoner of this family. But why would they do that?

Or, she was dead.

Finally, I drifted into a sleep filled with dreams taken from my childhood.

I woke suddenly from a memory, or a dream, of Claudia hiding under my bed, whimpering because my mother was throwing my shoes at the window, screaming that I never put my things where they belonged.

The room wasn't as dark as it had been when I'd fallen asleep. Was it morning?

It didn't feel as if I'd been asleep for very long. I turned onto my left side and adjusted the pillow. As I settled my head into the center, I looked across the room. The door was ajar. I gasped softly.

I knew I'd closed it before I went to bed. I knew, because I'd also turned the lock. It wasn't that I expected anyone to peek in on me, or to go prowling around the room while I was sleeping, but there was no doubt someone had been in this room several times, changing my passcode, going through my suitcase to find my real phone, and finally, taking the other.

Scrambling out of bed, my foot caught in the sheet, throwing me sideways, jamming my thigh into the nightstand. I winced. I rubbed the sore spot as I limped to the door, closed and locked it, knowing that locking it was futile.

Why had someone been looking in on me? Or was it worse? Had they come into my room and gone through my things again? But if that was the case, why hadn't I woken? I glanced at the clock. One-forty-five.

I returned to the bed and settled on my back, my head turned to keep an eye on the door. I had no idea how I was going to sleep now.

After a while, my neck grew stiff. I turned on my side, keeping my eyes fixed on the door, listening for the sound of a key, or footsteps in the hallway. The house was bathed in silence. My neck hurt and my eyes began to burn from forcing them open. Unlike earlier when they hadn't wanted to shut, now they kept drifting closed. But the thought of someone entering, even just to look at me, filled me with dread. Finally, I sank into sleep.

This time there were no dreams, but I woke just as suddenly. Through my sleep, I must have heard something, because again, the door was open. A cry of despair and fear pressed against my chest from the inside, longing to release itself. I wasn't a person who cried easily, but I felt more helpless every hour I was inside this house, confined within these walls.

I thrust myself across the bed and off the other side, lunging at the door. I looked down the dimly lit hallway, knowing it would be deserted. I closed the door firmly and leaned against it, breathing hard. It felt as if I'd run all the way from the lake and up the stairs, my heart was beating so rapidly.

I locked the door. I went to the sitting room and grabbed the armchair, pulling it toward the bedroom. It was heavier than I'd expected, which would be good for keeping the door closed, but I wasn't sure I could drag it all that way without damaging the floor.

When I reached the small step that separated the sitting room from the bedroom, I knew I wouldn't be able to lift it. I abandoned the chair where it was and looked around for something else to block the door. There was nothing. The nightstands were too heavy—massive pieces of solid wood. Finally, I got my large suitcase out of the closet and placed it in front of the door. The sound of it moving would be enough to wake me. It would send the intruder away, or at least they'd be slowed in their attempt to enter my room.

It didn't matter. I didn't sleep again for the rest of the night.

After a day spent enduring the constant hovering presence of one family member or another, I finally found myself alone on the back patio after dinner.

Leaving my glass of lemonade only partially finished on the table, I slipped out of my chair and almost ran around the pool toward the other buildings, secluded in gardens of their own. When I was out of sight of the main house, I slowed. It didn't mean no one could see me. And I had no idea if the staff was also tasked with keeping an eye on me, but I didn't notice anyone overtly following me.

I spent an hour walking around the property, looking for anything that might resemble a grave.

I finally found one.

FIFTY-SIX

RENEE

This grave was remarkably different from Tina's. The marker was a five-foot tall white marble pillar, prominently marked with the name of Daniel's father—Samuel Keller—and included the dates of his birth and death.

It was located inside an enclosure formed by four concrete walls, painted white, and surrounded by plants, situated between two of the other houses on the property. Houses that remained locked, the shades and drapes drawn, that no one ever talked about. At first, I'd assumed some of the staff lived there, but soon realized they were unoccupied. Greyson had his own suite of rooms in the main house, and the rest of the staff came and went each day. I wondered if they accessed that intimidating gate with their own remote-control devices, or if Greyson let them in. No one ever talked about that either.

The grave enclosure had an iron gate secured with a padlock. I'd had to peer through the narrowly spaced bars, but the gravestone was easy to read, even standing ten feet away outside the enclosure.

If I hadn't been searching for another grave, I might not have found it. When I first passed by, it had looked like a small, private garden, with a bench and a small reflecting pond. I'd thought it was a nice addition to the other gardens surrounding the two unexplained homes.

Finding another grave was both unsurprising and deeply upsetting. It did give me a few brief moments of peace because it didn't belong to Claudia.

When Daniel finally returned from Oregon, greeting me with a showy hug and a long, deep kiss while his brother watched with too much interest, I had no time to tell him about my discovery of his father's grave. Neither was there an opportunity to mention the midnight intruder. Daniel started talking faster than I'd ever heard him about all the people he'd spoken to about my role at the winery.

"Wait," I said. "I thought you were there to talk about a new variety of wine. We haven't even discussed this. Why were you making plans for me with strangers at another winery?"

"You knew this," Elliot said. "Why are you surprised?"

I wanted him to go away. As if he'd heard my thoughts, he grabbed his glass of wine off the end table and left the room.

I took Daniel's hand and tugged gently. "I need to talk to you."

He shook his head.

I continued pulling him after me, out of the living room, around the staircase to a small alcove under the stairs. I leaned close, speaking in an urgent whisper. "This is—"

"Not here. Later. Maybe. But not—"

"Someone came into our room in the middle of the night while I was asleep. Twice."

He kept his voice low. "If you were asleep, how do you know that?"

"They left the door open."

"Are you sure you didn't—"

"I locked it before I went to bed."

"You weren't dreaming?"

"I was not dreaming. The door was open."

"How do you know that wasn't also a dream?"

"Don't do this."

"Do what?"

"Act as if I don't know what happened to me. You weren't here."

"Okay. Sorry. I shouldn't have said that. But I thought we were going to... maybe the housekeeper wanted to check that you had fresh towels and soap."

"At almost two in the morning? The housekeeper unlocks the door to check supplies?"

"If my mother asked her—"

"Does she have a key?"

"I don't know."

"Who has a key? I didn't think interior doors had keys."

"I don't know. You can probably unlock them with a table knife or a screwdriver. I can't explain it. Was anyone in the room?"

"No."

"What do you want me to do?"

"You can start by believing what I tell you."

"I do. But I can't do anything about it now. Try to put it out of your head. I'm sure it was nothing."

"There are just so many disturbing things. I found your father's grave. Between those houses. What are those houses for, anyway? Who lives there? They look closed up. No one ever goes near them, and you didn't show them to me when we walked around the property. I don't get it."

He moved out of the alcove. "We really shouldn't be talking here."

He was right. I stepped into the entryway with him.

He turned back. "Do you want to see the house?"

Before I could ask about it, I saw Janice standing on the opposite side of the stairs, just outside the entrance to the living room.

Her sudden appearance made me wonder where she'd come from, how long she'd been there. Had she been closer, then moved away? Had she overheard?

"How was your trip?" She walked up to Daniel and lifted her cheek for a kiss.

After she'd received her kiss, and given him a long, affectionate hug, she smiled up at him. "Are you showing her the house? It's way past time, don't you think?" She smiled tenderly. She slid her hand into her pocket and pulled out a ring with three keys. "I'll go with you. I want to see her reaction." She gave me the same tender, eager smile.

Five minutes later, we were standing on the front porch of the first of the three houses. Janice unlocked the door and we went inside.

The house was beautiful. It was open and filled with light, nothing like the main house. It had obviously been built in the twentieth century and remodeled in the twenty-first. It was decorated to more modern tastes, without all the heavy draperies, dark wood paneling, and chandeliers of the historic chateau.

After we'd seen all the rooms, upstairs and down, we stood in the dining room. Janice beamed at me as if I were her favorite person in the world.

"What's in there?" I pointed to a door between the kitchen and the dining room.

"It's the wine storage room," Daniel said.

I walked to the door and pressed the handle.

Janice followed, placing her hand over mine. "There's nothing in there."

I opened the door. She was right. Nothing but a thick blue-and-cream-colored rug and three walls with wine racks, all empty. We stepped out of the room and Janice closed the door. We returned to the dining room.

Janice smiled at Daniel, then me. "What do you think?"

"It's nice."

"It was decorated to your taste."

"Was it? How do you know my taste?"

She smiled, tipping her head down slightly as if that question had an obvious answer. If it did, I had no idea what it might be.

"Why was it decorated to my taste?" I knew, but I wanted to hear her say it.

"It's for the two of you."

I gave her a stiff smile and a slight nod.

Her expression darkened, but she said nothing. Later, after we returned to the chateau and she'd left us alone in the living room, telling us to settle down while she asked Greyson to make tea, I leaned close to Daniel, speaking in a whisper.

"She expects you to live here with her forever?"

"It's an amazing estate. The lake, the pool. There's a staff that—"

"I would never live with your mother. Why would you—?"

Before I could finish speaking, and before Greyson had finished with the tea, Janice returned to the room. She stood just inside the doorway, glaring at me until I met her gaze.

"Families who love each other, want to stay close to each other. That's what's wrong with this culture. Families are broken and fractured and live hundreds or thousands of miles away from each other, so there's no support."

I kept my eyes directed at hers, as if we were in a battle for who was the weakest, who would look away first. I think I won, because she turned and left the room. At the same time, she was clearly the winner. She'd heard every word I'd said when I thought she was out of earshot, and she had all the power.

FIFTY-SEVEN

RENEE

I sat on a lounge chair sipping sparkling water. Abigail came out carrying a glass of red wine. She pulled one of the lounge chairs closer to mine and settled herself beside me, all the while keeping her delicate wineglass level, without splashing a single blood-red drop onto her white top.

"There." She took a sip of wine. "How are you enjoying the water?"

"It's a beautiful pool," I said.

"It's my favorite part of the garden." She sipped her wine. "I heard that my mother gave you a tour of your new home."

I gulped my water, even though it caused the carbonation to shoot painfully up toward my sinuses.

"Don't you just love it?" she asked.

"It's beautiful. It's sad that it's sitting there empty. It looks like it was built a while ago."

"Not that long ago."

"Who designed and decorated it?" I took another, much more sedate sip of my drink.

"It was done to Daniel's taste."

That was interesting. Not what Janice had said. Was it

done to mine? His? Or were both stories a lie and it had been designed for Claudia? Or someone else entirely?

"It's very different from his suite of rooms in the chateau. Were those also done to his taste?" I asked.

She lifted her sunglasses and gave me a hard stare. "Is there something you don't like about it?"

"No, not at all. But I suppose if I'm going to live there, I—"

"*If?* Are you getting cold feet, Renee? I thought my brother was the love of your life?"

"I didn't say that at all. I meant, it would be nice to add my own style. To feel like it reflects me." I sat up and placed my glass on the table between us. "Should we go look at it together and talk about it? I'd love to get your input. You have such great taste." I gave her a smile that felt stiff and dry. I hoped she didn't notice. "Wouldn't that be fun?" My voice sounded shrill.

Abigail heaved a sigh. "We can do that. Yes." She sipped her wine. She made no move to get out of her chair.

"Do you have time right now?" I asked.

She sighed, more gently this time. "You're a very impatient person. I thought we were enjoying the sun."

"It's getting hot."

"It's summer."

"Yes, but it's probably not good to be out in the heat in the middle of the afternoon. It's better in the evening, or morning." I wanted to add that drinking alcohol in the heat wasn't a good idea either, but I said nothing. Her habits didn't seem to prevent her from supposedly playing a key role in a multi-million-dollar wine business. If indeed she did. Maybe her brothers and mother did all the heavy lifting.

"You need to relax," she said.

"That's probably true. But I am hot, and I would love to walk through the house with you now, if you have time."

"May I please finish my wine?"

"Oh, absolutely." I leaned my head back. Maybe I could

find a way to work Claudia into the conversation. I *had* to find a way.

We didn't speak while she sipped her wine in the most laborious way possible, considering how she'd been sucking it down moments earlier. Finally, she placed the empty glass on the table. "All right. Let's go discuss how my mother's world-class decorator has failed to meet your expectations." She stood and smoothed her white top over the hips of her faded jeans, adjusting the thin straps to rest near the edges of her shoulders. "I need to get the key. I'll be right back."

She left her wineglass on the table. A moment later, she returned, and I followed her around the edge of the pool to the start of the pathway.

Inside the house it was cool. It took a moment for my eyes to adjust from the glare of midday light.

"What don't you like?" she asked.

"It's not that I don't like it. I just wanted to look more carefully, to think about how to make it more my own. We walked through fairly quickly when I was here with your mother and Daniel."

"Okay. Where should we start?"

We started in the living room, Abigail talking like a real estate agent, describing the construction of the house, the layout that had taken feng shui principles into account, the quality of the furniture, carpets, and window coverings. I asked as many questions as I could think of, not caring at all about the house, its furnishing, or the color schemes. I would never live there. All I wanted was to see if there was any trace of my sister in this place.

Had Claudia been walked around and told it was designed and decorated for her taste? Had she been told she would live here, permanently cut off from friends and her sister? Working for the family, living with the family, her entire being held captive to their whims and weirdness?

"When did you say it was built?" I asked.

"Why do you want to know that?" Abigail asked.

"It feels like it's been here for a while. Not that it's old. It just feels rooted. In a good way." I smiled.

She didn't return my smile. I wasn't fooling her. Did I dare to ask about Daniel's former fiancée?

"Did Elliot and Tina also—"

"I thought you wanted to talk about decorating. Leave Elliot out of this."

There was my answer. I followed her up the stairs. We walked through the bedrooms. I could hear that my questions were becoming more mundane. I sensed her growing irritation. I shouldn't have brought up Elliot. I opened closets and drawers. I checked lighting, I adjusted shutters and pulled the cords on mini blinds.

"What is the purpose of all this?" Abigail asked.

"No one has ever given me a house." I made my voice soft, meek. "I'm a little overwhelmed, to be honest. I just wanted to get a feel for it. To think about what it would be like to dream a little, I suppose."

That seemed to soften her.

We returned to the first floor and went into the kitchen. I continued peppering her with questions, looking around as if I were fascinated by the cabinetry, the countertops, the layout, planning how I would cook in this beautifully designed space.

"I guess the reason I asked when it was built..." I glanced toward the end of the granite countertop on the center island and then my gaze traveled to the baseboard under the cabinets beside the refrigerator. Something was...

"Yes?" Abigail asked. "What's your question?"

"I wondered because..." There was something on the baseboard. Red. Not red, but brownish red. Something splattered. A few small drops that looked like...

"What are you trying to ask?" Abigail said.

"I..." Was that blood? "I wondered..." I turned my attention to her. It couldn't be. The house was spotless. It must be. Had this place ever been lived in? It didn't seem so. Why would anything have spilled? And why did that look like blood?

"What's your question?" Her tone was sharp.

"The house seems older, but remodeled?"

"How on earth can you know that?"

I didn't know how I knew that. It was a feeling. I looked up at the ceiling, then turned my attention toward the bifold doors at the back. Very modern. You didn't seem them on older homes. But still. Maybe a creak I'd noticed on the stairs? Something about the smell of it, that it had been closed up for a very long time? That the ceilings were... they just seemed older, somehow. "I just wondered, that's all."

"Well, it was done for you. And right now, you're coming across as extremely ungrateful. I already warned you that my mother doesn't appreciate your lack of gratitude."

I met her gaze, trying not to let my eyes flick toward those spots. Blood. I was sure it was blood.

"Why are you so nervous?" Abigail asked.

"I'm not."

"You seem nervous and incredibly ungrateful. This is a beautiful home. Built and designed for Daniel and you. I think we're done." She started walking toward the entryway.

I desperately wanted to kneel on the floor and touch those spots, but if she returned and saw me, it wouldn't go well. I followed her out the front door and we walked back to the pool without speaking. When we reached the lounge chairs, she said, "If there's something you need changed in the house, please let Greyson know." She went inside and that was the end of it.

FIFTY-EIGHT

RENEE

I had to get back inside that house. I needed to find out if those tiny spots I'd seen were drops of blood. I knew in my gut they were, but I couldn't get my mind to agree until I saw them up close. Until I touched them.

I thought about asking Daniel to take me on another walk-through, but despite our growing closeness, despite feeling like I wanted to be around him more than I'd expected, I needed to do this myself. Elliot or Greyson were the only candidates who could provide access. Janice would harass me relentlessly, so asking her was out of the question.

Either man was likely to tell Janice not only about my request, but every word I said once I was inside the house, but I felt like I could manage Elliot better. Greyson was so reserved, so stoic in his loyalty, I trusted him even less than the family members. Maybe it was because he acted as if he was on my side in some way, when I knew he absolutely was not.

I found Elliot's office door closed. I gave it a loud knock and waited. He opened the door and stood looking down at me without saying a word.

"Sorry to interrupt your work, but it's almost lunchtime, so I thought you might have a few minutes. I have a strange request."

His expression changed and he looked eager to hear what I wanted to say the moment the word *strange* passed my lips. "Your mother and Daniel showed me our future house." I smiled, with a look that I hoped projected gratitude. "I wanted to take a quick peek at it again."

"Why don't you ask Daniel? Or my mother?"

"To be honest, I want to think about my own plans. Without other input. Everyone says it should reflect my taste. And I just want to take another look to think about what I really like. I was so overwhelmed before, and so appreciative, it's hard to remember everything. But your mother said I can make whatever changes I want. I just need to see it without other people giving their opinions."

He stared at me as if he didn't understand a word I'd said.

"To get a better feel for it. To think about decorating ideas."

"It's already decorated. My mother chose a style that Daniel would like."

"She said it was to suit my taste."

"Okay. Whatever. Let's not split hairs. What, exactly do you want?"

"I just want to dream a little." I gave him a simpering smile.

What was the deal with this house? Why would Janice lie about who she'd decorated it for? This was making me think it had been done for my sister after all. They were making such a show of it being for me, but after grandly walking me through it, they seemed to want me to forget all about it.

"Okay. Let's go." He grabbed his keys.

I was startled to see that he had a key to Daniel's house. "Do you have a tape measure you can bring?"

"A tape measure?"

I wondered if he'd never used one. He'd grown up with a household staff taking care of everything. He'd probably never moved a piece of furniture or hung a photograph. "It's a measuring thing that's usually metal and—"

"I know what a tape measure is, Renee. Why do you want one?"

"I have this really amazing chest that I want to put in the bedroom, and I want to—"

"Aren't you getting a little bit ahead of the game here? You haven't even planned your wedding."

"Your family showed me the house. Your mother said I could—"

"Fine. I'll ask Greyson." He took out his phone and sent a text.

Greyson met us in the living room, handed over a tape measure, and we walked to the house, winding through the grove of palm trees, past the plants that made parts of the property feel almost like a jungle at times.

Inside the house, I moved slowly through the rooms. I kept Elliot occupied with a flood of questions and comments and plans. I asked about the history of the house and received the same vague answers his sister had given me. I opened closets and stepped inside. I walked up and down the stairs. I studied the family photographs and asked about their childhood.

He seemed mildly confused, but not overly annoyed with my distracting chatter. There were two other closed-up houses, presumably waiting for Elliot and Abigail. I couldn't imagine three adults who wanted to live in their mother's backyard until the day she died. When she was gone, would one of them be upgraded to the main house? Would they fight over who got to take possession of the real prize?

Finally, I told Elliot I was feeling a little light-headed. I sat on the living room sofa. "Oh. I forgot to measure for the chest. Do you mind doing that while I rest for a minute?"

"You can do it another time."

"I really want to know if it will fit."

"What's the rush? You haven't even set a date for the wedding." He laughed. "It's going to be a while before you're living here. You have plenty of time to measure."

"Please. It will ease my mind if I know it fits."

He rolled his eyes, but he took the tape measure and left the room.

When I heard the creak halfway up the stairs, I darted into the kitchen. I knelt by the refrigerator and touched the stain on the baseboard. It had been a lot of trouble just to get a chance to put my fingertip on those tiny red spots. But I knew they were blood. I'd known when I first saw them.

I remembered my mother cutting limes, slicing her finger and screaming as the juice stung the cut. She leaped away from the counter and spun toward me. Toward both of us. I stood in front of Claudia, as I always did. Except when she wasn't there, when she ran, when she hid.

Sometimes, I thought she was behind me and suddenly I felt the movement of air, a coolness that said she was gone. She was so quick, my tiny little sister. There one minute, vanished the next.

Until that day, as my mother waved a knife that was far too large for cutting limes. Waved it at us, shrieking with pain and laughter.

"Why so scared? Little chicken shits. You have no idea what fear is, you little bitches."

She threw her head back, laughing. She waved the knife over her head. And then, her bleeding, juice-smeared fingers, sloppy loose from half a bottle of gin, lost their grip. The knife flew through the air.

And later.

Blood dripped on the floor and a small bit splashed on the white baseboard. I was the one who had cleaned it up. I knew what blood looked like. Large puddles of it, small drops. Wet blood and dried blood. Spatters and smears of it.

It felt as if I was seeing that same blood again. And again. Always. There was no doubt in my mind this was blood. I stood slowly and returned to the living room. There had never been any doubt.

Just as there was no doubt *why* there was blood in this house that had been decorated, not for Daniel, not for me, but for my sister.

FIFTY-NINE

RENEE

Now that I'd made a few tours of the house, which the Keller family had designed as my lifelong prison, I wanted to know about the other homes on the property. When I'd left the house after touching what I knew without a shadow of a doubt were drops of my sister's blood, I hadn't said much to Elliot. My throat was so constricted I could hardly breathe, much less speak.

After skipping lunch, drinking two mugs of tea, and taking a walk out to the lake, I'd finally recovered the strength to ask him more questions. I found Elliot in his office again. The door was partially open this time. His back was to the door, and he faced two large computer screens.

He was talking on the phone when I approached. "Sounds good," he said. "Appreciate it."

There were several seconds of silence.

"Yup. Yup. Excellent." This was followed by more silence as he listened, leaning back in his chair, clicking the mouse. The charts on one screen disappeared, replaced by a video feed of the bottling facility.

"You're a star," he said. "Talk soon."

He clicked the mouse. The bottling facility disappeared, and the charts flashed back in its place.

I knocked on the doorframe.

He whirled his chair around as if I'd shouted his name. "Hey. What can I do for you now?" He pulled out his earbuds and tossed them on the desk.

"It might be an awkward question," I said.

"Come in. Have a seat."

"It's quick."

"Have a seat," he said.

I stepped into the room and went to the small sofa near the windows. He stood and came over, taking the chair facing me. "What's troubling your pretty little head?"

"It's not troubling. I just wondered about your house. The house that was built for you and Tina."

"Oooh." He grimaced. "That's a loaded question. Why do you want to know?"

"I'm just trying to understand the setup. It's unusual. You have to admit that." I laughed.

"Is it?"

"I've never known a family that lived together like this."

"More families should. It's how things used to be."

"Is it?"

He shrugged.

"Did you and Tina live there?"

"Of course."

"And when she... when she died?"

He spoke softly. "I couldn't be there anymore."

"I can understand that."

"I don't really care what you understand. What's your question?"

Now I felt uncomfortable asking. I wanted to see the house, but he made it sound as if it were some sort of shrine to her. How could I say I wanted to go inside a place he might not have entered since she'd died? I wanted to walk around and look at their things, touch their furniture, and get decorating ideas from a place that was infused with his grief?

"Don't look so worried," he said. "You didn't upset me. I'm not going to break down crying. I'm past all that. I lost another woman, remember?"

"It feels crass to ask you now. I really can't." I stood.

"It's okay. I'm not fragile."

I started toward the door.

"You can't leave me curious." His tone was teasing, taunting, almost. "You have to tell me."

I turned back. "I just wondered if I could see it. I really appreciate how the house was decorated for me, or us. But like I said, I want to make some changes to make it more mine. And I wanted to see what yours was like."

"My mother decorates the houses as a gift for our *brides*. Or in Abigail's case—the *groom*." The sneering tone he used for the word *brides* sent a chill down my spine. Why had he said it like that? He made it sound like the women who came here were objects. Possessions of his mother's. Was I reading into it?

"I had the impression I get to make changes after Daniel and I are married."

Elliot burst out laughing. "After you're married?"

"Why are you laughing?"

He laughed harder. "Are you as clueless as you sound?"

"I don't think I'm clueless."

"Daniel is never going to marry you. Guaranteed." He stood. "I'm glad you came by for this little chat. Now you're not as clueless as you were."

I stared at him, waiting for him to say more. He held my gaze.

"Why isn't he marrying me?" I knew we were never getting married. But how did Elliot know? What was going on? I felt like he was going out of his way to make me squirm. He'd been so friendly when we toured the house. He'd acted as if the wedding was just a matter of time.

This was what Claudia had described in her email—he was trying to make me feel as uncomfortable as he possibly could. At least I didn't have an audience like she'd had. What did he want? Was this a brotherly competition, some way to get back at his older brother, or was it an outburst of unresolved grief because the man had lost two women he loved in such a short time? Because his mother refused to treat their deaths responsibly and had dumped them into wooden boxes and shoved them into holes dug quickly in the backyard?

"We shouldn't be having this conversation," he said. "And I shouldn't have said that. I need to get back to work. It's better for you if you don't mention this. To anyone." He returned to his desk chair and moved the mouse to wake his computer screens.

I stood there for another moment or two, but he didn't turn around. I wondered if he was even aware that I was still in the room. Finally, I left.

As I walked down the hallway, my head spun so wildly I thought I might have to place my hand on the wall to steady myself.

Why was he so sure Daniel and I wouldn't be married? Did he know who I was? Did he know this was all an act? Maybe he knew I wasn't going to live long enough.

If I vanished in the same way Claudia had, no one would know. My friends and former co-workers would ask questions, but they wouldn't know where to start because they knew nothing about Daniel and the Keller family. I hadn't told them what I was doing. How could I have made such a horrible mistake, to not let anyone know what I was doing, where I was going?

SIXTY

RENEE

When I finally got ahold of myself, I went looking for Daniel. I found him in the entertainment room watching a golf tournament. I sat beside him and reached for his hand. He took mine, but didn't turn his attention from the enormous screen facing the sectional where he was stretched out, holding a beer in one hand.

I'd arrived at this house of horrors wondering if Daniel might have been complicit in the murder of my sister. Now, I was close to convinced that Daniel was the only person here who stood between me and death.

It genuinely felt as if I'd fallen into a pit of vipers, one that I'd never be able to claw my way out of. Even if Daniel wasn't on my side, I still needed to pretend we were getting married. I needed to test the truth of what Elliot had said.

When a commercial started, I leaned close to him. "Now that I've seen the house, when should we start discussing our wedding plans? Isn't that why I'm here? To get to know your family and plan our wedding?"

"Great question." He squeezed my hand and took a swallow of beer.

"We should set a date."

He moved away from me and gave me a confused look. "Uhm, I guess if you seriously want to talk about that, you should speak to my mother about dates."

I sat up. His mother? I had to literally bite down on my tongue not to tell him what I thought about that. Could this man not make a single decision without asking Mommy? "Okay. Sure."

He patted my leg.

The golf game resumed. He took another swallow of beer, removed his hand from my leg, and turned his attention to the screen.

I stood, walked out of the room, and went looking for Janice.

She was in the kitchen, going over the shopping list with the chef. I cleared my throat softly.

Janice looked at me. "Are you okay?"

I nodded.

"There's no need to be so impatient. I'm almost finished here."

I nodded and coughed again, trying to clear my throat.

"Why are you so agitated? Do you have someplace you need to be?"

I shook my head. "No." My voice came out in a croak.

By the time they were finished, I'd regained my composure.

"Now, what do you need that has you so anxious?" Janice asked.

"I'm not anxious. It's just that I've been here a while now, and we haven't done any planning for the wedding. I was talking to Daniel, and the first thing we need to do is set a date. He said I should discuss that with you."

She folded her arms. "I've gotten the impression you have some serious hesitations about our family."

"I'm not marrying your family." I laughed. It was the wrong thing to say. And laughing was absolutely the wrong move.

She glared at me as if I'd ripped the strap on her top.

"That didn't sound right," I said. "What I meant was—"

"No, it didn't. Marriage is the joining of two families."

It was such an archaic idea. She acted as if two countries were discussing the pairing of their heirs for the consolidation of property and power. "I don't have hesitations about your family."

"That's a lie, Renee. You almost called the police on us."

"I wasn't going to call the police on you. I wanted to report—"

"Don't get bogged down in semantics."

I tried to smile, but my facial muscles refused to cooperate. "I don't have hesitations."

"You're still lying to me. You're excited about your new house, yes. But not so excited about living on our property. You're uncertain about working in the family business. And you seem morbidly obsessed with the unfortunate deaths of Elliot's wife and girlfriend."

I decided it was best not to comment.

After a moment, she uncrossed her arms and rested her hand on the counter. "Did Daniel mention you're expected to sign a non-disclosure agreement?"

"No."

"We need to protect the winery."

"You don't trust me?"

"It's not about trust."

It sounded like it was entirely about trust, but I wasn't going to argue that point either. There was no arguing with this woman about anything. She got what she wanted. She'd dictated everything for her children, and most likely, for her business, all her life. She was the winner.

"Are you going to be able to do that?"

"Yes."

"Good."

"And then we can set a date? I was thinking—"

"You need to ask Abigail to be your maid of honor. If she agrees, we can start making plans."

I gave her a limp smile. Another bizarre, senseless game. Was this just to force me to humble myself in front of Abigail? A formality? Or was there a chance Abigail might decline? Another game, pulling me further away from finding out what had happened to my sister.

Where was she? I wanted to stand up at the dinner table and scream at them. I wanted to get a shovel out of the boathouse near the lake and dig up every part of their vast piece of property, searching for her body. I wanted them to mention her name! They acted as if Daniel had never been engaged before, as if she'd never existed.

Maybe my search was hopeless. Maybe I needed to accept that fact and give up. I should use the wedding planning as an opportunity for escape—to save my own life before it was too late. To choose one of the many outings—shopping for a wedding dress, cake tastings, flower ordering—to run before it was too late.

I might never know what happened to Claudia. The final journey of her life, when I should have been there for her, tenderly caring for her remains, placing them someplace where she could truly rest in peace, might be gifts I would never give her. An obligation I would never fulfill.

But I could still escape with my life, and I was certain she would have wanted that.

SIXTY-ONE

RENEE

Wondering if the cloud of utter defeat that consumed me might be visible to Abigail, I walked slowly along the path toward the lake. The midday sun burned the back of my head, making me feel as if my hair was on fire.

Abigail spent quite a lot of her free time sitting in the gazebo, gazing at the lake. She often took out the canoe that was tied to the pier, paddling around the smooth surface of the lake for hours. I'd never seen anyone else use the canoe. I'd never even seen them set foot on the pier.

As I made my way to the edge of the lake, I hoped she wasn't out there now. I didn't want to sit in the gazebo waiting an hour or more for her to finish her canoeing before I made my request. I wanted to get this over with and move things forward. My hope, my flimsy plan when I set my sights on becoming the perfect woman for their family, had been to push them out of their comfortable complacency, forcing them to expose their secrets. Instead, my feelings for Claudia had overwhelmed me again and again, and I'd allowed them to push me close to my breaking point.

When the lake came into view, I saw Abigail standing on

the pier. She wore a large floppy hat, short shorts, and a crop top. Her feet were bare. She was halfway toward the canoe but had stopped and was looking across the water as if something had caught her attention.

I quickened my pace, wanting to catch her before she climbed into that precarious boat and began paddling away.

Stepping onto the pier, I spoke her name, hoping I didn't startle her and start the conversation off on a contentious note. It didn't take much with these people to put them in a mood.

She turned. "Hi, Renee. You look like you're in a hurry. Were you worried you'd miss a chance to go canoeing with me?"

I stopped, feeling as if I'd just stuck my foot in a large trap and the teeth were about to spring closed around my ankle, sharp metal spikes tearing my flesh, digging into my bone. "I wasn't—"

"Have you ever been canoeing? It's the most wonderful experience. I've loved it all my life. My father used to take me out all the time."

I gave her a grim smile. "I wanted to ask you a question." If I rushed this, how likely was it that I'd push her into saying no just to spite me? If I agreed to put my life into that canoe, and into her hands, would she agree to be the maid of honor in this charade of a wedding that was never going to happen?

"You buzz around, asking questions, worrying and fretting about everything," she said. "You act as if life is an endless string of problems." She laughed. "Do you ever relax and have fun?"

"Yes."

"When? Aside from a few hours horseback riding, I haven't seen you do anything fun since the moment you arrived."

"I've—"

"You never laugh. I don't even know what your laugh sounds like."

She was right. I hadn't laughed. There was nothing to laugh at here. "We haven't spent much time together," I said.

She shrugged. "I'm going canoeing. I know how to enjoy my life. Work hard. Play hard."

"That's a good philosophy."

"I didn't invent it."

"I know."

"Are you coming, or not?"

Surely, she wouldn't tip the canoe and try to drown me in the middle of the day. Would she? If I screamed, they would never hear me. Besides, wasn't the truth about drowning that it was a silent death? You don't actually scream; you just go under and suffocate, and no one hears you.

Daniel was in the house working. The whole family was there. But the whole family might be killers. One person in the family *was* a killer. Would they even care?

I could die in that canoe with her.

No. Abigail was the most innocuous of the entire group. Why would she kill me? She had nothing against me. It was the women who'd had the misfortune of falling in love with her brothers who died. Whether by their hand or their controlling mother's, I wasn't sure. But Abigail was the only one who had been moderately warm and welcoming to me. She'd tried to help me when I needed it.

She wasn't going to tip over the canoe and hold me under water. Besides, I was strong. I was in good shape from my trek through Thailand. Abigail thought it was hard work to lift three-pound weights, despite the appearance of her well-defined biceps. I could easily fight her off, if it came to that.

I walked to the end of the pier, slipped off my shoes at Abigail's advice that it was easier to maneuver inside the canoe if I was barefoot, and climbed down into the rocking boat. Abigail lowered herself in after me. She handed a paddle to me, picked up the other, and untied the rope. She used her paddle to give us a gentle push away from the pier.

As we glided out across the water, a surprising sense of

peace washed over me. The charm of canoeing was immediately obvious the moment I dipped my paddle into the water and took a stroke. The smooth, forward movement of the canoe, the ripple of the water around the sides of the boat, and the quiet slap of our paddles dipping in and out of the lake was soothing. There were no other sounds, making me feel as if I'd been transported to another dimension. I no longer felt trapped inside the walls of their property, even though I could see them in the distance. The endless arc of the sky made them appear smaller, less threatening.

When we were almost at the center of the lake, Abigail took her paddle out of the water and rested it across the edges of the boat. I was still paddling, which made the boat make a sharp turn. I stopped and we drifted, tipping slightly at the abrupt change in momentum.

Abigail was in the front of the canoe. Even though she didn't turn to face me, her voice was distinct. "What did you want to ask me?"

I didn't like the idea of posing such an important question to her back. I didn't like the fact that I was being pushed into it without the chance to approach the subject carefully. It would sound blunt and transactional, but now, there was no way around it. "I wanted to know if you would be my maid of honor."

Abigail began paddling again, pulling harder this time, as if I wasn't there. First, she took several rapid strokes on the right side of the canoe to turn us back toward the pier, then began alternating sides, her arms moving furiously. We pulled through the water quickly.

I dipped my paddle in, helping to propel us forward, wishing she would ease up on her effort and answer my question. I didn't have a good feeling about her sudden exertion, and her failure to respond to what I'd asked. Had she heard me? She must have. Nothing else explained her sudden frantic paddling.

Still, I wondered if I should ask again, if I should ask whether she'd heard, ask if she needed time to consider my request.

"I know we aren't as close as—"

"No," she said. The rhythm of her strokes didn't change.

"May I ask why not? I have to say, it hurts my feelings a little, that you're so blunt about it."

"I'm not a person who uses a lot of words to try to make someone feel better. If you don't like it, that's not my problem."

We were almost to the pier. She was maneuvering the canoe so that we came in with the side of the boat lining up to the side of the pier. She moved her paddle expertly from side-to-side, sculling so the boat didn't crash headlong into one of the pilings.

"I thought you might want to be in our wedding for your brother's sake."

"You thought wrong." She grabbed the rope and secured the canoe.

"May I ask why you don't want to be my maid of honor?"

She climbed out of the boat as if it were the easiest thing in the world to step out of the narrow, bobbing wooden pod. She extended her hand to help me up onto the pier. She adjusted her hat. Because of her floppy hat and dark glasses, I couldn't see her eyes, or much of her face.

"I can sense that you don't love Daniel. I don't know what your game is, but I do know you're not in love with my brother." Without giving me a chance to respond, she turned and hurried off the pier.

SIXTY-TWO

RENEE

Their games were unwinnable.

I was never going to find out what had happened to Claudia by pretending I loved this man, trying to plan a phony wedding, and acting as if I was slowly bonding with his family. Especially since I clearly was not. The only evidence of her presence in this place, I'd found on my own, without any of them speaking to me—something violent had happened in the gazebo, causing her to lose her precious bracelet, and something worse had happened in the kitchen of that honeymoon house, or whatever they wanted to call it.

And honestly, I didn't know for certain it was Claudia's blood. I assumed it was. It seemed likely that it was, but I had no proof.

This family was incapable of telling the truth, so why did I keep asking questions as if I might gain some insight into their behavior? Why had I deluded myself into thinking one of them would eventually trip themselves up and expose their secrets?

That afternoon, I went to the liquor cabinet and got Daniel's favorite bottle of whiskey. I tucked it into a bag that held a towel and sun hat I'd taken out to the pool earlier. I grabbed two of the heavy glasses that he used for sipping whiskey and two shot glasses, also burrowing them into the folds of the towel. I went up to his bedroom and locked the door behind me, despite knowing its ineffectiveness. I placed the whiskey and glasses on the table between the two armchairs in the sitting room.

At some point, Greyson had entered our room and moved the chair I'd dragged across the floor back to its original position. The chairs were arranged to provide a perfect view of the fairy lights decorating the garden below, and the stars that would soon be appearing in the clear sky stretched beyond, surrounding the thin sliver of the moon.

Next, I took the vial containing Janice's lorazepam out of my nightstand drawer. Using the thick heavy whiskey bottle as a pestle, I crushed several tablets, double what I'd been told to take, into a fine powder on the granite tabletop. Using a credit card, as if I were drawing lines of cocaine, I scooped it into the spare shot glass. I stored the powder and the remainder of the pills in my nightstand drawer.

After dinner, I suggested to Daniel that he and I should spend time alone in our room. I knew he expected that meant time alone in bed, but while his family clung to him and kept him in their orbit with questions about wine, winemaking, and the wine market, I slipped away and dashed up the stairs.

I dressed in a strapless dress that looked inviting but more formal than he might expect for an evening alone in our bedroom. I put the whiskey glasses and bottle on the table in the sitting room, pouring a partial shot for myself and a healthy two shots for Daniel. I mixed in the powdered lorazepam. For more than a few seconds I watched my fingers tremble as the powder remained visible in the clear liquid, but eventually it dissolved. The drink was mildly cloudy, but I was counting on the muted lighting in the room and the shock of watching me drink alcohol for the first time to distract him from focusing too intensely on his own drink.

When Daniel entered the room, I was ready.

I met him at the door.

He looked at my dress, glanced at the bed with the covers turned down, and then back at the two glasses of whiskey in my hands.

"What? I don't understand. I thought we—"

"No talking." I gave him a mildly seductive smile and handed the glass to him.

"You don't drink."

"I'm feeling a lot of stress, so I decided to give it a try. Just a little." I clicked my glass against his and let some of the gold liquid touch my lips. It burned and I performed a dramatic shimmy.

I hoped he would drink his quickly, that there wouldn't be any noticeable aftertaste, that none of the powder would linger, interfering with the silky-smooth alcohol. I took another sip, letting the whiskey touch my own tongue, and shivered again, with less drama this time.

Daniel laughed. "Too much for you?" He took a long swallow of his drink.

"Should we sit down?" I gestured toward the chairs. "The sky is beautiful."

He followed me to the sitting room and took the chair beside me.

"This tastes better than I expected," I said.

He took another sip and put his hand on my leg, his touch uncertain.

I placed my hand on top of his.

"Have you always liked whiskey?" I put the glass to my lips, teasing him as if I planned to drink more.

He took another sip of his drink. "I don't remember. My mother always served it as one of the after-dinner drinks at parties, and I drank it to look cool, at first. That's what I remember the most."

"Your mother has parties?"

"Sure." He took another sip. "We have lots of parties. For the winery employees. For other people in the industry."

"I had no idea."

He placed his glass on the table and turned toward me.

"Aren't you going to finish it?" I asked.

"Later."

"I was going to have a little more." I took another genuine sip.

He picked up his glass and downed the rest of it.

Smiling as I turned away from him, I placed my glass beside the bottle.

I tucked my feet up beside me and began talking softly about my canoe ride with Abigail. Within fifteen minutes, his eyelids were drooping. In another ten, his head had fallen forward and he was snoring. I woke him gently and suggested we get into bed. He looked eager, but also disappointed and confused as if he wasn't sure where we were.

Once he was settled in bed, I told him I needed to use the bathroom. I changed into comfortable clothes, put my hair in a ponytail, and came back into the bedroom a few minutes later. He was snoring again, much louder this time.

I dug through his dresser until I found the key to the house. I grabbed his phone and went into the sitting room. I waited, looking out at the stars and fairy lights. I would wait until after midnight to be sure the rest of the family were asleep before heading out.

Three hours later, as I approached the house where I was meant to live out the rest of my life, my earlier confidence had started to wane.

What did I think I was going to find? All I'd seen were those few tiny drops of blood. Under the pretext of checking the cabinet and closet space, the house had appeared to be completely empty. But still it whispered to me that it might be the last place Claudia had been. Was there something inside that might tell me where they'd buried her?

With my heart aching, tears filling my throat at the thought of searching for something I didn't want to find, but desperately needed to find, I inserted the key in the lock and turned it.

Inside, I felt a sense of calm, knowing I could explore without being questioned every step of the way, my movements scrutinized. Daniel's phone provided a flashlight, but I was trying to rely as much as possible on the dim glow coming from the outdoor lighting. I didn't think the light on the phone could be seen from the main house, but I wasn't sure if there was anyone patrolling the property at night.

I walked around the living room first, opening the drawers in the occasional tables, getting down on the floor and using the flashlight to look under the sofa and armchairs. I did the same in the dining room and pantry before making a thorough search of the kitchen.

I shone the light on the droplets of blood. I touched them. I searched all along the baseboard but there was no more blood. I wondered if there had been more, and it was cleaned up, but this was missed. I got to my feet and turned off the flashlight, dismissing the feelings of frustration bordering on despair that were creeping through my body.

I left the kitchen and opened the door to the small wine storage room off the kitchen. Daniel had only allowed me a quick peek, and Janice had seemed to want to skip that room altogether. I went inside and closed the door. Since there were no windows in here, I felt safe turning on the overhead lights. Recessed lights on the shelves designed to hold wine bottles at a proper angle also came on.

It was an enormous room considering all it did was store wine. Without counting, I estimated it would hold several hundred bottles. Who drank that much wine? I suppose if it was kept for years, replenished on a regular basis. Still, it seemed like a lot.

The large, ornate rug also seemed ridiculous. Why put such a nice rug in a room that was never used? Why have a rug at all? Maybe it helped with the climate control, although that didn't make any sense to me either.

Why was I thinking about rugs? I wanted to find out what had happened to Claudia in this house. I would never find her! I would never escape from this place. These people were monsters and whatever they'd done with her, they were going to get away with it.

I sat down hard on the floor, crossed my legs, dropped Daniel's phone beside me, and put my face in my hands. I leaned forward, my head spinning. I'd only had a few sips of whiskey, but because I never drank, the small amount of alcohol had hit me hard.

As my thighs pressed against the rug, I felt something poke into my flesh. I moved slightly, but whatever was under the rug was stabbing into my bone. I stood. I went to the edge and picked up the rug, pulling it back so it folded on top of itself.

The thick, blue and cream rug was covering a trap door that was about six by ten feet. The object that had been digging into my leg was part of a recessed handle, but the lock protruded slightly.

As my heart thudded faster, with my hands shaking, I dug in my pocket and pulled out Daniel's keys. I stuck one into the lock. It didn't work. I tried each one in succession. None of them turned the lock. I lay on the floor, pressing the side of my face against the trap door.

Was my sister down there?

SIXTY-THREE

RENEE

Sitting back on my heels, I stared at the lock. Would Daniel have a key? This was supposed to be his house, but no one would tell me how long it had been here. Did he know about this trap door? His mother had done the decorating. Unlike the rest of the house, the rug was more in line with her taste, reflected throughout the lavish, formal chateau she occupied.

Even if he did have a key, running back to the house and rummaging through his dresser for it risked waking him, or one of the others. If he had a key, shouldn't it be on the same ring as the house key? Unless he didn't want anyone accessing whatever lay below this floor. I shivered thinking about it, trying not to let any unwelcome images flood my mind. I needed to keep my thoughts on getting the trap door open.

I stood and went to the door, turned off the lights, and left the room. I returned to the kitchen and began opening drawers, looking for a knife or some other tool that would help me either break the lock or splinter the wood around it enough to lift up the trap door.

Yanking open drawers one after another, I felt my panic rising. Although it was completely furnished, down to vases on the tables, artwork, and photos of Daniel's family on the wall in the stairwell, every drawer and closet I'd opened on my previous visits had been empty. Still, I kept searching, flinging open cabinet doors, reaching into the back, feeling for anything, even a stray nail.

Finally, my luck turned. Under the sink in the downstairs bathroom was a small screwdriver. I grabbed it and returned to the wine room. I slammed the door, then froze, realizing I was becoming careless. Just because they were all asleep and the main house seemed very far away didn't mean I could start waving around the light on Daniel's phone and slamming doors.

I flicked on the lights, knelt down, and began chipping away at the wood around the lock. There was no way I was going to be able to pick the lock with a screwdriver. I was pretty sure I wouldn't be able to pick a lock even if I had the right tools. But I was not leaving this house without breaking through this door and finding out if Claudia's body was down there. It seemed entirely possible. I hadn't found her grave, despite searching the entire property. Unless they hadn't bothered to mark it with even a stone, as they had Tina's, or she was at the bottom of the lake, where else could she be? Especially with those drops of blood in the kitchen. Blood in a house that had never been occupied, in a kitchen where no one had ever prepared a meal.

The entire time I'd been in the room, I hadn't heard a sound. If, by some unbelievable miracle, she was alive down there, she would be so weak, she couldn't make a sound. It had been months. Unless someone had left water, and at least a small amount of food, she would be... I couldn't think about it. I needed to keep my thoughts focused entirely on digging the blade of the screwdriver into the wood, splintering it slowly, chipping away, destroying everything around that lock until I rendered it useless.

After twenty or thirty minutes of stabbing at the wood, digging the metal blade into it, ripping out sharp strips and tiny bits of chipped varnish, I sat back for a moment. My neck and back were damp, my hands ached, and I was breathing heavily. For all the work I'd done, there was only a small section of damaged wood around the lock, exposing the base of it.

I returned to work with an even greater frenzy, feeling as if I were stabbing a body, all the frustration and rage of the past weeks, filling my shoulders and arms.

I worked for another thirty minutes and saw more progress. In another hour or so I might be able to pull the lock free and hopefully lift up the trap door.

As I studied what I'd accomplished so far, I heard a sound. I gasped softly, holding my breath inside my lungs. I stood and moved toward the door, pressing my ear against it. The house was silent. All I heard was the thud of my pulse in my ear. I took a slow, quiet breath.

There was another sound. A door closing.

As quickly as I could, I shoved the splintered wood and flakes of varnish toward the trap door and pulled the rug back into place. I went to the door, flicked off the light, and quietly opened the wine room door. I stepped out and closed it softly behind me.

The light in the entryway was on. I backed up toward the kitchen, keeping my attention fixed on the hall that led to the entryway and living room. I carefully opened a kitchen drawer, placed the screwdriver inside, and closed the drawer. I ran my fingers through my hair and licked my lips to moisten them. I straightened my top and tucked Daniel's phone into my back pocket.

"Hello?" I called in a low voice. "Who's there?" I walked into the living room and stopped, feeling as if my heart stopped along with my feet when I saw who was standing there.

SIXTY-FOUR

RENEE

"What are you doing here?" Janice asked.

"I'm..." I laughed. "I wanted to be here alone, to think about my decorating ideas."

"Do you think I'm an idiot? Why are you really *here*?"

"I do want to decorate for my own taste and—"

"I mean, why are you here at all? In our home? With my son? It's clear you don't love him."

"I do. Of course, I love him. I love him with all my heart."

She laughed, a short burst of sound that was more like a shout. "It's very clear to me that you do *not* love him. I once loved a man with my entire being. You seem oblivious to that fact. I know love, and this—whatever you're playing at with Daniel—isn't it." She started walking toward me.

I took a few steps back. I wasn't sure what she was going to do. Why was she walking toward me? Her face was a mask. She didn't look angry or upset. She stared at me, occasionally blinking slowly, her lips pressed together.

"Tell me why you're here, Renee."

"I told you."

"I'm tired of your games," she said.

I laughed.

"You think that's funny?"

"Yes, I do. You and your children play a lot of games. Not me."

"Such as?"

"Giving me a house I didn't ask for."

"How is that a game?"

"It feels as if there are strings attached."

"Only in your mind. Because you don't know anything about love, and family. You don't understand loyalty."

"I think you have loyalty confused with control."

"You still haven't told me why you're here. Why you targeted my son. I'm assuming it's his money. But it feels like there might be more to it than that."

"I don't care about his money."

"Everyone cares about money."

"Maybe in your world."

"The only people who don't care about money, are people who already have it. Do you have a lot of money?"

"I'm not here to talk about money. I don't want Daniel's money. I don't want your money. I don't confuse love with money."

"Then tell me why you're here. Why do you love my son? Since that's what you're claiming."

"Because he's a decent man. He—"

"That's not love."

"I don't think I should have to explain my feelings to you."

"Why not?" she asked.

"Because I don't owe you anything."

"You're very smug."

I put my hands into my pockets. I wanted to take a step back. I didn't like the way she kept moving closer to me. I felt as if she might assault me. It seemed like a weird thing to do, and I was pretty sure I could fight her off. But why was she coming so close? Did she have a weapon with her? Was this the end for me?

If she did have a weapon, she wouldn't be able to pass off my death as an awkward, unbelievable suicide as she had with Faith.

What was she *doing*? She was so close now, I could smell her face cream.

"What do you want, Renee?"

"I want to marry Daniel."

"No, you don't. You came here with two phones. One is clearly a burner. So, you're up to something and I'm not letting you out of my sight until you tell me what you're doing here. I'm done with the charade."

I took a step back. My heart was racing. I took another few steps away from her.

"You're not leaving this house. So don't take another step, or you'll regret it."

The cold glint in her eyes, along with her words that I wasn't leaving the house made me so cold, I knew I wouldn't be able to take another step.

SIXTY-FIVE
RENEE

I yawned, knowing it looked genuine. "I'm so tired. I'm going to bed. I shouldn't have come out here without asking you."

"I told you, you're not going anywhere. You're trying to destroy my family, and I have a right to know why."

My laugh sounded harsh, but I didn't care. "How am I destroying your family?"

"My son has twisted himself into knots trying to make you happy. You're worried about one thing after the other. Paranoid about someone stealing your phones, about being held captive, of all things." She let out a short burst of laughter. "He can't do anything to make you happy. You have no job, yet you have no interest in learning about the winery and finding out where you might fit in to add value to our business. You obsess over people who have passed away, tearing open old wounds, and insist on acting as if their deaths are suspicious when it's none of your business. Your accusations cause pain for Elliot. Deep pain. So, you aren't going anywhere until you tell me what you're doing here. I've given you nothing but respect and I'm losing patience. I want to know what's going on and I want to know what you're doing out here in the middle of the night."

Had she come here planning to kill me? Did she want to find out who I was, and then she would shoot me? Or simply grab me and tie me up, then drag me out to the lake? She was wearing a thick robe over her nightgown. It was possible she had a small gun in one of those deep pockets where her hands kept disappearing.

I pushed my hair away from my face, leaving my hands on the sides of my head, as if holding onto my head might help me settle my thoughts and make a decision about what I should do.

"What happened to your fingernails?" Janice asked.

I dropped my hands to my sides. Chipping the wood away from the lock had damaged my nails, as I picked at the splintered wood, pulling it away from the door, prying up the pieces that wouldn't easily come loose. "Nothing."

"They're a mess," she said. "What have you been up to? Let me see." She reached for my hand, grabbing it before I could put it in my pocket. She studied my nails, gripping my knuckles so hard, one of them cracked.

I tried to yank my hand out of hers, but she tightened her hold on me, twisting my fingers.

"Tell me what this is about." Her voice was almost a whisper, but all the more threatening with its quiet tone.

I lurched backward, yanking my arm as hard as I could. I stumbled, pulling her with me. She lost her balance, dropping my hand and grabbing the back of the sofa to steady herself.

Continuing to move backward, I edged toward the kitchen, my thoughts on the screwdriver in that drawer. If she had a gun, a screwdriver wouldn't provide adequate defense, but if all she had was a knife, I had a chance. Maybe she had pepper spray. Maybe she had nothing.

Once I reached the kitchen, I'd have to turn my back to her, but so far, she hadn't made any other aggressive moves.

"Why are you so afraid?" she asked. "What's going on with you?" Her hands were back in the pockets of her robe.

I studied her, trying to determine whether she had a weapon in one of those pockets.

Shrinking away was the wrong thing to do. I needed to find courage. I needed to stop worrying about a weapon. If she was planning to kill me immediately, she already would have. She wanted to know what I was up to. She wanted to know why I was with Daniel, so even if she did want to send me into an early grave like the others, she was going to take her time with it.

By giving into my fear, I was losing my chance to find Claudia. If anyone had the key to that trap door, she did. Maybe that's why she'd been so reluctant to allow me back into the house after the first quick tour. Maybe it wasn't a house for Daniel and his bride after all, but simply a decoy. The decorating was so bland and generic, it was a laugh to believe the story that it had been done for anyone's *taste*. Certainly not mine, not Daniel's, and not my sister's. It might as well have been a model home for a real estate developer.

"I found something," I said.

"What did you find?"

"I'll show you."

"It's the middle of the night. I don't have time for silly scavenger hunts."

"It's in the wine storage room." I backed into the kitchen, trusting she would follow me.

She took a few hesitant steps toward me, then stopped. "The wine room is empty. Let's stop the guessing games. Tell me what's going on."

"Do you know what I'm talking about?"

"How could I possibly know what you're talking about? You're not making any sense."

"Then I have to show you. If you don't see it, you won't believe it."

She glared at me. "I'm tired. You disturbed my sleep. I have a full day tomorrow and I—"

"You're awake now. Go on." I nudged her toward the doorway.

"Please don't shove me."

"I didn't."

"Okay." As she passed through the kitchen, I held back, slid open the drawer, grabbed the screwdriver, and tucked it into my pocket, pulling my shirt over it, then bunching up the fabric to conceal the bulge. I hurried after her, catching up as she reached the wine room and turned to see where I'd gone.

It felt as if my heart had moved into my skull, the thudding was so loud. I tried not to think about Claudia's body lying below us. I tried not to think about what I would encounter when Janice unlocked and lifted up that trap door.

I opened the door, turned on the light, and we went into the room. "Under the rug." I bent over and pulled it back. "What's down there?"

She remained near the door, For the first time since I'd met her, the calm, superior mask that was her usual expression slipped ever so slightly. A look of terror flickered across her face. Her body stiffened as if she dreaded taking another step into the room.

I let the rug fall out of my hand. I looked at her and repeated my question.

After a long pause, she said, "I've never seen this before." Her voice was soft in an attempt to hide the faint tremor.

"How is that possible? You had the house built."

"I had no idea this was here."

This time, she spoke with more confidence, but I didn't believe her.

SIXTY-SIX

JANICE

Renee wore an arrogant, know-it-all expression. It wasn't unusual to see that look on her face. This girl was not in love with my son. She was not here to get to know us, to embrace my son's family and make us her own. She was up to something. I knew this because I've always had excellent instincts.

I'd wanted to hire a private investigator to find out more about her, but had finally decided that was risking someone outside our family knowing too much about our business. There are things I can trust my legal team with, and things I keep entirely to myself. There are things I can trust the employees who work on our property to take care of because healthy sums of cash buy lifelong loyalty.

But sometimes, there are situations you can't trust to anyone outside the blood ties of family. Investigating a woman who may or may not be in love with your son, a girl whom your son declares is the partner of his dreams, opens up a crack in the family's shell that can too easily be leveraged by the wrong person.

Perhaps I was cautious to the point of paranoia. But what

some consider extreme caution, others might call paranoia, to their eventual regret.

Now, as Renee faced me with that defiant look on her face, her ragged, bloodied fingertips, and the perspiration around her hairline, I wondered if I would be the one to regret my decision. Still, there were other ways to get the information I needed. She would never destroy us, no matter who she was or what she'd come here to do. Whether it was money she was after, or something else.

"I wonder who installed this?" I asked.

Renee laughed. "I'm not stupid."

"Of course not," I said.

"What's down there?" she asked, as if she expected me to confide in her.

"I have no idea," I said. "I didn't know this door was here until just now. I've never seen it."

"You had this house, including this room, designed and built. You knew it needed a rug. You chose the rug."

I nodded. "Yes, I chose the rug. But my husband worked with the architect to design and build these houses. I had nothing to do with it. I worked from diagrams and models to do the decorating."

"Unlock it. I know you have the key," Renee said.

She was acting as if she hadn't heard my explanation.

I couldn't unlock the trap door. I was not going to let her get the best of me. If she went into the space below this house, if she was allowed to speak with anyone outside our family after this, she would destroy all of us. She'd already proven her determination to do that.

She didn't understand why Tina and Faith had been buried here. She didn't understand anything. There was no way I would unlock that door for her. She was such a silly child, thinking she could order me to unlock it as if I took directions from her. I wanted to laugh out loud at the thought.

I slid my hands into the pockets of my robe. "My husband was a cautious man. He was so protective of our family." I looked up at the ceiling, closing my eyes for a moment. "I remember he talked about wanting a place to hide—a place that would keep us safe for months. He thought about climate disasters, of course. He thought about home invasions, the increase in lawlessness. But he also thought often about unforeseen dangers."

"I don't care about any of that. Will you please unlock the door? I—"

"He must have done this without telling me. It's the only thing I can think of." I opened my eyes and looked at her, trying to compose my features into an expression of nostalgia. It wasn't hard to recall my feelings of love for Sam. Those were close to the surface every hour of every day. I felt them whenever I looked at my children and saw reflections of him in their faces, their gestures, heard his tone in their voices. But even as I allowed those emotions to sweep over me, I kept my head clear. I needed to stall her. I needed to divert her attention and get her out of here.

I needed to finish this. I didn't want to. It wasn't really in me, but I had to keep my family safe. "It makes me feel as if he's here with me now. To think that he went ahead and did this. He died before he had a chance to tell us. It's been here all this time."

Renee covered her ears, as if the sound of my voice had assaulted her. After a moment, she let her hands fall to her sides. "Stop the lies. Open the door."

"I have no idea what would have happened to the key."

"I'll tell you why I'm here," Renee said. "Claudia is my sister. Was."

I felt as if she'd punched me in the throat. Her sister? How could that be? They looked nothing alike. Did they? Her *sister*? But Daniel had met this woman at our tasting room and fallen in love. How had he…? My brain couldn't put the pieces together. How was this possible?

"There's blood in the kitchen." Renee waved her arm behind her. "And she's down there. I don't know if it was you, or one of your sons who hurt her, or murdered her in this house."

I stared at her, trying to keep up. I could hardly take in what she was saying, trying to imagine how she'd managed to manipulate her way into my son's life, concealing the fact that she was Claudia's sister.

"And dumped her body down there, like you dump every woman's body, or else she was hurt and you shoved her down there, and now she's died after all this time!" Renee was screaming, sobbing. She was out of control.

She lunged at me, grabbing my arms, trying to shove her hand into my pocket in search of the key.

I pushed her away. She fell back against the wall, crying out as the edge of one of the wine racks stabbed at her shoulder.

"Calm down," I said. "I do not have the key. And I'm only going to tell you once—my sons are not killers. They had a tragic childhood. Abigail loved to scare us. She was a wild little girl." I laughed, remembering what a terror she'd been, but so full of life and such fire.

"She begged her father to take her out in the canoe. Of course, he made her wear her life vest. She stood up and started rocking the canoe, trying to scare him. It capsized." I felt my voice break but regained my composure quickly. "The boat must have hit his head as it went over. Because he never came up." I gasped, putting my hand to my throat. I never talked about it. This was the first time I'd spoken those words. This woman had forced me into this, and I hated her for it. Hated her with everything that I had. Crying softly, I continued. "My sons tried to save their father from drowning! It *destroyed* them when they failed to do that. So they may be a lot of things, but they are not killers!"

Renee stared at me. Any minute she would lunge at me again. She didn't care about what I'd lived through, what my boys had suffered, what we'd all lived through. She would attack me, digging through my other pocket, trying to get my keys. She'd started with the wrong pocket.

From the opposite one, I pulled out one of our kitchen knives that Greyson kept superbly sharpened at all times.

SIXTY-SEVEN

RENEE

I stared at the knife, the blade gleaming under the track lighting.

I had my answer to who had murdered Claudia, as well as the others. Now, she was ready to do the same to me, but without the subterfuge of trying to make it look like a suicide or an accident. What would she say when one of her children found my body? Or did they already know? Maybe that's why their behavior was so bizarre—knowing and hiding the fact that their mother was a cold-blooded killer.

"My children are not murderers!" She shouted it this time.

"Well, someone murdered my sister. She came here to be with the man she loved, and she vanished. The police can't find a trace of her. There are dead women all over this property."

Janice laughed. "They aren't all *over* our property. Elliot was involved with two troubled women who chose to end their lives rather than face their problems."

"I know that's not true."

"As for your sister, I don't know what—"

"She's down there." I slammed my foot onto the trap door. There was a hollow thud. "Open it." I lunged at her again.

She wasn't expecting it this time. She thought the knife

would keep me at a safe distance. She thought I was afraid of it. I grabbed both her wrists. She was a strong, healthy woman. But she was over two decades older than me. I restrained her arms easily, although her grip on the knife handle remained firm.

We wrestled in a slow, strained dance. My arms were stiff as I struggled to keep her from bringing the knife close to my body. I kicked at her shins, trying to knock her off her feet, but each time, she managed to move far enough away from my foot that I did nothing more than graze her bone.

As we continued to struggle, my arms began to ache. Her face was a contorted mask as I held her wrists upright, her elbows bent, trying to keep her hand straight so the knife pointed toward the ceiling. The light glinted off the blade as we moved, making me constantly aware of its presence, as it inched closer to my face.

Every time she made a sudden move, or started to twist wildly away from me, the blade turned in my direction.

Perspiration was building on the back of my neck and worse, on the palms of my hands. I felt them slipping on her wrists. She was stronger than I'd realized. Maybe I'd underestimated her because of her age. She was also determined— fighting for her life, her children's lives.

Once that trap door was opened, once I was free of this place, she would be exposed. No wonder her strength felt inexhaustible.

Finally, I was able to raise her arms slightly higher, moving my body closer to hers. I gave a furious kick at her ankle. She winced and lost her balance. She fell, landing on her left knee. She reached down to break her fall and loosened her grip on the knife. I bent her wrist sharply to the side and she dropped it.

I grabbed the knife and backed away from her.

I don't know what I looked like, but instead of coming at me as I'd expected, she cowered. "Give me the knife," she said softly. "It will destroy Daniel if you hurt me."

"I don't care."

She stood slowly, her hands out as if to keep me away. "You don't have it in you. You're not a killer either."

"How do you know that?"

She smiled. "I'm perceptive. How do you think I knew you didn't love my son? You're a very good actress. He believed you. My other children believed you. But I knew. The moment I saw you."

"Open the door," I said.

She shook her head.

I moved across the room, raising the knife so it was pointing toward her abdomen.

"We should talk," she said.

"No. I'm done talking. Open it or give me the keys."

She turned and rushed toward the door. I grabbed the back of her robe, pulling it partially off. With the fabric tangled around her shoulders and arms, she flailed, trying to break free. I yanked harder on the robe, pulling it down. I would get the keys out of her pocket myself.

She threw herself on the robe, gathering it in her arms like a swaddled infant.

Without warming, one arm shot out and grabbed my ankle. She pulled hard and I crashed to the floor, but I managed to keep a firm grasp on the knife as I fell.

She grabbed my legs and pawed her way up my body, trying to get to the knife. I twisted out of her way, turning on my side. She continued climbing on top of me, hitting my arms and shoulders, grabbing my hair, attacking in any way she could as she tried to regain possession of the knife.

A moment later, we had our arms around each other, our legs entwined, as we rolled onto the folded edge of the rug, wrestling and driving our knees into each other. She bit the underside of my arm. I screamed and tried to wriggle away.

After several minutes, I could hardly tell my body from hers.

Then, she had her hand around my wrist, trying to force the knife down toward my neck.

I fought her off, twisting in every direction. I managed to maneuver my way out from under her, and as she came at me again, grabbing for my forearm, turning the knife toward my face, I rose up and fell on top of her. I stabbed her once in her neck. She made a horrifying, animal-like sound, followed by a sickening gurgle, then fell onto her back, her head twisted at a horrible unnatural angle, blood pumping out of her body, soaking into the blue and cream rug, running across the white trap door.

I sat back, breathing hard. I looked at my hands and forearms. They didn't seem like my own—slick with blood. I still clutched the knife, unable to let go of it.

As my breathing slowed, I heard footsteps in the hallway. My breathing stopped altogether as I held the oxygen in my lungs.

The door opened and all the air came out of me as I looked up, leaving a painful cramp in my diaphragm. Any hope that I would now have help opening the trap door was gone.

SIXTY-EIGHT
ABIGAIL

At first, I didn't know what I was looking at. It didn't seem real.

When I'd opened the door of the house, I'd had a bad feeling. Now, I felt sick. But it still didn't seem real. It couldn't be real.

Before, I'd watched from my bedroom window as my mother crossed the patio, walking past the pool, the fairy lights sparkling overhead, turning her into a beautiful creature of the night, a goddess who had always been there, watching over me since I was a little girl. Protecting me from my worst impulses.

I watched her disappear from view.

I waited, thinking she'd walked down to the lake to think about Daddy. She did that sometimes. But she didn't come back. She was gone for such a long time and I didn't understand why she hadn't returned.

Then, I started to worry. I hurried down the stairs and outside into the cool night air. As I walked between the tall, thin palm trees, stretching up far past where I could see their leafy fronds in the darkness, I paused. The door to Daniel's house was open.

I moved slowly toward the door and pushed it open further.

I saw a light. I heard voices coming from the back of the house. My mother's voice. And Renee—the only other woman on our property. The others were all gone. At least, I thought they were.

Two of them were definitely gone. I knew because I'd looked at their dead faces. I'd seen Tina floating in the water, gazing up at nothing. I'd seen Faith when they carried her out of the wine cave. I had to see those faces. You never know if someone is really dead if you don't see their face, the eyes looking at nothing. Or maybe they are looking at something, it's just something you can't see until you join them on the other side. I don't really know, but I wonder about it.

When Daddy died, I wasn't allowed to see him. Mommy said he was gone forever. I would never see him again. He was there, and then, he was gone. He was sitting in the canoe and all I did was stand up to scare him a little. I didn't know it would tip over! He went under the water, and I never saw him again.

My mother said it wasn't good to look at his face because he wasn't there. He was dead. But I didn't know what dead meant, and if I couldn't see his face, how did I know he wasn't there? How did I know he was gone? He just evaporated.

That's why I needed to see their faces. I needed to see what dead looked like. I needed to see if they were really gone. Because I didn't want them in our house.

Now, I was standing just outside this room. It was all white —white walls and white ceiling. Specially made racks to hold wine bottles, painted white. Renee was sitting on the floor holding a knife. My mother was lying next to her wearing a white gown, but it was red. Wet and red. There was so much blood. There was blood on Renee's hands and her arms. There was blood on the rug and blood on my mother's arms and splashes of blood on her face.

I screamed.

I threw myself on top of my mother. I shook her. I grabbed

her shoulders and tried to lift her off the floor. I put my hand under her head and turned it gently so she was facing me, but her eyes were not looking at me. They were looking at that other place, somewhere too far away for me to see.

I screamed again. I was crying so hard I couldn't breathe. My mother took care of me. She protected me. I wouldn't be able to live without her. "What did you do? What did you *do*?"

"She was—"

"Why!?" I lifted my mother up, holding her close, putting my hand on the back of her head, pressing her face close to my neck. Her head kept wanting to fall away from me. "Mommy. Mommy. Don't leave me! Please don't leave!" She was so heavy. I lowered her head and upper body back to the floor and crawled away to the corner. I hugged my knees, crying. I was crying so hard I couldn't think.

What was happening?

"She killed Tina. And Faith," Renee said.

"She didn't!" I screamed. "She did not! She didn't kill anyone!"

"She murdered my sister. She's down there." Renee pounded her fist on a door built into the floor where she was sitting.

"Your sister? What sister? Who—?"

"Claudia!"

"Claudia's your sister?"

"She's down there. I need this open." Renee scrambled across the floor and grabbed my mother's bathrobe. She tore at it as if she wanted to pull it apart. "The key must be in here." She shoved her hand into the pocket.

I stood and took three steps toward her. I yanked the robe out of her hand, pulling her forward at the same time. She fell onto the floor, still holding the edge of the robe.

"Give it to me!"

"How can she be down there?" I asked.

"I don't know. I saw blood in the kitchen. Your mother must have—"

I kicked her shoulder.

She grunted, but she hung on to the robe.

"How did she get down there?" I asked. "I chased her from the lake. She was falling asleep but then she—"

"What?" Renee let go of the robe. She looked up at me. "You chased her from the lake?"

I slumped onto the floor. I buried my face in my mother's robe, inhaling the scent of her. Even with the disgusting smell of the blood, I could still smell *her*. My brothers would protect me. With my mother gone, they would keep me safe. I felt the tears bubble up again. For a brief moment, I hadn't looked at her bleeding, empty body and I'd forgotten she was gone! What was wrong with me? How could I forget? But my brothers would take care of me. I knew they would. It didn't matter if this girl found out about me. She would never get out of here alive. None of the others had. Tina didn't. Faith didn't, even if I wasn't sure how that happened, she still hadn't gotten out alive.

I didn't know what happened to Claudia either, but she hadn't left our home. Had she? It wasn't possible. She had to be here somewhere. The walls were twelve feet high. There was no way out. My mother made sure of that.

Was it possible Claudia was down there? Under that door Renee kept pounding on?

Claudia and I had been sitting by the lake that night. Putting those mushrooms that grew in the wooded area of the winery into her dinner had been a trial run. I wanted to see how her body responded, how fast she got sick. How badly she reacted. Of course, it wasn't at all the same as lorazepam, but it gave me a good idea of how strong she was, what she could tolerate.

Everything had been perfect. She was sipping her wine. The lorazepam was working its way into her body. She looked tired. It wouldn't be long before I would be able to lead her into the water and push her down like I had with Tina.

But then, everything changed. I became impatient and acted too soon. I suggested we walk to the edge of the lake, and I tried to push her into the water. She wasn't drowsy enough. Why hadn't I *waited*?

Claudia ran. She was a very fast runner.

Now, I moved my mother's robe away from my face. Renee was standing over me, holding the knife. "Did *you* lock her in there? You locked her in there and let her die?" Her voice quiet and cold, the point of the knife not far from my face.

"No. I chased her and she ran inside this house."

"Why wasn't it locked?"

I shrugged. "How should I know? We were in the kitchen. She wouldn't stop hitting me. Kicking me. She didn't understand, she was going to lose." I touched my face. I was crying. I looked at my mother and felt more tears coming.

"What happened?" Renee's face was too close to mine. Her breath was so hot.

"She fell. She hit her head on the counter." I shivered, remembering her slipping away from me, the look on her face. "Her head was bleeding. On the side. I thought she was... she wasn't moving." I didn't need to tell her the rest. She didn't need to know. It had nothing to do with her. I just needed to get the knife out of her hand so I could be rid of her.

"Why?"

"*Why?* Because I want my family! That's why. My brothers keep bringing these other girls here who aren't part of our family! They don't belong here. It's supposed to be the three of us. My brothers and me. Not all these other girls. Just me."

What a stupid question. Why was she asking me that? They were outsiders. That's why. They didn't belong in our family. They wanted to change us, to take my brothers away from me. I hated all of them. They wouldn't understand about my father, they wouldn't understand anything. My brothers might love them more than they loved me.

"I had to get rid of them," I said.

"What happened to Claudia? Why did you—?"

"I needed a tarp! And a wagon. To move her to the lake. When I came back, she was gone." My mother was here that night. I don't know how she knew, but she did. She always knew everything. She gave me a sleeping pill and put me to bed. How was I supposed to know what *happened* to Claudia? She was gone, that was all I cared about. Vanished. That was all that mattered. I didn't care where she *went*.

How could I get that knife away from Renee?

"You just shoved her down there to die? Letting her starve to death all alone?"

"What are you talking about?"

Renee stood slowly. She took a step forward. She raised the knife like she wanted to kill me.

SIXTY-NINE

RENEE

For half a second, I thought about killing Abigail with one clean stab of the knife. She'd tried to kill my sister! The only reason she'd failed was because she'd made mistakes and her mother had been forced to intervene. She'd become confused and Janice had removed her from the situation.

Killing Janice hadn't been a choice. I would have been dead myself if I hadn't. That knife in her hand was so close to my throat, I'd felt the sharp point of it more than once. As I touched my neck now, I felt hairline scratches on the tender skin.

When it was over, I'd been exhausted and unprepared for Abigail. But while she rambled, some of the things she was saying difficult to understand, my breathing slowed, and my heart steadied itself.

As she talked, it wasn't entirely clear what had happened to my sister. But one thing was clear, Abigail had made a careful and deliberate plan to kill her. Then, she'd knocked Claudia to the floor and left her for dead. Somehow, Claudia had ended up in the space below the floor where I now stood, but whatever had happened—it was Abigail—trying to rid the world of anyone who would splinter the tight-knit cluster of Janice and her three, traumatized children.

Abigail looked at me with pleading eyes.

I lowered the knife.

"You think she's down there?" Her voice was a hoarse, frightened whisper. Disbelieving.

I didn't want this monster in the room with me when I learned the answer to that question. I didn't want her beside me, not her or anyone else in this horrid family, when I lifted that door and faced my worst fear.

"I don't know."

"Do you want me to help you open it?" she asked.

I looked at her. Even at this hour, her beautiful eyes had touches of liner and shadow, making them dramatic and captivating.

How could I be rid of her? And why was she being so kind? So suddenly concerned about what I wanted? Her tone so gentle? She must be raging with grief over the loss of her mother —the center of her life for as long as she could remember. This woman lying dead between us was such a strong force in her daughter's life, it was almost as if she'd implanted her very psyche inside Abigail's mind. I wasn't sure Abigail could think for herself at all.

I forced her out of my mind and put my thoughts on Claudia, on thinking about what I might find when I opened the trap door. I allowed the tears to flow into my eyes.

"Maybe Daniel..." I waited, hoping she would pick up the thread.

"Should I get him?"

I nodded, but she didn't move.

"The police."

"What? Why would you want the police?" Abigail asked.

"Your mother locked her down there and left her to die." I

heard a whimpering sound come out of my throat. "Don't you realize that?"

She gave me a look of such hatred, I knew that if I didn't still have a tight grip on the knife, holding it close to my side, she would have driven it into my heart.

Unable to control her fury, she sneered. "If the police come, they'll arrest you for killing my mother."

"She attacked me. She was going to kill me."

"We'll see about that." She moved toward the door. "I think you're right. Daniel needs to see this. We need him to get the door open anyway. Obviously, you weren't able to." She eyed the splintered wood that lay around us. "I'll get him. You can't go into the house with blood all over you like that." A moment later, she was gone.

When I heard the front door close, I hurried down the hall. I locked the door before walking slowly, with dread pulling at each step, back to the room with the trap door.

Stepping carefully onto the blood-stained rug, I looked at the body on the floor. I now had the time to search the pockets of Janice's robe for the key to the house and also, I desperately hoped, the key to the trap door. I stuck my hand into the extra-ordinarily deep pocket where she'd concealed the knife. It was empty. I tried the other pocket. Also empty.

That wasn't possible. I straightened and held the robe by its hem, shaking it hard, expecting the keys to fall from an interior pocket. Nothing emerged. I twisted it around, feeling all along the seams. It had to be here. I'd locked the door behind me when I entered the house. How would she have gotten inside? Unless there was a side door I didn't know about? But I'd heard her footsteps in the entryway.

Spreading the robe on the floor, I knelt and studied the inside for a small pocket that had a closure of some kind. Still nothing. I ran my hand across the fabric, feeling for a hidden slit that might reveal a pouch, just large enough to hold a few keys. There was nothing.

I stood and kicked the robe to the side.

Janice was wearing a nightgown. A casual glance told me there weren't any pockets. But maybe, like I'd expected in the robe, there was a small slit somewhere with a tiny pouch designed to hold a tissue.

The horror I should have felt at stabbing this woman now engulfed me at the thought of touching her body, probing for a pocket and the key I had to have. I couldn't return to the house without entering the space that lay below the floor. I had to open that trap door. Now.

I touched her hip, feeling a shiver run up my arm at the softness of her flesh, the stillness of it beneath the thin fabric. I felt up and down her left hip, searching for a pocket. Nothing.

Squeezing my eyes, closed, I moved her slightly to reach her other hip. I opened my eyes as her body slumped more than I'd expected. A thick silver chain around her neck was exposed. Putting one hand over my mouth, I used my thumb and index finger to lift it away from her skin. On the end were three keys.

Holding my breath for no logical reason except that I felt ill, I slid the chain around until the clasp was exposed. I undid it and carefully pulled it away from her neck. I stuck one of the smaller keys into the lock and it turned. I grabbed the recessed handle and lifted the door, standing as I heaved it open.

A well-constructed staircase descended into a dimly lit room.

Before I could place my foot on the first step, a voice spoke. "Who's there?"

My sister was only thirteen years old, but the look in her eyes when she saw that knife, dripping with lime juice and blood from my mother's cut finger, flying through the air, was the steely cold look of an adult woman.

Claudia cried when my mother called us *chicken shits* and *little bitches.*

She'd heard those words a hundred times, and she'd cried a thousand times.

"Why doesn't she love us? Why does she say those bad things?"

"We have to ignore it."

"That's not how moms talk to their children."

"It's the alcohol."

"It's her," Claudia said. "You can't blame alcohol. She hates us." More tears formed in her eyes and spilled down her cheeks.

"It is the alcohol. She's different when she's not drunk."

Claudia looked at me, her eyes red around the edges, the pupils so large, her entire irises seemed solid black. "Was it alcohol when she shoved my hand in her puke because I didn't want to clean it up?"

I nodded, afraid I wouldn't be able to find any words to answer what she might say next.

"Then why did she scream at me to grow up when I cried? She wasn't drunk then."

"She's sick."

Claudia nodded.

When she was little, Claudia hid from our mother. When she was little, I kept her safe. That's how it had always been. I felt good that I was able to protect her. I liked it when she wrapped her tiny arms around my neck. I didn't like it that she was so scared she had to search for places to hide, but I was proud of myself for keeping her safe. Even if it made it worse for me sometimes. Most of the time.

I couldn't look at her eyes when they turned nearly all black like that. It felt as if she wasn't really looking at me, that she was looking somewhere else, her mind was somewhere else, she was seeing something else. Or someone else.

Then, as that knife flew through the air, landing in the floor, the tip spearing the linoleum, standing upright, almost as if there was another person in the room, standing beside us, I saw Claudia's eyes grow dark like that.

Our mother sucked her finger. "Fucking hell!"

"You shouldn't be using a knife when you're drunk," Claudia said.

My mother slapped her. Hard. So hard, there was a cracking sound that was louder than the sound of her hand on Claudia's flesh.

Claudia made a noise that was half cry, half grunt. For a minute, I thought she might have stopped breathing.

"Don't you talk to me like that. I wouldn't need a drink if it wasn't for your mouth and all the money you bleed out of my bank account every fucking day of every fucking month. The only reason you're here is because your so-called daddy wanted to try for a boy. Now, he's gone. My money's almost gone, and my life is long gone. All I have is you two and your ungrateful mouths."

I expected Claudia to cry. Or scream. Or lunge at my mother with her fists. She'd done those things before. But she didn't do any of them.

She pulled the knife tip out of the linoleum, walked slowly to my mother, and shoved it into her stomach.

Instead of protecting her like I always had, instead of helping her, I fainted. I don't know if it was the blood, or the shock. When I woke, my mother was lying on the floor. A huge puddle of blood surrounded her, spreading slowly across the floor. There was blood on the cabinets and blood on Claudia.

Everything turned black again.

In the end, I did take care of Claudia. I helped her figure out the right things to say when the police and the social workers came. And I said the same things. She was a child. Our mother attacked her with the knife. Claudia was terrified. We didn't have to lie about our mother being drunk. The autopsy proved that.

They still put Claudia in a mental health facility for several years. She needed therapy, they said. She needed to talk about what she'd lived with, they said. She needed to process what had happened. She needed to heal from her trauma.

I don't know if she did any of those things, but when she was eighteen, she was released. She seemed content. Adjusted. Mostly normal. As if I knew anything about what it meant to be normal.

SEVENTY-ONE
NOW: CLAUDIA

When I heard loud voices and thumping, I didn't think it was Janice opening the trap door to bring me the small amounts of food and water she carried down the stairs every few days. This was something else.

Living in a windowless room, all alone, not knowing if I would ever leave, not knowing what day it was, when it was night, or how long I'd been down here, my mind wasn't right. The things I'd remembered and imagined and feared tortured me in ways I couldn't describe. But even with that, there were times when I managed to find a sliver of hope.

I could hope that somehow, in a way that I couldn't imagine, even knowing it was beyond impossible, Riley would remember how I used to hide when we were small. How I hid from our mother, and how Riley always found me. It was silly, acting like I was a little girl now. But it did make me feel hopeful and keep me from scratching at my own skin, pulling out my own hair, sobbing until I couldn't breathe. It was all I had down there as the days and weeks blurred and then dissolved into nothing—no day or night, no time at all. Nothing but the door above me opening just when I thought I might never see a human being again, and Janice stomping down the stairs, dropping a box of supplies on the floor, then turning around to climb quickly back up, slamming the door closed, and securing the lock.

"Who is it?" I called again.

"Claudia?"

"Riley!" I lunged toward the stairs and tripped, almost falling. An enormous, burning sob tore through my body like molten lava that could no longer be held inside the earth.

A moment later, my sister was down the stairs and in my arms.

We held on to each other so tightly, for so long, I thought we would never peel our bodies apart. We cried and sobbed; we spoke incoherent words, trying to express our terror that was almost beyond words.

Finally, we let go of each other and looked in each other's eyes, exchanging weak, tear-filled smiles.

She looked around the room. "Wow."

"Isn't it strange?"

"Janice said her husband built it as a disaster shelter," Riley said.

The space where I'd been held captive, five rooms, actually, wasn't too awful. There was a large living area with two sofas and three easy chairs, a dining area separated by a railing, a galley kitchen, and a TV with loads of DVDs. There was a small bedroom with a double bed, and another room with three small beds for children. The bathroom had a shower and tub as well as a stacked washer-dryer. The man had been crazy prepared for a long-term disaster because the fifth room was filled with bottled water and packaged food, all of it expired over a decade ago.

"Tell me everything," Riley said.

"I want to get out of here. Then I'll tell you."

"There's... when you go up, you need to be prepared."

I looked at her, already moving toward the stairs. I wanted

to get out of this underground apartment before someone closed that door and we were both trapped down here forever.

Riley grabbed my arm. "Wait. She's dead. I killed Janice. Her body is up there."

"Oh." The sound came out of me in a short puff of air, as if all the stale air in the basement room had been sucked out. For a moment, I couldn't breathe.

"There's a lot of blood. And her body is right at the top of the stairs."

I nodded. Together, we climbed the stairs.

We tried not to look as we made our way to the door and out of the wine room. We went to the living room where it was still dark. We sat on the sofa, holding hands, feeling the warmth of each other.

Riley squeezed my hand. "Tell me everything."

"Everything?"

"What happened. How did you get locked down there?"

"She tried to kill me." It seemed so long ago now. Almost a dream.

"Who?"

"Abigail. Just liked she killed Tina."

"And Faith?"

I squeezed her hand, leaning my head back on the sofa. I felt light-headed. The fresh air in the room, after all those months in that tiny apartment. It was large, for what it was, but also so small, sometimes I felt there wasn't any air, I felt I was choking, even though I knew I wasn't.

I didn't want to tell her about Faith. Not yet. She was so happy to see me, to know I was alive. She would be so upset, maybe angry that I'd killed her. I hadn't meant to. Faith promised to keep my secret. I thought she was my friend, and then she told Janice. I begged her to tell me why she'd done it and all she did was stare at me with those empty eyes. Just one more person in this horrible family who wanted to take Daniel away from me.

I shoved her down the wine cave stairs before I even had time to think. It just happened. It was almost the same as it was with my mother. My whole body filled with pain. All that hurt had to go somewhere. Just like with my mother, I felt as if I was watching my body do something it had to do.

When it was over, I wasn't even sure who had done it. Me.

I didn't want to tell Riley. Not yet. It was too soon. She just found me. She would let go of my hand and I'd be all alone again.

"Abigail put something in my wine," I whispered. "She tried to push me into the lake, but I wasn't as drugged as she thought I was. I started running and she chased me. I ran to this house. I thought I was far ahead of her, that I could hide here. But she found me right away. She was hitting me and scratching at my face." I touched my skin. The marks were gone now.

"She shoved, and I fell. I guess I passed out. Obviously I did, because when I woke, I was..." It felt as if someone had their hands around my throat. I put my own hand there, trying to peel their fingers away. "I was down there."

Riley let go of my hand and put her arm around my shoulders, pulling me close. "A few days later, I think it was a few days, Janice brought me food. And some water. And she kept doing that."

"Why did she keep you down there?" Riley asked. "What was she planning to *do*?"

"I don't think she even knew! I asked her, but she got really upset. She told me to stop talking, to be grateful I was alive." I moved away from Riley. I ran my fingers through my hair, pushing it away from my face.

"Janice knew Abigail had killed Tina," I said. "She knew she was trying to kill me, so she was trying to keep me safe." I laughed. Riley didn't. "She didn't want her boys to know their sister was a killer, maybe? She didn't want me murdered, but if she let me go, when people found out what her daughter had done, she would have lost Abigail."

Riley rubbed my arm.

"She couldn't even let her children out of her sight. She would never let one go to prison. Never. She spent her whole life making decisions without ever second-guessing herself, but with me, she couldn't decide what to do. It almost seemed like she was as trapped as I was."

We sat quietly for a few minutes.

"Daniel is coming soon," Riley said. "With the police, I think. Abigail went to get him."

I started shaking.

"What's wrong?" She put her arm around me again, but the shaking wouldn't stop. "Claudia, are you okay? What's wrong?"

Would they find out? Would Riley find out? Was I supposed to tell them what I'd done? It didn't seem fair. "I just can't believe I'm finally out. I'm finally free. It was so, so much like before. Being locked up."

"And Faith? What happened to Faith?"

Was she guessing? Did she *know*? "She just... I was locked down there."

"She died a while ago. Quite a while ago. Probably before Abigail tried to kill you," Riley said.

I started crying.

Riley put her arms around me, pulling me close, as if she was trying to hold me together. "I know. I know. It will be okay."

"Why are they calling the police? Will you be arrested for killing Janice? Will I?" My voice was shrill. It sounded like I was screaming. I didn't want the police to come. I wanted to leave this place with my sister and never see the chateau or any of these people ever again. Why was Riley so calm about calling the police? She killed their mother! The police weren't going to like that. Neither were Janice's children.

"Faith told Janice I had a secret. She was going to tell them I was locked up in a mental health hospital. If she told them, they wouldn't have let Daniel marry me!" I started crying harder. "I know. I *know*. Now it seems... I don't know why. I loved him so much. I thought I did. It seems so long ago. It feels like nothing but a bad dream. But back then, I wanted him so much. I couldn't let them find out. I couldn't understand why Faith would do that. Just for spite. Or something. Maybe because it's so stressful living here, being an outsider, being hated and judged. I didn't mean to."

SEVENTY-TWO
RILEY

The darkness was starting to fade by the time I heard a key in the front door. Claudia and I were still seated on the couch. At the sound of the key, her hand trembled inside mine. I wasn't sure if it was because she feared what might happen to me, or because she saw her own future with absolute certainty.

This was what had made me decide to drug Daniel, to go alone when I came back to this house. And yet, when I'd first seen her face, touched her hand, looked into her eyes, when she'd cried, I hadn't been able to ask the question burning inside me. The question eating at the back of my brain that I'd silenced since the moment they'd carried Faith's body out of the wine cave. The question hovering over two lines from one of Claudia's emails that had clung my memory.

Faith told Janice I had a secret. If she tells them I was locked up, my life with Daniel is over.

Claudia had gone on to write that the one person she thought she could trust, the woman who seemed to be in a position similar to her own had betrayed her in the cruelest way. She'd written half a page of unanswerable questions, begging to know why Faith would have done this to her, why, when Faith promised she would keep her secret, would she betray her like that?

Now I knew that Claudia had broken under the fear of being exposed, the terror of losing Daniel. All the games and gaslighting inflicted on her by his family, driving her to fear for her own life, but still longing to marry the man she loved, had pushed her to the breaking point. I'd had a bad feeling about it.

Now, the key was turning in the lock. The door was opening.

I heard voices.

Daniel and Abigail. Elliot. Other voices that belonged to the police officers. A moment later, they were in the living room, all of them standing in a row, looking down at Claudia and me. There wasn't a caring expression on any of their faces, although I wasn't sure why I'd expected that.

Elliot and Abigail started toward the doorway, in the direction of the wine room and their mother's body.

One of the police officers told them to stop, while the other gave us their names and titles, making everything feel slightly chaotic.

"I'm Detective Anna Yarborough and this is Detective Tim Kroeger," she said. "There's a lot to sort out here, so let's get started. The medical examiner is on her way. Until then, I need everyone to stay out of the room where the victim's body is located."

"I need to see her!" Elliot said. "You can't stop me from saying goodbye to my mother." A moment later, he was gone, despite their loud demands that he wait. Detective Kroeger hurried after him, with Abigail right on his heels.

By the time they'd forcibly brought Elliot and Abigail back to the living room, two uniformed police officers had arrived. They separated the five of us and began asking questions. The police officers took basic information, and the detectives rotated through the rooms where they had each of us sequestered to ask more probing questions. Questions were often repetitious, trying to back us into corners that would elicit information we were trying to hide.

While they questioned us, the medical examiner and her staff took photographs of Janice and the wine room and the rooms below ground. They collected blood and other evidence. We heard their voices, but not the things they said. We saw nothing, not even the removal of Janice's body from the house.

In the end, the detectives believed what I told them about how Janice had come at me with the knife, how I'd fought for my life. They were inclined toward physical evidence more than they were toward stories of imagined threats to a semi-reclusive family's way of life. And I had physical evidence. The scratch marks from Janice's knife lined my neck from my jaw to my collarbone. I had bruises on my face and arms and legs where she'd hit me during our lengthy struggle.

They saw Tina's grave. They saw Faith's grave.

And because they had evidence to support what I'd said about Janice's attack with the knife, they believed what I told them about my discovery of Faith's body.

But the relief I felt was short-lived. Because Abigail admitted to killing Tina, they were inclined to believe her when she insisted she hadn't murdered Faith. She'd wanted to. She'd planned to. That almost eager confession on her part might have been what made them believe her, as she sobbed and ranted about not wanting any other women to *break apart* her original family. She didn't want those other women in her house. She wanted to keep the childhood bond she'd had with her brothers unbroken throughout their lives.

It was Faith's *destiny*, Abigail said, to drown in the lake. Just like Tina had. Like Claudia was supposed to. But before Abigail could make that happen, she'd watched in horror as my sister shoved Faith down the stone steps into the wine cave.

They arrested Abigail. After her sobbing, near-hysterical

confession, she appeared almost catatonic as they guided her toward the front door. She didn't say goodbye to her brothers. She didn't even weep in silence or show any signs of fear. She simply walked out the door without a backward glance.

Then, they arrested my sister.

She was not stoic, and neither was I. We cried and held on to each other. I whispered in her ear that I would find a way to help her.

"You can't," she said.

"I will. Haven't I always?"

She nodded, but when she left, she looked terrified. And defeated. "I thought I would be free," she whispered.

As they pulled her away from me and put plastic restraints on Claudia's wrists, placing her arms behind her back, I cried out in pain, as if it had been done to me. Claudia took it without making a sound.

Daniel's face was also twisted with pain. "It's not right," he said. "She should get help. She's had mental health issues. She's done—"

"Stop talking," I said.

"How do you know?" Claudia cried out. "How do you know? Did she tell you?"

The police officer shushed her. A moment later, they were gone.

The detectives had been very thorough.

But as the saying goes, you don't know what you don't know. There was one question they didn't ask. And because it wasn't asked, there was one secret they didn't uncover.

SEVENTY-THREE
RILEY

The police were gone, taking my sister and Abigail with them. Claudia had gone from one prison to another. I was free to leave, but now, I didn't think I would. Where would I go?

Nothing had turned out the way I'd expected, which made me realize that I'd given very little thought to how it might turn out. All I'd wanted was to see my sister's face again, to hear her voice, to touch her hand, and watch her smile.

Now, she'd been taken away from me once more. They kept taking her away from me. Of course, that was because of the things she'd done, but she was driven to those things by forces outside of her, by terrible people, cruel people. And it didn't change how I felt having her ripped out of my life. She was gone and I was alone.

The two brothers and I stood in the living room of the chateau. Greyson was hovering in the hallway leading to the kitchen, watching and waiting, as he always was. I wondered if he was unsure of his role, now that Janice wasn't there, telling him what to do every minute of the day.

Elliot sank onto the couch, covering his face with his hands. I thought he might start sobbing. Instead, he rubbed his hands across his face, stabbing his fingertips at his hairline, tugging his hair forward as if he might be trying to pull thoughts out of his head.

Daniel and I remained standing. He caught my gaze, but we didn't speak. Both of us seemed to be waiting for the other. I supposed he was also wondering what would happen now.

After several minutes, Elliot lurched off the couch. "I have no idea what I'm supposed to do. But we still have a winery to run, so I might as well do that." He walked out of the room without waiting for a response, increasing his pace as he reached the doorway leading to the offices, as if he was frightened of getting a response.

"Let's go out by the lake," Daniel said. "We can talk without being overheard."

Why was he still concerned about that? I followed him out the door and we walked in silence along the path to the gazebo. We sat down and looked out at the lake. The water was like glass, the sun golden and shimmering in a cloudless sky.

"Claudia thought it was disturbing that you like to sit here and look at the place where your father drowned," I said. "Doesn't it bring back terrible memories of that night? Or make you feel sad?"

"Why? It's peaceful. It's not as if he's out there."

"But doesn't remembering what happened ever make you relive the panic of not being able to get to him in time?"

"It was night, so we couldn't see anything. It was an accident." He shrugged.

I shivered. I inched away from him and drank in the dark blue water, letting its gentle lapping sounds soothe me. To me, it was beautiful. At the same time, it made me slightly afraid of who this man really was. I thought he would offer a deeper explanation, but after several minutes of silence, I realized he wasn't going to say any more about it.

"Why are you still being so careful? Coming out here to talk so no one will hear us?" It was an agreement we'd made—never speak about the true nature of our relationship. Ever. I'd come close a few times, when the gaslighting and games inside that house got the best of me, but either I'd caught myself before I was overheard, or Daniel had stopped me in time.

Daniel had first contacted me shortly after Claudia vanished. There aren't that many Riley Gatlins in Washington state, so I was easy to find. He told me he hadn't been truthful with the police when they'd come to inquire about her stay at Chateau Noir. He explained that if he'd broken away from the party line his mother had outlined and told the truth, that Claudia had vanished from their property, his family would have closed ranks. They would have protected each other as they always had. His mother's first-class attorneys would have blocked the investigation at every turn.

Because the police informed them that Claudia's phone had pinged multiple times in San Francisco after she'd stayed at their home, there was no cause for searching the property. There was no reason to question his family beyond a basic inquiry about whether they'd seen her or heard from her since.

"If I bring home a new fiancée," Daniel told me, "it will disrupt my family even more than Claudia's presence did. They don't coexist well with outsiders, and they aren't expecting someone new so soon."

I laughed when he said that. Despite my unspeakable dread that something terrible had happened to Claudia, I laughed out loud. "You aren't serious. You can't be."

"I am. My family is... I can't describe them."

He didn't have to describe them. I had a very good idea of what his family was like, thanks to my sister's long emails.

Although, it wasn't until I lived with them that I realized, I'd had no idea at all what they were really like.

"It's the only thing I can think of." Daniel's voice broke and he paused for a breath. "One of them killed my brother's wife. And I think... I'm so sorry, Riley, I feel physically sick telling you this, but one of them might have killed your sister. There's no other explanation for her disappearance. Even though her phone pinged in San Francisco, I don't think she ever left our estate.

"If you come here, I have to hope that whoever it is will feel threatened by someone new, an outsider. They might slip, lose their self-control. They might say something about her, I don't know. It's a long shot, ridiculously long, but I don't know what else to do. And if I don't do *something*, if our lives go back to normal, my mother and siblings will settle in and continue on as if it never happened. As if Claudia was never here at all. And I'll never find out. You'll never know what happened to her."

Thinking about the carnage I'd witnessed in the past twenty-four hours, it appeared as if his plan had worked. But it made me realize it was a flimsy plan, almost no plan at all. We hadn't given any thought to the details of how it would actually play out. Another death was certainly not in the plan. My sister arrested and charged with murder was absolutely *not* in the plan. Although, to be fair, that had happened before I'd arrived. Before the plan came into being.

I felt as if I'd made a deal with the devil. Daniel had shoved my sister into a family that was so far beyond dysfunctional, the word hardly described them. He'd also gaslighted her in the worst way, right alongside his mother and the rest of them. His cruelties were both large and small. He'd nudged her to choose an engagement ring that was almost identical to the one belonging to her dead sister-in-law, then watched in silence as his family tarnished her enjoyment of it.

When I read Claudia's email about the curating of the rings

—pre-selected and sized for her—it had been so obvious to me. And yet, he'd allowed her to doubt herself, to question her own ability to make a decision by putting on a lavish and flamboyant display that clouded her mind.

The most horrible part of it was that he hadn't gaslit her because he was unconsciously reacting to his own childhood trauma. He did it because he'd tried to concoct the same plan with her as he had with me. This man had targeted my sister as if she were a pawn to be used in his pathetic attempt to escape his family, keeping the lucrative winery, but breaking his mother's iron-clad grip on his life.

He met my gentle, fragile sister and was immediately captivated by her. But when she was vague about a gap in her life story, he went digging. Once he found the story of our mother's murder, it wasn't difficult to piece together what had happened, and to figure out Claudia's part in it. He didn't even need the mental health hospital to break their patient confidentiality.

I didn't know for a fact which details he'd managed to uncover, but I knew in my gut that enough of our horrible childhood, especially my mother's death, was gruesome public knowledge. I knew because Daniel had offered a peek at his barely there conscience. He'd objected when they arrested Claudia for killing Faith. He started to insist she needed *help*, not punishment. He almost let it slip that he'd already known what Claudia had done when she was thirteen.

But Claudia never told him about that. She hadn't even told Faith *why* she was in a mental health facility. What I didn't know was whether Daniel targeted her because he thought she might disrupt the status quo in his family, or if he thought she might be driven to commit murder again. Maybe he thought that was the only way to stop Abigail. Maybe, he'd wanted his mother out of the way permanently.

It was hard to know what was inside that man's tortured, twisted, manipulative head.

This was a man who took his sweet time getting out of bed when his mother screamed that his father and sister were drowning.

Daniel put his arm across the back of the bench where we sat inside the gazebo. "I'm still being careful because I don't want Elliot to know about our arrangement."

"Why not?"

"We were telling the truth when we told you he's fragile. He has a lot of guilt from when our father drowned. For some reason, he blames himself."

I nodded. Fragile was one word for it. Angry might be another. What would Elliot do if he found out that Daniel was the one who had set this all into motion? That if Daniel hadn't planned an elaborate charade to find out what had happened to Claudia and Tina, their mother would be alive. Abigail would still be with them.

An awareness of how much power I now had surged through me.

He moved his arm so it was touching my upper back. "But also, I wouldn't mind continuing our charade. What do you think? You and I—"

"Sure. I could stay for a while. Maybe a long while." I moved closer and leaned into him.

"And our charade? Not a charade anymore?"

"Maybe, yes."

"I'd like to get to know you better."

"One thing you should know about me, is that my sister is everything to me."

He laughed softly. "I know that."

"It's important that we get her the best defense attorney available. And that we—"

"Done."

"You would do that?" I looked up at him.

"I owe you. Both of you."

If that didn't confirm that he'd targeted Claudia, I don't know what else would, short of him telling me outright.

EPILOGUE

RILEY

Lying in bed beside a man I was quite sure was a sociopath didn't make for drifting into a peaceful night's sleep. I wondered how long I would be required to do this before he hired a first-class defense attorney for my sister.

I didn't think I was being overly optimistic to believe an attorney with the right experience could get Claudia either a few years in a mental health hospital, or even better. After all, it was only the word of an admitted killer who claimed to have seen Claudia push Faith down the stairs to her death. And my sister was as good a liar as I was.

She'd learned how to lie when I taught her what to say as we sobbed over our mother's bleeding body. Locked up in the place she was, her mental condition observed every hour, she'd become an even better liar. She learned about lies of omission, keeping her secrets from the other patients. She'd lied to staff when they asked if she'd slept well. Sleeping well was considered a sign of good mental health and she knew it was important to reassure them. She'd lied to staff therapists, telling them she never had dreams or any thoughts at all of self-harm, or harming others. The memories of her mother's abuse and violent death were fading.

Lying awake wasn't a terrible state to be in, because I had more plans to make.

Finally, it was too much. I slipped out from beneath the blankets and out the bedroom door. I glided down the staircase that now felt like an old friend. Coming around the corner into the main hallway, I saw that a light in the kitchen already on.

When I stepped into the kitchen, Greyson stood at the counter. A mug of tea, steam rising from the surface, was waiting for me on the bar. He smiled.

"How did you know?" I asked.

"It's not easy to sleep under these circumstances. Unless you're a sociopath."

I slid onto one of the chairs and wrapped my hands around the mug. "Thank you."

He picked up his own mug of tea and took a sip. "Why are you still here?"

I looked up at him. His gaze was steady, curious. But there was something else, as if he might be waiting for an invitation, or calibrating what he would say, depending on what I said.

"Daniel is paying for my sister's defense attorney."

"He owes her that."

I nodded and took a sip of tea. "And I guess you could say I'm making plans, trying to figure out my options. It's a delicate situation." I gave him a tentative smile.

"I have a delicate situation myself," he said.

I took another sip of tea.

He put down his mug and rested his hands on the counter, leaning forward slightly. "I think I can trust you."

"You can."

"I've observed, in my very limited experience of the world, that all of us are broken. The ones you can trust are those who learn something when life breaks them. Those who don't, can't be trusted."

"That makes sense."

"I'm not who you think I am. I'm not who Janice told everyone I was."

"Oh?"

"I'm her son. Her first son."

I wrapped my lower legs around the legs of the chair, thinking I might slide off as the words flowed from his lips with his usual calm, steady tone, as if he were asking me if I wanted a second cup of tea.

"You don't believe me," he said.

I did believe him. I absolutely believed him. I immediately saw the resemblance in the shape of his mouth and his hairline. How had I never noticed before? "I believe you."

"She had an affair before Daniel was conceived. Sam found out about it before she told him she was pregnant. So of course when she told him she was—he didn't believe for a single minute that I was his.

"Sam couldn't accept me, but he allowed her to keep me. He said they would tell people they'd *taken me in*—whatever that means." He laughed, without a trace of bitterness. "The child of some obscure employee who had died in an accident, or some murky story along those lines. I would be raised as a family employee."

"It sounds like Sam was as charming as Janice."

Greyson laughed. "Apparently, she bided her time. She wanted to change all of that, to make me part of the family. They were fighting about it the night he drowned and I over-heard them. She was really upset. I was eleven and she said it was getting too late. If they didn't tell me soon, I would be too old, the others would be too old, to make that kind of change to the family. But Sam said absolutely not. And then he died."

"That must have been awful." I closed my eyes for a

moment. Searching inside to see if I felt any empathy for Janice. I felt a light flutter of sadness for her, but it didn't last long.

"I couldn't ask her about it right away. Obviously. And then I couldn't for a long time. The grief. The way they all reacted. And I was a kid. It took me a long time to get the courage. I was fifteen before I did. She treated me well. I had the same tutors as the others, but that meant I was also a virtual prisoner like the others."

"I'm really sorry."

"Like I said, we're all broken. In one way or another."

"Some worse than others."

"When I finally confronted her, she promised she would tell them, promised I would become one of them." He laughed. "Although as the years went by, a part of me wondered why I wanted that. I wanted equal share in the winery. It seemed only fair."

"Absolutely." I sipped my cooling tea.

"So, I've been waiting. And waiting. And waiting."

"Was it worth it? Just for money?"

"For a long time, it wasn't about money. Or ownership. Or anything like that. I wanted to be recognized. I wanted to be part of the family. They were my half-brothers and sister. She was my mother."

I nodded, feeling tears in my eyes. I blinked them away.

"But you didn't have friends. Girlfriends?"

"I did. I have. Employees at the winery. I'm not a complete prisoner." He laughed. "But I'm also not very well acclimated to society. It's comfortable here."

I nodded.

"It became a habit. Or something. She kept telling me it would be *soon*, kept giving me hope. Telling me she had to find the right way, the right time. Hope, slightly deferred, can carry someone for a very, *very* long time. Longer than you can imagine. You hardly notice the years going by."

Greyson and I talked until three in the morning. He asked for my help. If I went through with my charade of a marriage to Daniel, which he clearly wanted, I would be in a position to ensure Greyson got what he deserved.

I told him I had nowhere else to go. We had that in common.

* * *

A few days later, when Daniel, Elliot, and I resumed eating our evening meals in the formal dining room, I didn't have the hubris to sit in Janice's or Abigail's places at the head or the foot of the table, but I absolutely wanted to. Instead, I took my seat at the side. Daniel and Elliot also took their usual places— Daniel beside me and Elliot across from me. The throne-like chair at the head looked particularly out-of-place, drawing our attention to it as if she refused to let us go.

Greyson served our dinner of grilled prawns, wild rice, and a spicy white corn dish. He refilled Daniel's and Elliot's wine-glasses. He placed the bottle on the table and left the room.

I took a sip of water, turned, and offered a demure smile to Daniel, then the same to Elliot across the table.

Elliot sat back in his chair and took a large gulp of wine. "It doesn't feel right," he said.

"It will," Daniel said. "We're free."

"Are we?" Elliot swallowed more wine. "The whole family is gone."

"It wasn't much of a family," Daniel said.

"But it was ours." Elliot stabbed a prawn and shoved the entire thing into his mouth, as if he wanted to cork his throat to prevent any words he might regret from coming out.

His leering bravado was gone. He'd been a creep, but maybe all he'd been was a very damaged man who was trying to out his sociopathic brother—a man who stayed in bed when his mother screamed that his father was at the bottom of the lake.

Elliot looked lost and uncertain about how he was supposed to behave, about his place in the world and his place at the table, and his relationship to his brother. Possibly, he was equally uncertain about his relationship to me.

As if he'd read my thoughts, he chewed and swallowed the prawn with difficulty, eager to speak. "Who's in charge?"

"Why does anyone need to be in charge?" Daniel asked. "We're brothers. We'll continue in the roles we had before. We'll work out the rest as we go."

Elliot picked up his wineglass and swirled the contents, eyeing it with suspicion.

I pushed my chair back. I stood and walked to the head of the table. I pulled out the throne-like chair and settled myself within its strong arms. Daniel gave me a hard stare. He opened his mouth, but before he could suggest I didn't belong there, Greyson returned to the room. He pulled out Abigail's chair and sat down.

I waited for Elliot to place his wineglass on the table. I gave him a gentle, protective smile. "Welcome to *my* family," I said.

A LETTER FROM CATHRYN GRANT

Dear Reader,

I want to say a huge thank you for choosing to read *Welcome to the Family*. If you did enjoy it, and want to keep up to date with all my latest releases, just sign up at the following link. Your email address will never be shared and you can unsubscribe at any time.

www.bookouture.com/cathryn-grant

Families, whether they're formed by blood, marriage, or kindred spirits, are endlessly fascinating to me. They're the source of incomparable love but can sadly be the birthplace of unbearable pain. I don't think I'll ever grow tired of writing about the secrets, betrayals, and the triumph of love and hope over the darkness that sometimes lurks in family life.

The siblings in this story have become such a part of my life, I feel as if they became members of my extended family.

It's always an unsettling experience to say goodbye to a group of characters when I write the final page. I love knowing that they've also lived with you for a short time, and I'm so honored that you invited them into your life.

I hope you loved *Welcome to the Family* and if you did I would be very grateful if you would write a review. I'd love to hear what you think, and it makes such a difference, helping new readers to discover one of my books for the first time.

I love hearing from my readers—you can get in touch on my Facebook page, through Instagram, Goodreads, or my website.

Thanks,

Cathryn

www.cathryngrant.com

 instagram.com/cathryngrantauthor
 facebook.com/CathrynGrant.Writer

ACKNOWLEDGMENTS

It's been a thrilling creative experience working with Helen Jenner on *Welcome to the Family*, my first novel with Bookouture. At times, the process felt close to something magical as our vision for the book became so perfectly aligned. I'm incredibly grateful to have such a talented editor and team who are as excited about my story as I am.

To my family, for absolutely everything, always, especially for listening to me talk far too much about murder and crimes of all sorts.

Most of all, to my husband, who has read, and reread every word I've written. My first reader, my biggest fan, my soulmate. Thank you for all the cups of coffee, tea, and bowls of popcorn. The man who wonders about the *why* behind crime stories as much as I do.

And to my readers. Thank you for reading. You will never know how honored I am that you choose to spend your precious time escaping into the lives of the characters I create.

PUBLISHING TEAM

Turning a manuscript into a book requires the efforts of many people. The publishing team at Bookouture would like to acknowledge everyone who contributed to this publication.

Audio
Alba Proko
Sinead O'Connor
Melissa Tran

Commercial
Lauren Morrissette
Hannah Richmond
Imogen Allport

Cover design
Jo Thomson

Data and analysis
Mark Alder
Mohamed Bussuri

Editorial
Helen Jenner
Ria Clare

RAISING READERS
Books Build Bright Futures

Dear Reader,

We'd love your attention for one more page to tell you about the crisis in children's reading, and what we can all do.

Studies have shown that reading for fun is the **single biggest predictor of a child's future life chances** – more than family circumstance, parents' educational background or income. It improves academic results, mental health, wealth, communication skills, ambition and happiness.

The number of children reading for fun is in rapid decline. Young people have a lot of competition for their time, and a worryingly high number do not have a single book at home.

Hachette works extensively with schools, libraries and literacy charities, but here are some ways we can all raise more readers:

- Reading to children for just 10 minutes a day makes a difference
- Don't give up if children aren't regular readers – there will be books for them!

- Visit bookshops and libraries to get recommendations
- Encourage them to listen to audiobooks
- Support school libraries
- Give books as gifts

There's a lot more information about how to encourage children to read on our websites: **www.RaisingReaders.co.uk** and **www.JoinRaisingReaders.com**.

Thank you for reading.

www.ingramcontent.com/pod-product-compliance
Ingram Content Group UK Ltd.
Pitfield, Milton Keynes, MK11 3LW, UK
UKHW040402290825
7630UKWH00004B/102